The Empty Net

Michael David Lannan

Trafford Publishing, a Division of
Trafford Holdings Ltd.

© 2002 by Michael David Lannan. All rights reserved.

No part of this publication may be reproduced, stored in a retrieval system, or transmitted, in any form or by any means, electronic, mechanical, photocopying, recording, or otherwise, without the written prior permission of the author. Any similarity to any persons living or dead is coincidental and not intended.

For information contact the Publisher or the Author at mdl@mobile.rogers.com.

National Library of Canada Cataloguing in Publication

Lannan, Michael David, 1960-
    The empty net / Michael David Lannan.

ISBN 1-55369-401-5

I. Title.

PS8573.A5856E46 2002	C813'.6	C2002-901658-4
PR9199.4.L35E46 2002		

TRAFFORD

This book was published *on-demand* in cooperation with Trafford Publishing.
On-demand publishing is a unique process and service of making a book available for retail sale to the public taking advantage of on-demand manufacturing and Internet marketing.
On-demand publishing includes promotions, retail sales, manufacturing, order fulfilment, accounting and collecting royalties on behalf of the author.

Suite 6E, 2333 Government St., Victoria, B.C. V8T 4P4, CANADA
Phone   250-383-6864   Toll-free   1-888-232-4444 (Canada & US)
Fax   250-383-6804   E-mail   sales@trafford.com
Web site   www.trafford.com   TRAFFORD PUBLISHING IS A DIVISION OF TRAFFORD HOLDINGS LTD.
Trafford Catalogue #02-0214   www.trafford.com/robots/02-0214.html

10   9   8   7   6

The Empty Net

This book is dedicated to my parents who made it all possible, my wife, Arleen, for her unwavering support, my brother Jeff, the funniest person I know, my brother Greg for his strength, my sister Kathy for her example of dedication, and my family and friends who make the journey that much more interesting and bearable.

To Rudy,

a lovely person and a scholar. Hope you enjoy at least some of it!!

The Empty Net

Eddy Walsh loved to play Hockey.

Ice Hockey, ball hockey, air hockey, broom ball hockey, it didn't matter as long as it was some sort of hockey, he would play. The competition, companionship, physical exertion and euphoria of success, the sheer poetry of the game, what could be better. He was an active boy and loved to do anything physical, but hockey was special.
Oh sure, like most young boys he played baseball, soccer and some other sports, and was successful at them, but Eddy Walsh found they all paled in comparison to his beloved game of hockey. Baseball was too slow and graceful, football was too structured, slow and contrived. Basketball, enough said. Tennis, bowling, soccer, swimming, it was great that the girls and elderly had some activity to do, but they weren't hockey and they weren't for Eddy. Eddy was raised on Hockey. His earliest memories involved playing with mini hockey sticks on the living room floor and watching *Hockey Night in Canada*. If Eddy was well behaved on the Saturday, which was rare, then he would be allowed to stay up late to watch the second period of the hockey game. Eddy loved watching the games, in black and white, on the small family T.V. Eddy would curl up with his pillow and a blanket on the hard wood floor, surrounded by his family. He loved how the announcers made the game seem like magic. The theme song grabbed him first, then the player introductions and then the game itself. Eddy would mimic the arena announcer for hours, repeating goals and penalties and making the other announcements that he could hear in the background on the television. He thought the coolest job in the world was the job of being the arena announcer. Eddy loved it when the players fought. Trying to pull the sweaters over each others head, the wild swinging of fists, the emotion, and sometimes the blood and gore of a one sided win. Just like the crowd at the game, he would yell louder when a fight was on then when someone scored a goal.

The Empty Net

Kinda of strange, but kinda true. His parents would tell him that fighting was not part of the game, but Eddy knew different. Eddy knew different a lot of times.

As if under a powerful spell, by the start of the third period of the hockey game, eyes heavy and the begging and pleading unsuccessful, Eddy would drag himself to bed. He would hum the theme song to himself as he fell asleep.

Before Eddy was six years old he could name all the players on the original six N.H.L. teams. He didn't know the names of the Provinces, States or their capitals, but, they weren't going anywhere any ways. His parents and family kidded Eddy about how much he loved hockey, but they were secretly very proud and pleased. It was good for boys to have a hobby and an outlet to let off their male aggression. Besides what could be more Canadian than being a young hockey fanatic.

Eddy had a bed shaped like a puck and stick, pyjamas with team logos on them, sheets and pillow cases with his beloved Montreal Canadiens logo on them, and an N.H.L. light. Eddy had loved the habs ever since he could remember. He didn't know exactly why, maybe it was the beautiful colours of red, blue and white, the fact they won the Stanley Cup a lot or the fact they spoke a different language and just somehow seemed different than the other teams. It was all of no consequence, he was crazy about them and it didn't matter why. As he got older he also learned to hate the Maple Leafs. Their fans were loud, obnoxious nut cases that really had nothing to cheer about it. It's not like they were winning anything. The leaf fans always talked a better game than their team played. The leafs were always the hottest team in the league in October, but were never seen or heard in April when the hardware was being given out. Win or lose, it didn't matter, the media loved them and weren't shy about it. It got so Eddy didn't know if he loved watching the habs win, or the Toronto Maple Leafs lose, more. When the habs would regularly defeat the leafs it was fantastic. The leafs were the favourite of the local kids in the neighborhood and other than Bobby Gage, his best friend, there were no other habs fans in his town, none that he knew of. He had a habs sweater, red gloves and a habs hat. He proudly wore them all over town and to school, even when those troubled leaf fans snickered at him. What did he care. The leafs had never won the Stanley Cup during his life time and at the rate they were going, there was no risk they ever would. The habs had won them regularly and made a tradition of it. They expected to win and then set about to do so. Just making the playoffs was not good enough. Second place was simply the first loser and they could take no consolation in that position. Eddy always felt certain teams were beat before the season started, just by listening to them talk. If their goal was not to win the Stanley Cup, then why were they wasting their time competing. The leafs to him were the epitome of the attitude. It always surprised him how people could be fanatical even about obvious losers. But, even Eddy realized that you couldn't just have one team in the league, you needed some victims for the habs.

In his room Eddy had a table top hockey game with the metal players that always jammed or fell over, and had the long metal rods that you had to manipulate to work the players. He also had an air hockey game in his room. The biggest problem Eddy had was finding someone to play with. When he couldn't find anyone to play, he would beg his younger brother Shannon to play one of the games with him. Shannon didn't like to play hockey with Eddy for several reasons. He didn't really like sports, he hated losing all the time when he did play Eddy, and he hated the fight with the corresponding game flipping by Eddy, if he ever was winning. Eddy was not a good sport when it came to losing, or when it came to winning for that matter.

Eddy was the older of two boys in his family. His little brother Shannon was almost two years younger than Eddy and they were polar opposites of one another. Eddy was athletic, street smart, arrogant, adventurous, and mean spirited, Shannon was a sweet, intelligent, well spoken, reserved boy who seemed to lack in self esteem. Both boys had no shortage of desire or commitment to hard work. Luckily, they also had a stern disciplinarian father, Gerry, who would get after them if they ever showed signs of losing the commitment to succeed in whatever they were doing. Of course success of any kind never seemed to be enough for Gerry. If Shannon got an "A" on an assignment at school then the father would ask why he didn't get an "A+". If Eddy scored three goals in a game, the father would ask why he didn't get four goals. This drove the boys crazy, but also helped to secure their bond with one another. They didn't understand why the father did what he did, they just knew they didn't like it. It didn't motivate the boys and only served to make them resent their father. The two boys busted their tails in almost everything they did. Shannon took pride in everything and always tried to do his best. Eddy only tried his best in sports and other things he liked. It was obvious at a young age that school was not one of those things Eddy liked. Many boys would have been bitter, rebelled or just given up, but not the Walsh boys, they just kept going. The reality of seemingly never being able to satisfy the demands of their father became their norm. It was expected so there were no surprises.

    Shannon did well in school, of course never well enough for Gerry, but his teachers liked him and he was no trouble in the classroom. Shannon was quick to raise his hand anytime the teacher needed a volunteer. He would clean the blackboard, clean the chalk brushes outside, get paper, take messages to the offices, anything that was needed, he would do. The other kids in the class thought he was a bit of a kiss ass, but didn't say anything to him or Heaven forbid do anything to him, for fear of Eddy. Eddy cast a large shadow in the school yard, whether or not Shannon appreciated it. Eddy was not a great student. Grade after grade, he hardly got by. If the school policy wasn't to basically pass everyone and move them up the ladder, he would have failed several grades. He was above average in size and so holding him back would have done nothing but strike fear into the hearts of those poor punks in the grades below him. Eddy was a funny guy, who could be likable and that was his only redeeming virtue. Some kids in his class were odd, acted odd and did odd things, Eddy was always creative and that counted for something. He was a practical joker and liked to pull pranks as often as he could. One year the teacher was trying to show the class how the water that people use and rely on was being polluted by phosphates and other pollutants. Eddy loved that word phosphates even though he didn't really know what it meant. The teacher put a sheet of wax paper at the back and on the outside of the classroom fish tank and dimmed the lighting to show what phosphates did to the quality of the water. The class got the point despite how it was lamely displayed. Eddy could do better. He went home that night and looked up phosphates in the dictionary. While Eddy didn't care about school he would certainly pursue subjects that were of interest to him. Eddy discovered that phosphates were produced by detergents that people used on a daily basis.

The next morning the teacher was aghast to see soap suds coming out of the air filter and spilling over the top of the tank. Now that was an environmental disaster. As visual and compelling as it was, the teacher was not impressed. She looked at the dead fish and looked at Eddy and quickly determined that it had the mark of Eddy to it. Eddy readily confessed, and his legend grew. The teachers did not like for one minute his deviant acts, but they did appreciate his honesty after the fact. Eddy had to clean the tank out and promise to pay for the dead fish. Luckily for him they were not very expensive and so his mother gave him the money to give to the teacher. His mom was great in trying to insulate or at least protect him from the father when she could. Deep down the father would have appreciated the prank, but he would have been angry because he had to part with the funds to pay for it. Gerry Walsh did not like to be parted from his hard earned money for no good reason. Heck, he didn't even like being parted from his hard earned money for a good reason.

"Eddy you should focus more on what is important and less on hockey and playing jokes on people." Miss Turner admonished him. She was his teacher two years in a row and saw some potential in Eddy. She was afraid he was simply going to continue to take short

The Empty Net

cuts and end up with no values, or at least the wrong values, and no work ethic. She liked him and didn't want to see him fail in life. It was a message that Eddy would hear over and over from various teachers during his academic career. Eddy would tell them all the same story, he was going to play in the N.H.L. and be rich and famous. He didn't need education or their help. They could save the motivational talks about education for some poor loser that needed it.

  The Walsh family lived in a small post war town that had many streets that looked alike. They had a front yard, back yard, garage and road out front, all they really needed. They were neither rich or poor, had everything they needed and even some of the things they wanted. There were about 10,000 people in town, so everyone knew most everyone else. That was good and bad, but when everyone was young it provided them with a certain sense of comfort. Kids could play outside, explore the area, and trust adults. What a world. Kids could be kids. The town had a theatre, a few streets with stores, a baseball field, cenotaph, an ice cream store, two indoor hockey rinks and five out door hockey rinks. Not too mention the thousand or so outdoor rinks people had in their back yards. When it got cold in town there was no shortage of places to skate or play. There were about fifty kids on Eddy's street, so there was always someone to play with. The kids thought it was great to always have someone to play with, and enough kids so that when they had trouble with one or were fighting with another, they could avoid them for awhile and still have someone else to play with. Gerry was Scottish, although his family had been in Canada for about 200 years. Everybody could still tell he was Scottish. He was cheap, or frugal as he liked to say, had a temper, which he said was simply being assertive, and loved to tell people how things should be. He never did have an explanation for that particular trait. He was an intelligent man, with an incomplete formal education, athletic, competitive and unhappy. He pictured his life different than his reality and somehow when sharply focused it was difficult for him to handle. He enjoyed his children and spent lots of time with them. He never talked to them much, but he spent the time with them. It was an odd dynamic, but no more odd than other things happening in the life of the Walsh family. Despite there only being four people in the Walsh family their life was full and very busy. The house was active and there was always something going on or about to be going on. The town was dominated by the mill where about 60% of the working adults were employed. As went the mills fortune, as went the town's fortunes.

The father worked at the mill, but Eddy and Shannon had no idea what he really did there. He would often complain about the "dummies" he worked with, or for, and they could see that he was often tired from working too much, but they didn't know what department he worked in or what his role was. It was something that they instinctively knew not to discuss with the father. The boys liked the mill because it was a huge place with lots of big smoke stacks and every time they went there they got a gift. That's what it seemed like to them, anyway. The mill had an annual Christmas party were all the families would get together. The party was actually held over four weekends and the day you went was determined by your last name. The office people and other "suits" had their own day. There would be movies, popcorn, pop, treats and Santa Claus. Every child under twelve would get a Christmas present from the company. That was the best part of being the kid of a mill worker and was an event that was eagerly anticipated by all the kids. Unfortunately for the kids, after a large contract was lost to some over seas company, the age for gifts was reduced to nine. Eventually, due to competition, the market, the times, for whatever reason, the Christmas parties were canceled. Shannon felt particularly ripped off because he was younger and hadn't gotten as many presents from the company as Eddy had.

As stern as Gerry was, their mother Kathy was the opposite. She was Irish and gentle, the epitome of kindness and sweetness, always there for the boys and anyone else that needed to talk. In a town were most mom's stayed home, she was the one sought out by other kids to tell their troubles and bend an ear. She loved the role which became a life long one. She was not athletic, but did take interest in the sports the boys were involved in. Both parents were tee-totalers and they seemed to get along fairly well. The house was a modest one with lots of toys, food and love. The boys never lacked for anything, but weren't exactly known as trend setters in the neighborhood. Of course there were few trend setters in this town.

The Walsh's had their children later in life. Mrs. Walsh was almost forty when Eddy was born, Mr. Walsh was slightly older. They considered their boys to be miracles and tried to treat them accordingly. Although they were older than the parents of Eddy and Shannon's friends, age never prevented them from actively participating in their children's lives.

Eddy enjoyed nothing more than getting into trouble and making Shannon the fall guy. Shannon had been blamed for so many pranks that Eddy had pulled it was embarrassing. Not that Eddy minded Shannon taking the heat for them, it was just that Eddy wanted the attention and really wanted people to know that he was the creative genius behind some classics and not Shannon.

The next door neighbours of the Walsh family were a family named Milton. They had two girls and two boys younger than the Walsh boys. They were shy, withdrawn kids, but were very nice to the other kids. Their parents were "alky's", whatever that was. They would get a delivery from the Beer truck once a month. They liked to drink and then throw the bottles around the house. The kids spent most of their time outside looking after themselves. The father worked at the mill and the mother was at home. They said that the father had been hurt somehow in the War and was never the same. Sometimes the mother would come out onto her porch and start screaming at the world. She really hated when the kids, even her own, would play ball hockey or football out on the street. She did not seem to have a high tolerance for noise, unless she was making it.

The Empty Net

Eddy's street had a lot of trees on it. Mostly ones with big leaves that disappeared in the winter. If kids weren't sitting in them then they were climbing them. It was a great street, but kids never look at their surroundings and appreciate how beautiful it may be. They simply enjoy it without thinking much about it. Only when the child becomes an adult do they start to analyze the physical and monetary details of their youth. Many of the trees on their street had little orange berries on them, the same size as a small pea. The berries fit perfectly into the little pea shooters almost all the kids carried with them. Eddy loved to load up with the berries and then start shooting against the front window of the Milton house. It wouldn't take long before Mrs. Milton would be at the window yelling and screaming. Eddy would press the attack despite the response. When she disappeared from the window Eddy knew she was on the way out. He would hide behind the bushes at the side of her house and then shake them when she was on the front yard. She would then run towards the bushes, often falling over before she got there. Sometimes other kids would join in the fun. It was only later after Mrs. Milton had died that he thought about how sad her life and that situation was. Years later he hoped that the Milton kids had never seen him taunting their mother, but they probably had. Just another thing Eddy should be sorry for but probably wasn't.

Eddy and Shannon loved the different seasons because their mom had a theme for each one. The Easter theme would start in March, no matter when Easter was going to be. The inside of the house would be decorated with bunnies, Easter lilies and other appropriate items. Outside there would be baskets strategically placed in the bushes, giant plastic carrots beside the porch and a couple of plastic bunnies on the lawn. The other kids would tease them about the Easter set up, but the boys knew everyone really enjoyed it. When Easter finally came, the inside of the living room looked like a candy plant had an explosion that was contained by the Walsh house. Chocolate bunnies, chocolate eggs, chocolate bars, chocolate cookies, chocolate candies, white chocolate, dark chocolate and milk chocolate. Their mom must of thought they needed a lot of chocolate to take them to the next theme which was Thanksgiving. Thanksgiving was great. Turkeys, horns of plenty and funny looking corn adorned the inside and the outside of their house. Big fancy bows were tied onto the trees. The boys never knew exactly what the bows were for, but they looked okay. The Thanksgiving meal was the best meal of the whole year. Turkey, roast beef and a ham competed for the families attention as the main course. Stuffing, potatoes, yams, corn, peas, carrots, rice, buns and gravy helped round out the table. There was never even enough room to put all the food out at once. Every year they had a week's worth of left overs despite eating so much they would almost get sick. After dinner Mr. Walsh would thank Mrs. Walsh for a wonderful banquet and then blame her for making him eat too much.

The Halloween season started immediately after thanksgiving. The funny coloured corn and other decorations would make way for ghosts and goblins. Fake pumpkins, goblins, ghosts, skeletons, witches and other scary imagery engulfed their space. On Halloween night they would light the candles in the four or five scary pumpkins they had cut up and would turn on the eery music. Three hours and a hundred and fifty kids later it would be all over. The kids would empty their loot on the kitchen table so that the parents could sift through it and throw out the undesirable candy. The boys would protest of course, but they really didn't want pink coloured popcorn that had become loose at the bottom of their pillow case "bags" any way. Mrs. Walsh must not have enjoyed Halloween as much as the other seasonal themes because the decorations disappeared without a trace within a couple of days.

The Christmas season was the best and started in mid November. Not only were there the predictable decorations on the windows and throughout the house, there was a sled on the roof and a lighted Santa Claus and Reindeer on the front lawn. The staircase was decorated, the fridge was decorated, they even started wearing candy cane looking socks and Mrs. Walsh wore various Christmas theme ear rings. It was over kill to say the least, but it had a warm comforting feeling to it. Mr. Walsh didn't seemed to care, although once in late November he asked his wife where the Christmas decorations were. If it was optional that people would put up decorations for the other special occasions, it must have been mandatory to put them up at Christmas. Every house and most businesses had jolly displays from late November until the second week of January. When it snowed, which it did often in the winter, the decorations took on a surreal glow. It was a magical and stimulating time of the year. Sometimes downtown a person could walk around in the snow looking at the displays and fancy scenes displayed in the store windows and hear Christmas carols playing in the background. It was truly a celebration for the senses and a special time for people of all ages. People acted differently at this time of the year, how could they not!

    Eddy and Shannon could hardly contain themselves waiting for Christmas morning. It was near impossible going to sleep Christmas eve. They would leave a glass of milk and a plate of cookie's out for Santa and a couple of big carrots for the reindeers. They would then scamper into bed and try and get some sleep. The Walsh family had a rule that no one could get up before 7:00 a.m. and the kids had to wake their parents up first, before going into the living room. The rule worked better in theory than in practice. One year the Milton's must have been celebrating Christmas early and their shouts of joy and good tidings woke Eddy up. Not being able to fall asleep again he inched his way quietly into the living room. He was amazed by the amount of presents. He looked closely and discovered that each family member had a neat pile of gifts under the tree. He looked at his, but couldn't tell what they were. One present had a little run in the tape holding the package closed. Eddy decided to help it out and pulled the tape back a little more. He found he could open the present to see inside and tell what it was. He would then put the tape back on and return the present to its original place. How brilliant. He saw a present for Shannon that couldn't be fully wrapped. He could see that it was a fire truck. "Wow! so cool, I love it". Eddy paced the living room thinking about the fire

The Empty Net

truck. It was from Santa Claus and looked great. He knew he had to have it and thought about how he could get it. He decided to take a tag off one of his presents from Santa, a pair of gloves, and put it on the fire truck. He put Shannon's tag on the gloves and made sure the presents were in the proper pile. Enjoying the spirit of the season he was able to fall back asleep quickly.

Shannon woke first and excitedly got Eddy out of bed, together they woke up their parents. The parents loved Christmas because of the joy and innocence expressed by the children. It was truly touching. Shannon got to open his presents first because he was the youngest. When he opened his second pair of gloves from Santa his mom got nervous and started whispering to the father. She couldn't understand what had happened. Had she put the wrong tags on the presents, did she forget to put all the presents out, she was becoming a wreck. Shannon was quite pleased with his new gifts and ran and gave his mom and dad a big hug and a kiss. He was a sweet boy who was appreciative of anything he was ever given. In contrast, and not wanting to wait any longer, Eddy started to rip through his gifts. He would hardly even look at them before moving onto the next one and ripping it out of its wrapping. He looked so excited when he opened the fire truck from Santa. Shannon looked a little envious because he was the one that had asked Santa for a fire truck, not Eddy. As soon as he opened it his mom came running over to the tree. She started to explain that Santa must have put the wrong name on the gift because it was actually for Shannon. "How do you know Santa was getting Shannon a fire truck, mom?" Eddy always seemed to have the answer or at least the question. "Well, I had a talk with Santa, and I just know." His mom wasn't all that convincing, but Eddy knew the score. He negotiated some terms of use for the fire truck from his mom, and then gladly carried it over and gave it to Shannon. Shannon was so happy he didn't put the toy down for a week and even slept with it for a few days. The parents looked at each other and said "thank God", a phrase they seemed to repeat fairly often. Eddy got away with his trick and was sort of sad he did. He liked the attention, even if it was negative. He thought he was creative, but didn't bother repeating the Christmas trick in the future.

Eddy had a lot of ideas, especially when it came to pulling a stunt or trick on someone else. He wasn't mean spirited even though many of his pranks were. He never intentionally would set out to hurt anyone, but he also never stopped to think first about the potential outcome. He was just interested in pulling off the prank.

One of Eddy's favourite pranks was the one he played every May on the old lady down the street, Miss Dunn. Miss Dunn was a woman of about sixty years that had never married or had family. The only thing she had was her cats and her garden. She prided herself on the championship Tulips she grew. Day and night she would be out fertilizing, watering, picking at them and talking to them. It was an odd relationship to say the least.

The growth of the tulips and their peak always seemed to coincide with the annual May 24th holiday, fire cracker day as the kids called it because there was always fireworks associated with it. Usually, there was a craft display in the park, dog and fancy bike competitions, and all sorts of games that were usually free. The day culminated with fireworks.

Miss Dunn had about thirty tulips in neat rows out in front of her house. She was on a hill so the tulips could be seen by all the neighbours. She also had about 100 tulips in the back yard, but no one ever saw them. Her back yard was huge and surrounded by trees. As he did each year at that time, Eddy got up early and went down the street to Miss Dunn's house. All was quiet in floral land. He gently placed a firecracker in each tulip along the front row. Prior to leaving the house he had carefully tied a wick to each firecracker so they could be placed about 10 inches apart from one another. He then lit the ten foot wick and watched as it slowly burned. He then got Shannon to go up to the house to ring the door bell, as he pealed across the street to hide in the bushes and watch the show. Just as Shannon was about to

The Empty Net

ring the door bell, the door opened, out came Miss. Dunn. "Hi ! Shannon, how are you?" Just as Shannon went to answer the first explosion hit. Eddy was always in awe with how far the tulip shrapnel would fly. Boom, there goes another. The wick had held and was working like a charm. Like a well rehearsed symphony orchestra, the tulips were playing their part wonderfully. Miss Dunn had started to cry by the second explosion and totally broke down by the 20th. She wasn't even on the porch to see the 30th one bite the dust. For someone that went through the same tulip misery every year, Eddy thought she would handle it much better than she did. When the noise stopped and the smoke cleared, Eddy remembered that Shannon had been busted by Miss Dunn. What would he say to her, was he safe? Eddy noticed that Shannon was comforting the old Lady. Shannon helped her back into the house and then came out and started to clean up the mess. What the hell was that all about?

By the time Eddy got home, the telephone conversation between Miss Dunn and his father was over. Eddy did not like the way the prank was unraveling. Sensing that his father was really pissed he decided to take a different tack. He wouldn't blame Shannon, like he did for everything else. He wouldn't even deny it. Instead he started crying like a school girl, "I'm sorry, I didn't mean to, I won't ever do it again." Hey this might even work. As the black two inch wide leather belt hit his backside, he figured out, it had not. "Oh, that hurts." His father didn't have to say anything to him, Eddy understood. Shannon eventually came home and he blasted Eddy, in the meek way only he could. "Well so much for that ritual", this getting older thing seemed a shame if you had to give up pranks like that. It was one of the few times that Shannon seemed genuinely upset at something Eddy had done and he told him so. Eddy pretended to be the tough guy and laugh it off, calling Shannon lots of names, but somehow, somewhere, Shannon's disgust registered with him. Despite his image and tough persona, Eddy loved Shannon and wanted his little brother to respect him and like him, but not necessarily be like him. Eddy saw Shannon before bed that night and promised he wouldn't destroy those darn tulips of Miss Dunn in the future. Shannon was pleased but not altogether convinced. After that day, Shannon started spending a lot more time at the house of Miss Dunn. He raked her leaves, cut the grass, watered the garden, helped with groceries, and basically did anything she needed. Shannon was like a bunch of United Way agencies rolled into one. The parents thought it was great and wondered why Eddy couldn't do something nice like that for someone. Eddy and Shannon had a typical yet unique relationship. Brothers get into trouble as only brothers can. Because there was less than two years age difference between them, they were able to do many things together, when Eddy allowed it of course. The brothers would get along famously for hours at a time, then with no warning, and for no cause, they would be going at each other. It would start with the whining then one might take something that belonged to the other. Within seconds, it would turn physical. Eddy would get Shannon in a head lock and start giving him head nuggies. Sometimes Shannon would get Eddy so mad that Eddy wouldn't think things out. Once after a minor dispute outside, Shannon poured a glass of juice on Eddy and sprinted to the door. Eddy was not impressed as some purple sugary stuff oozed its way down his neck and back. Luckily for Shannon it caught Eddy by surprise and he was not able to catch him before he had locked the screen door, with himself safely inside. The outside door to their house was a metal screen door, with glass on the outside and screen on the inside. When it got warm you could raise up the bottom glass and get a nice breeze through the screen. Eddy banged on the screen door yelling at Shannon to open it. Shannon knew Eddy could not get it open and became braver by the second. He got so bold as to put his face up against the glass and make faces at Eddy. Eddy could take it no longer. He hauled back with his fist and smashed that glass as hard as he could. The pain was immediate. The blood was profuse. Eddy still had a souvenir piece of glass lodged in his hand when their mom came to the front of the house to see what the noise was all about. Shannon was crying uncontrollably, the sight of all the blood on Eddy made him scared. He thought his older brother would die and it was all because of him.

The hospital was not a new experience for Eddy, both he and Shannon had been there many times before. He was usually not happy to be there, but today was different. He didn't mind the blood, in fact that was kind of cool, but the glass piece in his hand hurt and he wanted it out. The Walsh family, minus the father who was working, quickly made its way to the emerg. The triage nurse seeing all the blood and sensing something was not quite right, ushered them right into an examination room. Within minutes some old guy, smelling like rubbing alcohol, had made his appearance and was now going to make everything okay.

"Gee, that shouldn't be there", the doctor said as he pointed to the piece of glass. Mrs. Walsh looked at Eddy with that please don't say anything back look she often shot him. Eddy passing up a wonderful opportunity, nodded in agreement with the doctor and said nothing. The glass was removed and the hand and knuckles were stitched. The pain started to subside and Eddy started to think of how he was going to explain this one. He knew his mom would be okay with it, but wondered how his father would respond at having to buy a new piece of glass for the door. Of course, it wasn't like the door would be fixed immediately, it would probably stay in it's glorious state for many weeks or even months as a testament to the foolishness of Eddy and the frugalness of the Walsh family. The next day when the father woke up he spoke to Eddy and Shannon about the door incident. He was really quite surprising in that he didn't get too mad. He didn't want the boys hurting each other and gave them a speech about protecting each other and being a force against others. What a surprise. The boys acted like the door incident never happened and never spoke of it again. The father was funny that way, they never knew what to expect.

When he should have been angry, he wasn't, sometimes when he shouldn't have been angry, he was. The boys could never figure him out and after awhile gave up trying.

Not long after that incident Shannon came home from the park with a cut lip and bloody nose. Eddy was furious, "who did this to you." Shannon didn't want to escalate the problem, but finally relented and told him it was Joey Martin. He didn't exactly tell him what happened, but that was probably because he was just so upset and hyperventilating. Joey was a big kid two grades above Eddy. Eddy didn't care who the kid was. He got on his bike and rode to the park. Joey and his friends saw him coming and started to gather around and laugh. As Eddy got off his bike and started to walk towards Joey, Joey said "Hey buddy, how is your little brother?" Just as he got the word brother out, Eddy nailed him with a right jab to the nose. Joey bent over quickly. As if possessed, Eddy smashed him on the back forcing him to the ground. When he was on the ground Eddy pounced on him and started flailing away at the poor carcass of Joey Martin. After what seemed like hours, but was really only a couple of minutes, Eddy grew tired and stopped. Joey had started to throw up and Eddy didn't want any of that action. Joey's friends were silent, like statues. None of them had attempted to help Joey even though they were all older and bigger than Eddy. Eddy wondered about their loyalty and gut's as he got on his bike and rode home. It was the last time Eddy or Shannon would be challenged by those that hung out in the park.

When Eddy got home Shannon asked what happened. Eddy told him that Joey wasn't feeling well enough to talk and left it at that. Shannon would find out the truth tomorrow at school. Later that evening Shannon told Eddy what had happened. Shannon had gone to the park to see if his friends were there. They were not, just the big kids. Shannon got restless and decided to climb up on the bars that held the swings up. It was easy for a good climber to get up them, but not so easy to get down. After about twenty minutes it became obvious to everyone that Shannon was stuck. Joey offered to help. Shannon didn't know Joey, but had recognised him from school. Joey and a couple of his friends tried to reach up to help Shannon down. Shannon had leaned too far to one side and fell off. Joey sort of caught him in the air upside down. If it hadn't have been for Joey, Shannon would have landed very hard on his face and probably have broken his neck. "Yikes", why didn't you tell me that Shannon, Eddy demanded. He was really angry now and also felt a little silly because he had just left some guy half dead in the park because he had tried to help his brother and may have even saved his life.

The next day Eddy tried to approach Joey at school. Joey saw him coming a couple of times and ducked into vacant classrooms. He didn't want anything more to do with that psycho. Finally, Eddy caught up with Joey. He said in his most sincere voice how sorry he was for the misunderstanding and the beating he had inflicted on him for nothing. Eddy even offered to have Joey kick his ass, if and when he felt better. Joey thanked him but declined the generous offer. Joey was now Eddy's project and every day he did something nice to him. Eddy would bring him chocolate bars, pop, chips and all sorts of other snacks. They became sort of pals and all was forgiven.

Eddy was pleased that it ended as it had. Even though he was very happy that he had put a beating into an older and bigger schoolmate, he knew the kid didn't deserve it and so it was wrong. Although in the future Eddy would be more discreet, he was always quick to take action if someone had hurt or threatened his little brother. Eddy was now fanatical about protecting his family.

Chapter Two

Bobby Gage lived down the street from Eddy and they were best friends. They had started school together and been in the same class every year. Sure there were only two classes per grade at their school, but it still was pretty rare that two friends would always be in the same class every year. Bobby said it was fate, he being of the spiritual bent, believed in that sort of stuff. He would talk about destiny, greatness and responsibility, and Eddy would talk about random acts of destruction, getting by and total freedom. They did everything together and it was a rare day that they weren't together playing or hanging out. Bobby was just as athletic and driven as Eddy was. As an only child Bobby's parents showered him with anything he wanted. Eddy liked that because whatever was Bobby's seemed like Eddy's. Bobby didn't mind, he was spoiled and he knew it. The other big difference between the boys was that the Gage family had a little dough and so they could indulge their kid. Mr. Gage worked at a radio station in town. He sort of ran the joint and every once in awhile he would have to go on the air when a disc jockey didn't show up for work. There was also talk that he had inherited some money at some point and they used that to supplement their income. Who knew, who cared! The Gage family was always kind to Eddy and to him that was all that mattered. The two families had an open door policy. The boys went freely between both houses. Where ever they happened to be at dinner time, that is where they ate. Sometimes if they were playing late, they would just sleep at which ever house they were at.

     Eddy and Bobby loved the winter because they could play ice hockey, they also loved the summer because they could play road hockey. In the summer Eddy had a tent set up in his back yard that would remain for the whole summer. Bobby and Eddy tried to camp out at least three times a week when the weather was nice. It was neat in the tent for the two boys. The smell and feel of being outdoors, the freedom of being in charge, yet only a twenty second walk to the washroom or fridge. The parents did not check on them and so they

The Empty Net

were the masters of their domain. Not bad for young kids. Nothing was as it seemed, however, and the tent was no exception. The boys liked the tent so much because it meant that at about two in the morning they could wake up and wander the neighborhood. They would walk the streets in the area, inciting the local dogs to near riot, readjusting the location of sprinklers that were inadvertently left on all night and testing the odd door bell. It was such an invigorating experience, like a drug, they needed more and more. In the beginning wandering the streets for an hour and ringing one door bell was a huge adrenalin rush, enough to satisfy their joint craving. Then it would take four hours of wandering and trying to ring every door bell on a street. That was tough, but so rewarding. Often the police would show up in the area and the boys would flee the law by heading to the park and hiding or jumping through the friendly backyards. This was their place, their kingdom, they knew every nook and cranny, where to go, where not to go. They would never get caught, especially by some 250 pound officer of the law, on foot, not from the area. Eventually though, as with many things, the prank became lame, the rush had evaporated, and they were just tired of being tired all day. The tent then became a place of true slumber for the two adventurous home bodies. Eddy and Bobby played on two hockey teams each winter, together of course. They would play with kids their own age, as well as with a team of kids a year older than they were. Unfortunately for them, the way things worked in this town was that the older boys and the men's leagues got the indoor rinks and the younger kids got the outdoor rinks. Playing indoors was like a right of passage reserved for those that had endured y ears of freezing outdoors.

    At times Eddy actually dreaded having to play on those outdoor freezers. It would get so cold on the ice, with the freezing wind blowing, and no protection from the elements, sometimes Eddy would cry. When a players shift was over they would skate to the unprotected bench and freeze a little more. Only the parents stayed warm. They had a glassed in area where the change rooms were located at the end of the rink. It wasn't the greatest place to see the game, but it was a warm, popular spot.

Conditions on the ice could change drastically during a game. On occasion a forward would be on breakaway and either get blown over by the wind or the puck would disappear in some snow piling up on the ice. The ice was so hard you only had to get your skates sharpened once all year. Once Eddy and Bobby went to their rink on a day the big boys were practicing there because the indoor rinks were booked. After about twenty minutes pucks began to break in half. Guys would shoot them against the boards and they would break apart because of the cold. The goalies must have had fun as there was rubber flying in every direction. Eventually the coach restricted them to wrist shots because of all the broken pucks, then when that didn't work, just had them skate.

Even when the player bundled up and wore ear muffs and a hat outside of their helmet it would still be cold. Sometimes kids had so much warming paraphernalia on their head you could hardly tell if they were wearing a helmet or not. The younger kids dreamed about getting older just to play inside. To tease them and keep them motivated the younger kids would play two play-off games in the indoor rinks every year. It was like Heaven. The warm dressing rooms, walking on a rubber mat to the ice and then the look, feel and even the smell of the indoor ice. It was incredible. It was like playing in the N.H.L. No freezing wind to contend with, no snow pockets on the ice, it was truly amazing and almost made playing outdoors worth it. If freezing for a few months was what it took to get to play indoors, Eddy could do it.

It was a cool day that April morning with the locals complaining and the weatherman moaning. The local kids couldn't have cared less. Ball hockey ruled and they would play in cold, heat, rain, snow, anything. When the mailman was stuck inside because of the weather, they were out playing ball hockey.

Pass the ball Gage. Bang, another perfect pass and it's top shelf. Walsh from Gage, something the Ludstone Drive street kids heard over and over. Somehow the two pals always ended up on the same team. They would perform like a pair of synchronized swimmers, always knowing where the other one was and what they were going to do.

What could be better than two best buddies, Eddy Walsh and Bobby Gage killing the day playing the game they loved. Inseparable almost from birth, they dreamed about playing together in the N.H.L. someday, and together they would put in the time and effort to make it happen.

Hockey cards were the local neighborhood passport. Every kid had hockey cards and would bring them out and play, show or trade them whenever the opportunity would arise. The favourite games were "knock down" and "farthies". With "knock down" a kid would line up five or six cards against a wall so that the cards were standing up on an angle. From about six feet away, anyone that wants to chance it can fling a card towards the wall. If they knock down the card then they keep it, if they miss or the card doesn't fall, then they lose it. It was kind of a sucker's game, the key was to be the kid that had their cards against the wall. They would win three to one on a regular basis. Little kids would almost never be that kid, unless they were playing with kids even smaller than they were. Usually, it was the biggest kid that had the honour, but there was some rotation. It was a great way to build up your card collection. "Farthies was more balanced in terms of who could win. There was no "house" in that game. Any number of kids could play. Whoever got their card closest to the wall won all the cards. Eddy loved playing both games because he won no matter what. He would practice flicking cards in class, getting them to land perfectly on someone else's desk. He was also able to build up his collection through trades. Because he hated the leafs, and every other kid loved the leafs, he would trade his leaf cards for three or four other cards. He had every player on every team, except the leafs. He would get stuck with them when he won games or bought new packs, but he would never trade for them. Eddy had such a big collection of hockey cards that he kept it in two shoe boxes. He would only carry sixty or seventy cards with him at a time. They were the duds that he didn't mind losing. No one really knows when it happened, but at some point growing up, hockey cards became yesterday's news. Cards magically disappeared, ending up, who knows where? Any one that was fortunate to keep their cards may have ended up with a valuable collection as they became the rage of collector's many years later. Eddy had no idea where his cards went, but suspected that his mom got sick of seeing them in his closet month after month, unused and eventually threw them out.

As carefree kids, the day to day goings on of the world were of little relevance to the ball hockey players of the Ludstone area. The only thing that effected them was a ball going down the sewer opening or a slow moving car that interrupted their game. That really pissed them off. When a car came into sight someone would yell "car". Like ants at a picnic, the players would scramble to the side of the road, and the goalies would drag the nets as far as they could to get them out of the way. Instinctively, when the car past, the process would reverse. Someone would yell "game on" and the action would resume. Sunday's were the worst day of the week for being interrupted with cars everywhere. Why did big people drive so slow on Sunday's, the kids all thought. "There is lot's of room, you are not going to hit me, keep driving you wanker." In the winter it was so fun to shoot a block of ice or some snow at the stupid humans driving by in their fancy cars. The funny looks they gave the players in their rear view mirrors, as if they had been violated. Usually, games would start at 8:00 in the morning and last until 6:00 or 7:00 at night depending on the light and the parents. Players would come and go throughout the day, with nothing ever being said. People knew, somehow, which team they were on. Everybody knew each other well enough that teams were easy to pick. It was like magic, except for a couple of players that no one wanted, or if no one was in the mood to play goal that day. The two or three players no one wanted were usually younger and related

The Empty Net

to another player. They would go home crying, and a few minutes later their mom would be yelling from the porch for their other son to come home for a minute. Everyone knew the score and the drill was always the same, so after awhile you just let the kid play, besides they came in handy when the ball would fly past the net and down the street. Someone had to get it. Ball hockey was a common sight on the street, winter, fall, summer and spring. Even when they played ice hockey in the winter they would still save some time for ball hockey.

In the cold months the orange hard plastic ball would be like a rock. With only a baseball glove, some small shin pads and a goalie stick, it was often difficult to get some sucker to play goal. On days were they were absolutely desperate they would invite Gerry to play. "Mr. Walsh, would you like to teach us how to play?" How could he refuse, after all he had played a couple of games of semi-pro, so he was as close to a former N.H.L. player as this neighborhood had seen. Eddy, his brother Shannon and Bobby weren't thrilled with dad the goalie, but it did beat shooting on a net with a sweater hanging down. Gerry was always on the kids to play tough and to play through any pain they had. His favourite line was "walk it off." It didn't matter if it was a bruise, a cut, or a dislocation, walking it off was the cure-all. There was not a lot of equipment required for ball hockey. Basically, a pair of hockey gloves, or as most kids got by with, a pair of winter mitts, and a plastic blade stick. The kids would drive their mother's crazy by using the stove to warp their plastic blades. It was a fairly easy process. Cut the broken blade off the stick, attach the plastic blade and screw it on, heat up the blade and put a nice warp into it. Eddy had a warp that made the stick look like a boomerang. No stick measurements on this street. Forget the backhand, it was impossible, but the speed and movement you could get on a slap shot defied the laws of nature. A few of the cool kids refused to use plastic blades, preferring old wooden game used sticks instead. They would get the blade so worn down that it would be less than two inches high. Whoever said size didn't matter had never seen one of these gems. Those worn down sticks with a two inch blade could make remarkable shots. The problem was, you couldn't take a wrist shot or back hand with them, they were simply made for the slap shot. It was also hard to pass with them, so guys on the team didn't like seeing them on their side.

Eddy was on the street shooting at the net when his dad came out to play. "Warm me up" the old man yelled at Eddy. "Let's see if you can shoot". Eddy fired a couple of shots toward the net. "You shoot like a girl" he heard. "Oh! good". Eddy was so pissed because by now all the street was out ready to play. He didn't like being embarrassed, especially by his old man. "Move closer if you have to." Eddy stepped on his blade, as though somehow changing the curve would magically make the difference. Maybe he was really trying to break the blade so he wouldn't have to continue to be humiliated. "Hurry up" the kids were getting restless. Eddy got the ball, faked a slap shot and then let go a snap shot. It was as if life was in slow motion, the ball speeding towards the father's groin area, the loud noise he had never heard his father make before, the wet patch on the front of his father's pants.

Until that day he had never heard his father swear, was his dad just making up for lost time or had Eddy really hurt him. Hearing the vulgarity from inside the house, Eddy's mom came out to help walk the old man back into the house. As he stumbled up the porch, a faint voice was heard to say "walk it off". As Gerry the goalie went into the house the kids went crazy with laughter. Eddy could only laugh a little. Would his dad be mad at him, would he be pleased that he had improved his shot, who knew. Eddy ran into the house to see what was happening. His dad was lying down groaning and looking a bit pale. "Nice save dad." The groans were somewhat louder and sounded like words, but not words Eddy understood. "Eddy, I think you should play outside with your friends and leave your father to rest", his mom suggested wisely.

Eddy wouldn't know for several more years what it was like to stop a blast to the "rocks", but he instinctively knew it wasn't a good

The Empty Net

thing. It was hard to get a goalie for a couple of weeks after that incident, but eventually things returned to normal and goalies were once again plentiful, although Gerry never played goal for them again. No one could remember after the incident ever hearing "walk it off" or "play tough" again either. Growing up together Bobby and Eddy played on the same team for five years and looked forward to, and talked about playing together for ever. But as they got older Bobby developed into a premier puck handler with enormous offensive skills. Eddy had developed into a good defenceman, but was not the player that Bobby was. The two never really talked about it or compared themselves with one another. They each played a different position, so comparisons were silly. People were talking about Bobby as a can't miss prospect since he was 12 years old. Two things happened that year to change everything. In a practice one day during a line rush drill, Bobby came down the right side and in the high slot cut to his left so he could get a good shot on net. Bobby had toyed with Eddy and the goalie all practice and Eddy had seen enough. In frustration, as Bobby blew around him again Eddy swung his stick and chopped Bobby down. Bobby wasn't known as a screamer, until that day. Any one in or even near the rink knew something was wrong with somebody. Bobby's new elbow pads couldn't hide the fact that his right arm seemed to be in two parts now. The blood soaked sweater confirmed there was a problem Eddy was greeted with a "fuck you" when he entered Bobby's hospital room. He didn't know if Bobby was kidding or if he was really mad. When a can of pop sailed next to Eddy's head, he figured it out. Bobby was indeed pissed at him. Rather than make things worse Eddy left. He thought he heard Bobby's mom give him a fuck you on the way out. He was surprised by her mouth, but Eddy didn't think it was wise to stick around and discuss it.

Bobby was out for the season, eventually the cast was taken off and after two surgeries the pins were removed from his arm as well. Bobby and Eddy didn't talk the rest of the year. No more sleep overs, no more watching games together or playing Nintendo. Whatever friendship they had was done.

    Eddy felt sick about it. He would cry at night when he thought he was alone. His mom knew something was wrong, but Eddy wouldn't talk about it. After a week of not seeing Bobby in their fridge, Eddy's mom knew what the problem was. Without Eddy knowing she called Mrs. Gage and spoke to her for about two hours. The two mother's saw each other often, but didn't share the same friendship that their children did. There were certainly times when they all got together and there was no problems between them, they were just different people with different friends.

    Eddy's mom was shocked to hear what had happened. She had heard that Bobby hurt himself, but she didn't know it was her Eddy who did the hurting. Eddy's mom convinced Mrs. Gage that the boys were like brother's and their relationship shouldn't come to end like this. Reluctantly, Mrs. Gage invited Eddy to come over and play with Bobby that evening. Eddy arrived at the Gage house at about 5:30 p.m. and could feel the tension in the air. He said hi! to Mrs. Gage, with no mention or apology for the "fuck you" and met Bobby on the basement steps. They nodded at one another and went downstairs. They didn't say anything for about twenty minutes. "I'm sorry Bobby, I didn't mean to hurt you." "You broke your stick on my arm, butt breath, what the hell did you think would happen?" The banter went back and forth deteriorating by the minute. "You were just pissed because I'm twice as good as you and you got sick of me flying past you all the time ," Bobby said with that mean, pointed tone that couldn't be mistaken. So it was out, someone had dared to make the talent comparison. Eddy called Bobby a wuss and said he hoped his arm fell off. The two exchanged "fuck you's" as they headed up the stairs, and as he left Eddy thought he heard a faint "fuck you" from Mrs. Gage. "What's wrong with that dame" Eddy thought, always with the bad language. As he walked home, Eddy was angry, then happy, then he ran into his

The Empty Net

room where he cried the rest of the night. His mother and father and even Shannon left him alone until the next day. At breakfast Eddy advised that Bobby would not be coming around anymore and that they were no longer friends.

Eddy's mom was sad and started to cry as she sprinted from the kitchen. It was the end of an era. Her little boy's first buddy, his blood brother and now they were enemies. Mrs. Walsh was angry at Mrs. Gage for not doing more to help the situation. She hated to see her Eddy get hurt. Eddy and Bobby were never civil to each again. The life they had was over, things would be different from now on.

At first Eddy was lost, just moping around the house, not really knowing what to do. He seemed to have a lot of free time on his hands now. As days turned into weeks and then months, the sting of the Gage incident diminished. Eddy started to get on with his life, but he vowed to never allow himself to open up to someone again, as he done with Bobby. As Eddy grew older he never did forget that hurt, and promised himself that he would never open up to anyone again.

In June when they moved to Toronto so Bobby's dad could work for a big television station, their fate was sealed. As time passed Eddy forgot about Bobby, or at least he didn't think about him every day. Whenever someone would knock on Eddy's door to get a hockey game going, he could not help but think about Bobby.

Chapter Three

As Eddy and his friends moved up the academic ladder to grade seven, and then grade eight, their interests became diverse and their behaviour became less predictable. They were all getting older, more mature. Gone were the long days lost in sports. The old gang seemed to be less cohesive and their numbers had dwindled. Some had moved away, some had learned to read and write and now put school on a pedestal. Eddy would get so frustrated trying to get a good ball hockey game going now. He would knock on door after door and find few takers. Most of the time he was reduced to shooting balls into an empty net on his driveway. If the condition of the garage door was any indication, Eddy was not a sniper. He would play for awhile and then quit and just sit around dreaming of days long past.

In the evenings, if the weather was nice, some of the kids would ride over to the ice cream shop and just hang out. Most of his grade eight classmates now smoked and many had boyfriends or girlfriends. Eddy wasn't quite ready for that yet, but had tried the odd cigarette. It was getting dark on a Saturday evening when Eddy gave up on the idea of getting anyone to play hockey with him so he decided to walk down to the school to hang out. There were already about twenty kids there when he arrived. Some were in his class, some were older and a couple of others he didn't know. One of the older kids he didn't know offered him a smoke. Not wanting to feel like a jerk he accepted it, acting like he had accepted hundreds before. That first drag was earth shattering. He felt shaky, sick, plugged, sad, remorseful and dizzy all at once. The second drag was less dramatic. The third felt good and by the fourth he figured he was hooked. He finished the smoke and butted it out on the side of the school building. The other kids looked at him like he was cool and more importantly one of them, whatever that meant. Some of the other kids choked or coughed, one kid threw up. Obviously not regular smokers. The crowd mocked them in the "crowd" way, and lowly the rejects slipped into the night. Before

The Empty Net

the night was over Eddy had mooched about four other smokes. He liked the sensation and the peer approval didn't hurt either. When Eddy got home, he passed his father in the hallway. He had forgotten where he was and what he had been doing. "Where the hell where you?" Eddy was startled, "what do you mean?" "You know damn well what I mean, why were you smoking?" Eddy was anxious but wanted to stand his ground, after all, he was basically an adult now and could do what he wanted. "Some kids were down at the school and they gave me a smoke, I had never tried them before and wanted to see what it was like". That sounded very reasonable, Eddy thought. "You stupid moron, with every thing you know about smoking, you would be stupid just to even try it, did you like it?" "Ah! the million dollar question." "Yah! It wasn't too bad". Mr. Walsh was not impressed. "Fine, fine, you want to be the big shot, 13 year old Mr. Cool guy. Okay Mr. Cool, lets go outside for a minute. Wait for me on the porch".

Eddy had no idea what the father was up to now. Was he going to wrestle with him on the front porch? Was he in Eddy's room now packing up all his stuff. The suspense was excruciating. Finally, the father arrived on the porch with something in his hand. "Try these". His father passed him a small cigar with a white tip on the end of it. He told Eddy to put it in his mouth as he lit it. "Take some puffs on this", the father said sternly. He hovered over Eddy with a certain knowing smirk on his face as Eddy puffed away on the little cigar. It may have been the rum flavouring, it may have been the wine dipping, but these little "cubans" were special. He finished the first one in about five minutes and asked the father for another one. Eddy hadn't seen his father that angry in many years, not since he took that shot in the rocks, pretending to be a goalie, so many years ago. "No more allowance for you boy, it is cancelled immediately." "Don't think I'm going to work hard just to pay for you to smoke." "Are you going to drop out of school as well" the father demanded. "What the hell does that have to do with anything?" Eddy demanded back. "Don't let your mother find out that you are a chimney, and keep the damn things away from your brother." The best intentions of Mr. Walsh were a bust, and went up in smoke. He wanted to show Eddy that smoking was really stupid, but didn't know how to get through to him.

Within a few days Eddy realized that smoking cigarettes was stupid. They weren't for him. Not as long as those little "cubans" were available. He was smart and didn't want to spend money for both. From then on he only smoked the cigars. They were more money than the regular smokes, but they were worth it. Eddy never gave any cigars to anyone else. He developed a new aversion to the "bumming" process. Besides they were too expensive and after all, Eddy was a Walsh. Eddy became known as the cool cigar smoker guy. It was a pretty good bet that he was the only one in grade eight that smoked cigars. Eddy loved the smoking culture. He carried a lighter that had that strong lighter fluid smell to it. It had a cowboy scene painted on the metal and fit nicely in his jeans. He loved pulling it out, flicking it on his leg to open the metal lid and then flicking it back to spark the flint and get it going. He would practice the motion trying to get faster and faster at it. The local kid's, smoker's and non smoker's, were equally impressed. Eddy would use his jeans as an ash tray when needed and kept his cigars under his ball cap or in his sleeve.

The peer groups and social structure of Eddy's world began to change rapidly. There was now a gang or group of guys that was no longer based on how good they were at sports. Jocks didn't seem to hang out together anymore or dominate the school yard. The new cool groups were mostly guys that had longer hair, smoked and had all the latest music. They wore funny, baggy clothing and liked to hang with their girlfriends and talk. The world was changing and it was hard for Eddy to change with it. There were no rules, no signposts, no one knew what was expected or what to do, how to act.

As if the physical changes weren't hard enough, now Eddy and his friends had to deal with the cultural changes that were taking place around them. Sure it was great to have new freedoms and that sense of coming into your own, but it was a huge trade off. The carefree times

The Empty Net

of youth were passing, painfully, for ever. No more could Eddy go to the park and lie on the grass all day doing nothing. It was physically possible, but not the new reality. The bike rides, innocent games, horseplay and frivolity were now replaced with a new, less innocent type of frivolity.

The grade eight class was excited as the night of their first real dance came closer. This was not going to be some strange event held at the school gym, during the day, with the lights left on. No this was at a rented hall, with a couple of chaperones, but not too many, no lights and lots of mood. Eddy like most of his class were going stag. Eddy wasn't sure what to wear and wished that Bobby and he were still friends so he could talk to him. Bobby was always the snazzy dresser and the one that Eddy relied on for fashion advice, such that it was. But that was wishful thinking and had all been ended with a wild swing of Eddy's stick and solidified with Bobby's move to Toronto. Eddy finally decided to wear jeans and a red lumber jack shirt. He swiped some of the father's cologne for good luck, and thought he was pretty hot stuff. Shannon gave him that confidence booster only a brother could, "have fun you fag."Great, Eddy couldn't wait for Shannon to go through the same experience so he could be just as helpful. There was quite a mob gathered out front when Eddy arrived. Some of the kids he didn't even recognize. Some of the guys were in suits and some of the young ladies were in dresses. Of course some were dressed in jeans and looked like bums, sort of like him. It was interesting to see how different some of the kids looked compared to inside the classroom, and how differently they acted.

Eddy slapped down his $ 5.00 and made his way into the hall with some of his friends. It was pretty cool. It smelt really good as the mixture of perfumes and colognes, both expensive and cheap, permeated the hall. Eddy stood against the wall with most of the other guys at the dance. Just like in their ball hockey days, teams seemed to be magically forming. All the guys on one side of the hall and all of

The Empty Net

the young ladies on the other side of the hall. There didn't seem to be much movement between the two camps. Each side unsure of the other and not wanting to make the first move.

Eventually, some girls, brave girls, went to the centre of the dance floor and started to dance with each other. Hey that was alright, Eddy thought. Before too long some guys had joined the ladies on the dance floor and were strutting their stuff. Eddy knew hockey, Eddy knew sports, Eddy didn't know dancing. There was no one to teach him, no shows to learn from. Evidently he was not alone. He couldn't believe what some of the kids were doing on the dance floor. By the time 11:00 p.m. rolled around, no one really cared, anything seemed to go and no one knew what they were doing, nor did they care about what the others were doing.

Eddy was approached by Susan Green, a girl in his class. He never really gave her much thought in school, but here, with the lighting, the mood music, her short dress, revealing blouse and manicured hair, she looked good. She had long blonde hair, blue eyes and wore glasses. Her glasses were not flattering, but when she wore her contact lenses she was pretty hot. Susan had a nice developed body and looked much older than her thirteen years. She asked Eddy to dance. He said sure and then took his time as the fast dance music came to an end. He really wanted a slow dance and as fate would have it the next song was slow, very slow. He wrapped his arms around Susan and the two soon became one on the dance floor. He didn't know exactly what to do, so he ran his hand down her back and slowly onto her bum. He squeezed her bum and she didn't seem to mind. It felt good so he continued as long as he could. He would have kept going but he was too conscious of the sensation coming from his pants. "Shit" this was no time to make "wood" and not being too modest, it was obviously noticeable. Susan just pulled him in closer and didn't seem to mind. Eddy was falling in love. He suggested that they go outside and Susan readily agreed. They went out to the back of the hall, behind the parking lot. They found a fence that they could lean against. He pulled her closer and they started to kiss. Oops, he still had gum in his mouth. He spit it out and they continued. Neither knew what to do, but it seemed to come natural. After kissing for about twenty minutes, Eddy put his hand on Susan's breast, she moaned. He must have fumbled for ten minutes trying to undo her top and bra. He didn't want to get stopped so he took his time. If this had been a hockey game he would have gotten a couple of delay of game penalties. Finally, he had arrived. He couldn't believe how soft and firm her breasts felt. Her nipples quickly got bigger and this intrigued him even more. By now the two love birds were lying on top of one another. They continued to move and kiss as Eddy groped her breasts.

Without warning it happened. She must have rubbed up against him one too many times. His shorts were full and already things were feeling sticky. How could it have happened, he thought. After the eruption he stopped kissing her and put his hands down. "Why are you stopping?" "Did I do something wrong?" Susan didn't understand. Eddy said he had to be home by midnight and should be getting home. Susan told him he could have a ride because her father was coming to pick her up. Eddy sheepishly declined and with no further explanation he raced to get home. Susan didn't understand, but then again neither did Eddy. Eddy got home and cleaned up. The next morning he phoned Susan and talked to her for four hours on the phone. They talked about everything and nothing. Half of their conversation was silence, but they heard each other loud and clear. They started to call each other everyday, sometimes three or four times a day. Eddy had his first girlfriend. It would be official when he met her parents and she met his. He had told his mom about Susan, but not his father. His mom was supportive but seemed a little sad for some reason that Eddy couldn't understand.

The only sex advice that Eddy had ever received from his father was something about staying away from them all or they would end up killing you slowly. Eddy assumed that it was great advice that had probably been passed down from generation to generation, but he didn't know what the hell it meant. He just assumed it would all make sense at the appropriate time. Oddly, it never did.

Eddy and Susan spent the rest of grade eight together. They did everything together, much to the disappointment of Eddy's other friends. They kept experimenting with the sex thing, and Eddy got better about not soiling himself. They didn't go all the way though, that could wait. Susan helped Eddy with his homework and settled him down in class. He was like a new Eddy. He didn't do much concrete for Susan, but she loved being around him and that was enough. Susan was a very mature, classy and intelligent young lady. Anyone that met her could tell that she had that certain refinement that only the well heeled can produce. She knew how to act in public and spoke like a college graduate. She wanted to be a teacher so that she could help others. She had a secret dream of opening her own school somewhere in a poor region, perhaps teaching the poor the secrets of the rich. She wasn't contemplating anything extreme like a school in the jungles of Guam, just a simple set up in a poor district. She was restless and wanted to do something important. Eddy was happy about that because he didn't think they played hockey in Guam. She a had a love for humanity that had been acquired from her family. The graduation was a blur for Eddy and Susan. They could only see and hear each other. Their parents liked it, especially Eddy's. Gerry was so pleased that the boy had gotten grade eight under his belt. After the graduation, the couple skipped the grad dance to be with each other. Little did they know that Mr. Green had invited the Walsh family over to their house so they could get to know each other.

Susan's father was a well to do lawyer, quite a contrast to Mr. Walsh. The Green house was huge, fully furnished and paid for. Clearly it was on the other side of the tracks from the Walsh family. James Green and Gerry Walsh did not exactly hit it off. No matter, they sat and drank while watching the football game on the coloured television. That is the great thing about being a guy Eddy thought, you can bond with any guy just by saying nothing. No matter how opposite

The Empty Net

and different as long as there is a television, sports, dames or booze, guys have it made.

The ladies were so much different. Mary Green and Kathy Walsh got along famously. They went into the kitchen and sat for hours talking, with no booze in sight. Eddy didn't know what the deal was, but was glad that they were getting along. Eddy and Susan made their way between both groups and eventually disappeared to the basement. They played pool, watched t.v. and made out. Life was good. The Green family had known affluence for many generations. They were the type of the family that could tell you what the great, great, great grandfather had done, and who he had done it with. Eddy hardly knew what his father did, let alone the father's grandfather. They wore inherited jewellery and hung pictures of previous generations throughout their impeccably maintained homes. Their well manicured lawn was perfect and kept moist with the built in sprinkler system. The gardener didn't hurt, but really wasn't all that necessary. He was simply there as a symbol of the power, position and opulence of the Green family, serving no real purpose.

When the couple finally made their way upstairs all four parents were now ensconced in the living room and were talking. They were talking about high school and hockey. There were two high schools in town, the public one and the Catholic one. Eddy assumed he would go to the local public high school because it was closer to his house. Mrs. Green disclosed that Susan would be going to the Catholic high school, because they thought it was better and because it was closer to their house. Eddy hadn't even given high school any thought, especially which one he would go to. Sure he went to a Catholic grade school, but what did that mean anyway. All of a sudden Eddy had to start to start thinking seriously. They had to enroll in the high school of their choice within the next week. Eddy couldn't stand the thought of not going to school with Susan, and he knew that the Catholic school had the better hockey team. When Mrs. Green spoke of getting Susan fitted for her kilt, his decision was made. "I'm going to the Catholic school too", Eddy proudly stated. His father was surprised, his mom

The Empty Net

was pleased and Susan just gave him a big hug. Later he thought about taking the bus every day and wearing a uniform, but figured it was only for four or five years so he could do it. Eddy talked to his buddies and most were going to go the local high school because of the distance. Eddy regretted their choices but remained firm in his resolve. Only in time would Eddy recognize how good a choice he made that day. His life would have been so different, so unimaginable had he just gone to the local high school.

    The last day of grade eight was a sad one for Eddy and his friends. There was a lot of hugging, kissing and crying. People were signing people's year books, putting in their phone numbers and promising to keep in touch with each other. Even before the ink was dry, Eddy doubted if anyone would really keep in touch. Some of the people he hadn't spoken to in eight years, why would they start to call now? It didn't matter, it was comforting in the thought that others cared, or at least could pretend they did. Eddy was scared but really looked forward to moving on to high school. It was time to take the next step.

    Some of the kids in Eddy's grad class were going to be working in the summer. Eddy thought he could wait at least another couple of years and since his parents didn't push him to be cheap child labour, he decided to enjoy the freedom while he could. The only thing that bothered him was now some of his friends were not around during the day, or when they were around they had lots of money to spend. Eddy was jealous of the money but not of the working part of the equation. As his friends were buying new bikes and other neat things, he would tell them how much working sucked.

    His message never sunk in with them, but Eddy insisted on trying to enlighten them anyway. Shannon was much more practical when it came to money than Eddy was. Despite his younger age and limited experience he understood that it cost money to buy things, and he understood that he liked to buy things. After consulting with his mother, Shannon decided to get a paper route. He had heard that one

The Empty Net

of the older kids in his school, probably in Eddy's class, was getting rid of his paper route and that it was for sale. Shannon met with the fellow and arranged a fair price, they then contacted the newspaper and advised them of the change.

    It was technically illegal for the paper boy to sell his route, it didn't belong to him, it belonged to the newspaper. But for as long as anyone could remember that is how things worked. Shannon got his buggy and newspaper bag and was all set. He was smarter than the bigger, and obviously dumber paper boy because he arranged the turnover to be on the weekend that collections had to be made. That meant that Shannon would be collecting for papers he hadn't delivered, which was fine, most of it went t o t he newspaper any ways, but he would get all the tips for doing nothing. The tips was where the real money was. Shannon got off to a good start. His route paid for itself within the first month. Capitalism was a great thing. Sometimes Eddy would help with the papers, of course he would always be handsomely rewarded for his efforts. Usually it was when Shannon was sick or involved in something at the school that he needed the help of his big brother. The fees charged by Eddy to help him out were excessive, or "extortion" as Shannon called them, so he didn't ask too often. Shannon did other things too like collecting pop and beer bottles for the deposit money, running lemonade stands and various other kid businesses. Anything for money, if it wasn't too bad he would do it. Eddy was the opposite, he liked the money but not the effort in earning it.

Chapter Four

During the summer before grade nine, Eddy had pretty much the same routine. He would get up at around 11:00 a.m. have lunch, talk to Susan on the phone for about an hour, then go to the gym to work out. He would work out for about two hours, alternating between the bike, the upper body and the lower body. His main focus was to build his upper body so that he would be stronger on the puck.

Most of the guys at the gym were older than Eddy, some were unemployed men, some were men from the mill. Eddy wondered why some guy in his fifties would pretend to be something he wasn't and spend the day in the gym. Sometimes the older guys would give Eddy a hard time about using the equipment or why he was there, but they weren't too bad and most liked the cocky kid.

Eddy was working the bench press when some roid monkey started to give him a hard time. This guy, Bones, was about six feet three inches tall, had mostly no hair, eyes that were bulging out of his head, and arms that didn't quit. "Get the fuck off the machine dufus." Eddy was scared and didn't know what to do. He pretended not to hear him. "Hey dipshit, I told you to get off the machine". Eddy could pretend no longer. "Fuck off and wait your turn you meatball", Eddy could hardly believe the words coming out of his mouth.

It happened so fast Eddy didn't know what was happening. Bones had grabbed him by the throat and smashed him about six times in the face before Eddy lost consciousness.

Eddy remembered waking up in the hospital with his mom there. How did his mom get there? Was it all a dream? Eddy looked in the mirror and knew it wasn't a dream. His nose was broken and his face was badly bruised but there were no serious injuries. It was a novel experience for Eddy as it was the first time he had been really pummeled.

Bones had been arrested at the gym after getting stomped by some of the muscle heads who did not agree with how he treated the

The Empty Net

young hockey player. When the police arrived to arrest Bones they laughed when they saw him. Bones was no stranger to the police and was on a first name basis with most of them.

Susan started to cry when she saw Eddy come to her door. "Oh my God, what happened to you". Eddy explained what had happened. She sort of got mad at him. She suggested that he should have just gotten off the weight machine and given it to the guy. Eddy hadn't even considered that. He wasn't going let anyone push him around, despite the odds. If you start to give in, when does it stop?

When Mr. Green came up the stairs and heard what had happened, and saw Eddy's face, he suggested to Eddy that a lawsuit may be in order. Mr. Green said Eddy could sue the club for not having better security and Bones for the actual assault. Mr. Green thought he might get about $ 20,000.00, mostly from the gym. Eddy didn't know if that meant his share or what Mr. Green would get. He was less certain of getting anything out of Bones. It had to do with who provoked whom, if there were witnesses that would come forward and then it would really depend on if Bones had any money or not. It could be expensive to move the case forward and could take several years. But as Mr. Green stated and everyone present agreed, justice should be done.

Gerry Walsh thought the lawsuit idea was the best idea he had heard in a long time. How fortunate that his boy got pummeled in a place that may be responsible. Gerry could taste the dollars. At dinner that night Gerry talked about how they could use the money. All of the sudden the money acquired a communal flavour to it. Gerry was clearly getting too excited so Eddy calmly announced that there would be no lawsuit. He didn't believe that was the way to go and he would deal with it his way. After all it was him that was going through the pain. Gerry could not finish dinner, he felt weazy.

The police came over to the house for another statement and to take some pictures of Eddy's face. They told him that Bones had just gotten out of jail, had a lot of prior convictions, and would be going back to jail after this trial, if convicted. Eddy thought long and hard before he made the short trip to the other side of town. The house at the end of the lane was a shit hole. There were a few busted up cars in the driveway, a couple of motorcycles towards the garage and garbage all over the lawn. If there was a Mrs. Bones, she was not a good housekeeper. There was no bell to ring so Eddy just sort of banged on the door.

"You took a chance coming here, maybe I should just finish you off and claim you were trespassing". "Maybe you should shut the fuck up and listen to me". As Eddy spoke he thought here we go again. Instead, Bones said "I'm really sorry kid, I was juiced up on steroids and I had no idea how old you are". "You are a really big kid." Eddy sensed a turn for the better. They exchanged chit chat for a minute or two before Eddy got up the nerve. "Sir, I think we should settle this matter here and now, I don't think you want to go back to jail, and I don't know that I want to wait five years to complete a law suit. "Cut to the chase kid". "Fine, fine, whatever you say, I want four grand cash and one of those motorcycles over there." "Are you nuts kid, those are Harley's and worth a lot of money, besides you probably couldn't even drive one." "How much time do you think you will get to drive them in jail, besides you will teach me." After some more back and forth posturing, Bones finally relented, "one of the bikes and two grand cash, that's it". "Done" said Eddy as they shuck hands. Eddy was ready to shit himself. What had he just done. He wasn't even old enough to drive yet, let alone an 1100 c.c. Harley Davidson. Bones went into the house and came back with the two grand cash and signed over the motorcycle ownership. Their business complete, they said goodbye to one another. Bones was clearly impressed by the young kid and his nerve. He thought Eddy was tough, street smart, and he certainly knew how to hustle.

Eddy didn't realize how heavy the bike was until he tried to get it home. How would he get the thing home, it was so heavy. Oh! well, Eddy thought that was probably the least of his problems. He would treat it like an intense workout and do his best until he had nothing left to give. He tried every which way to get the thing moving. He sat on the seat and tried to push with both legs, only problem was they hardly touched the ground. He got on one side, with his knee on the bike and pushed with the other leg, not bad. Finally, he simply held on to the handlebars and pushed it beside him. As he arrived at his house drenched in his own sweat, Shannon came running out. "What the hell is that?' "That is my new ride" Eddy said proudly. "You are so dead when the ancestors see that". Shannon was probably right, but Eddy really had not given that a whole lot of thought. Eddy put the bike to the side of the house and got some stuff to clean it up. It was the most beautiful thing he had ever seen. The chrome and vivid colours, the naked virgin painted on the gas tank. The sound the engine made was unlike anything he had ever heard. It was so great to own a hog, even if he couldn't drive it yet. Eddy's father finally arrived home. "What the hell is that" he said. "That is my new bike, I told you I needed one, but you said we couldn't afford one, so I got one myself." "Ha, ha, smart guy, who's is it, and where did it come from." Eddy leveled with the old man. I went to see Bones and made a deal with him for the pain and suffering. "He gave me $ 1,000.00 and the motorcycle." The father was kind of impressed. He knew the bike was worth at least ten grand and to get a grand in cash as well, not bad. The father had to be the father though and told Eddy that the money should go in the bank and the bike should be sold. "I will put $ 900.00 into the bank and the bike we will put on blocks until I get my licence." The father reluctantly agreed. Eddy could hardly believe it. He thought his dad would go crazy and make him take it back. He would have told him it was actually two grand if he knew he would respond this as he did. His mother was more concerned with the bike than anything else. She made Eddy promise that he would never ride it, at least until he had his licence and went to some training course for motorcycles.

    Eddy agreed, like there was some alternative and they all went out to look at the bike. They had to admit it was pretty nice looking. Just like the bikes in the movies, except they were always driven by the bad guys. Eddy's father built a nice wooden shed in the back yard to store the bike in. They went together to a garage and learned how to

The Empty Net

properly store it and look after it. Eddy was very pleased. Shannon was very jealous, but in his usual way, didn't say anything. The father treated the bike like it was his own.

Eddy contacted the police the next morning to tell them that he had changed his mind and did not want to testify at the trial of Bones. The cops were perturbed, to say the least, about this new turn of events. "You will testify, Eddy, make no mistake about that," the cop barked at him. "No officer, I will not testify, be clear on that, and if I'm forced to do so then I will tell the Judge that it was my fault for starting the trouble." "You little bastard, get out of here". Eddy then went to the fitness club and had a good chat with the manager. Eddy told him that his lawyer, Mr. Green, had suggested that Eddy could get at least $ 30,000.00 out of the club, maybe more. But Eddy really liked the club and the guys in it and didn't want to see it come under financial strain. Eddy said he loved working out there and would like to keep working out there in the future. He mentioned the money a couple of more times, before the Manager interrupted with a suggestion, "how about a life time membership for free?" "That sounds good, but do you think I should talk to my lawyer first?" said Eddy. "I don't think there is any reason to do that, how about I throw in a permanent locker for you, and five hundred cash." Eddy was starting to like this little game. "I hate to come alone, could you throw in five one year memberships and make it a grand." The Manager readily agreed and disappeared for about twenty minutes to get some paper work in order. When he came back he had an envelope with the one year memberships in it, the lifetime guest pass, and a grand secured by an elastic band. He also had Eddy sign a release that he wouldn't sue the club in the future for the injuries he had received from Bones. Eddy was happy to oblige. He stuffed the grand in his pocket, another grand no one would ever k no w about, thanked the Manager and left. Eddy was so pleased, one beating equaled $ 3,000.00, a Harley, a lifetime fitness membership, a lifetime guest membership, a permanent locker and five one year memberships. It

The Empty Net

was certainly worth the short term pain, perhaps there was somewhere else he could get beaten up. A bank or a jewelry store might be an interesting and rewarding site for his next beating.

Eddy tried to open up a bank account, but the bank wouldn't let him. He would either have to get his parents to open the account for him, or he would have to have a social insurance number. Eddy thought how stupid it all was. It was his money and he wanted to store it in the bank. What a strange place with stupid rules. Eddy vowed that they would never see his money, ever, and went home and hid it in his room. He would work on a more permanent storage site later, unless he decided to spend the money first.

Eddy ran into Bones by accident a few days later. Bones told him that the police had dropped the charges and thanked him again. As tough as Bones was, he was genuinely pleased to not have to go back to jail. "If you ever need anything kid, you call me." Eddy had a new friend, a violent, dope dealing, extortionist that probably was involved in other things that Eddy could not even imagine, but a friend none the less.

As the summer went on Eddy got bigger and stronger and his relationship with Susan grew. She loved hanging around the rink to watch him work out on the ice each afternoon. Eddy was not the best guy on the ice but most were grown men, and he was the youngest one there. He had bought her a nice friendship ring and so officially she was his girl. She would show all her friends the ring her boyfriend gave her. She rarely took it off.

Chapter Five

Two weeks before high school Eddy got his course schedule in the mail. He immediately called Susan, who had also just received her schedule. They had five classes together and two classes not together. Not bad, they were both very pleased. There was also notice that the hockey team would begin try outs in a week. Eddy was excited. He would dedicate that last week to getting ready. No more girlfriend or cigars, for the week any way.

    The school had one hockey team and they had not tasted success in many years. There were no grade nine or ten kids on last years team, and only a few grade eleven kids. It would be very difficult to make the team, but Eddy didn't care, he knew he would make it. Eddy had used some of the assault money, as the family called it, to buy new skates, the best skates on the market. He had broken them in and they were great.

    The first time Eddy went into the Crusader's dressing room he was impressed. They had a big logo painted on the wall as well as pictures of former teams. There was also carpet on the floor which was nice when you were walking around with your skates on. It was so much nicer than the rooms he had used in the past. But as nice as the room was, the inhabitants of the room were not. A couple of guys smirked when Eddy entered the room that first time, one guy openly laughed, and one guy seemed to spit in his direction as he walked by. As Eddy got changed he could sense that some of the other players were keeping an eye on him. The veterans were particularly curious. Who was this kid and what was he doing here? Eddy was so nervous he thought he was going to toss his lunch. He couldn't wait to get on the ice, because there he felt comfortable and at home.

    Danny Goren was the kind of teammate that no one really liked and no one really knew how he made the team. He wasn't very big, he wasn't very fast, he didn't score a lot and he was annoying as hell. Small and fast was okay, big and slow was okay, big and fast was the best and small and slow was no where. Danny was in grade twelve and

The Empty Net

in his second year with the hockey crusaders, so was pretty much guaranteed a spot, even though he hadn't played much the year before. Danny had the annoying habit of whistling, just like a real whistle. He thought it was a gift. The previous year he had gotten three penalties for his whistleing during the game. Danny would wait until the other team was breaking in towards his goalie, at the appropriate time he would whistle, hoping to stop the play because everyone would think it was off-side. He got away with it a few times. The refs would think that it was someone in the crowd and so he only got those three penalties, even though he deserved about fifty of them. Danny's other bad habit was his penchant to stir up trouble and then disappear. He would come in from behind during a stoppage in play and nail some kid in the back. The crowd would gather on the ice, Danny would slither away, and someone else would be left to fight his battles. Guys didn't mind standing up for one another, but didn't like when someone started a fracas and then took off. Some day Danny would have his style come back to haunt him, and Eddy thought he might just be the one to speed that along. Eddy had assessed the lineup and thought he could make the team, if the coach had an open mind. He figured it would be at Danny's expense or one or two of the other guys that seemed to be on the bubble. There were no other grade nines or tens trying out, so any new kid, other than Eddy, would basically be replacing someone his own age. After two days of skating drills, the players were finally divided into two teams. They would have three exhibition games in the next two days and then the team would be picked. The skating drills had gone very well for Eddy, he was one of the nicest skaters on the ice, but wasn't one of the fastest. That bothered him immensely and so he set out to figure why. He read books and magazines about skating in the hopes of reading some miraculous cure. He did see an ad for a professional skating assessor. For only $ 395.00 they would come to your rink, video tape you doing some skating drills, assess you and provide you with a custom made program to improve your skating. If you weren't happy, you could get a refund. Eddy thought that was a great idea and a nice way to spend some of the assault money, that no one knew he had. Eddy made the call, the experts would be there in a couple of months. Eddy was a little bummed out, but he knew he could wait. If Danny Goren's legs moved as fast as his mouth, he would have been a great hockey player. It seemed every time Eddy was on the ice, there was Danny. Maybe the coach had arranged it that way, maybe Danny had arranged it that way, or maybe it was just fate. Danny taunted Eddy at every opportunity. The thing that bothered Eddy the most was that the guy wasn't even creative in his taunts. The usual rookie comments but nothing very good. Hockey players enjoyed good taunting and some pests had reduced it to an art form. But Danny was no Picasso and soon his rambling's wore on Eddy.

  Towards the end of the second game, Eddy could take no more. Danny came in from his defence position and tried to crash the net after a stop in play, but Eddy intervened. Danny laughed and said "want to go rookie", Eddy didn't give any cute response, he just grabbed him by the sweater, brought him in closer and started swinging away. The coach and two captains broke it up but not before Danny was a mess. He was pointing to his mouth, as if to tell the trainer/stick boy that he had lost some chicklet's, but it was hard to tell with the blood coming out. Eddy went to the bench, Danny went to the dentist. With his two front teeth gone it looked like Danny's whistleing career was over. No one would miss it, no one cared.

  After the game the coach took Eddy aside, Eddy thought he was toast. It was the first time the coach had really spoken to him. Eddy didn't even know if the coach had even seen him. "Congratulations Eddy, you are on the team, I can't promise you how much ice you will get, but you will play". Eddy was so excited, he thanked the coach and ran to the pay phone to call Susan and then his mom.

  His mom was very happy for him, because he had worked so hard, but she was also worried for him because the other players would be so much older. Susan was very happy because as the girlfriend of a hockey player, the entry into grade nine would be made that much easier. When they got off the phone, she immediately got back on it, calling all her friends. The players that had made the team, skated and worked out about four more times before school was to start. With each passing day the team treated Eddy better and it was clear they had respect for him. Eddy felt great to be part of a team that would be together for awhile. He figured that by making the team in grade nine that by the time he was in grade twelve he would dominate the league. After each practice the team would go out for pizza or something else to eat. Eddy, being the youngest rookie had the distinct privilege of paying for that first team building meal. He didn't mind as it made him the centre of attention and besides he certainly had the money, thanks to Bones. The next day it was a rookie in grade twelve who had to spring for the grub, Eddy could now enjoy. The team went bowling together and also went to a movie. Eddy was very impressed with the time the team spent together. The guys were great offering Eddy advi c e and promising to get him old tests if he needed them, what ever he wanted or needed, someone on the team could hook him up. It was quite an advantage over all the other grade nines that didn't have nineteen older buddies with connections.

    Coach Reilly had been the Crusaders coach for about fifteen years. No one knew if he had a first name because everyone including the parents and fellow teachers called him coach. Coach had played junior hockey and had a pretty decent career. People said that he could have gone on to play in the N.H.L. if he had wanted to, but he decided on University and teacher's college instead. The rumour was that in his last year of University he got his girlfriend pregnant so he didn't have much choice but to think of a long term way to support his newly created family. It must have been a good choice, now he was the head of the phys ed department, head hockey coach and still married to his University sweetheart. Coach was a good practice coach but would lose his cool during games. Over the years he had been suspended many times for various lapses in his sanity. On one occasion he did not like a call the ref made. He yelled at him relentlessly. When the ref gave him a bench minor penalty he threw all the water bottles on the ice in the ref's direction. When the ref tossed him out of the game he absolutely lost it and threw the stick rack on the ice and then a nearby garbage can. The crowd loved it, the athletic association suspended him for two months.

Coach always looked after his players and did what he could for them. He tried to get them scholarships and was always trying to get scouts up to see them. He would always be hounding business people to provide things for the team. As a result of his hard work they had free sticks, tape and some equipment. Coach did play favourites and if you were one of them, your life was easier. The coach believed that loyalty was rare and seldom put to the test. He preached team loyalty and looking out for one another. He ran tough practices but the players all agreed they were creative and very instructional. He was known as a straight shooter. Eddy and Susan went together to get their school uniforms. The clerk seemed like a sweet man, he certainly knew his business but his lisp made him a little difficult to understand. He looked after Susan first. When he had Susan all decked out properly in his estimation, he told her she looked divine. Eddy would have been jealous, but this fellow was no threat. As the man put a measuring tape between Eddy's leg, pushing up against his crotch, Eddy became a little uncomfortable. The man made a lot of little noises to himself and said "yes" a lot. When everything was the right size and the pants had been pinned up, the man told Eddy he looked gorgeous. Eddy didn't know whether to drop him, say nothing or thank him. They thanked him as they left with parts of their uniforms. The rest would be ready at the end of the week. Eddy hoped he wouldn't grow out of the uniform and have to go back to the store to get measured again. Eddy paid for his uniform himself, from the assault money. He was pleased and it made him feel grown up. The father was ecstatic and thought it would be a good tradition to continue.

Eddy was pleased that he knew what he would be wearing everyday. A navy blue sports jacket, white shirt, tie and grey dress pants. No more competition or last minute early morning mad rush to find something to wear. He also really liked Susan's kilt and couldn't

The Empty Net

wait to get into it. He also wouldn't have to compete with all the other kids to see who could spend the most money on clothes from the big city. Eddy was not exactly a clothes horse in grade school and his parents did not believe in spending a lot of money on fancy jeans or shirts that would last the same amount of time as the cheaper no name ones. Even with his new found money Eddy wouldn't have been able to subsidize his family clothing budget because his parents would have become suspicious. The morning of the first day of high school Eddy thought he was going to be sick. He had so many emotions and was so nervous he didn't think he would make it. He had a shower and threw his uniform on. His mom made him a nice breakfast, none of which he could eat. He had a glass of grape juice and that was it. He forgot his lunch in the fridge, grabbed his hockey bag and off they went. His mom, who had just recently received her driver's licence, decided to drive Eddy to school. They didn't take the same route that the bus would take so it didn't take very long to get there. When he arrived there seemed to people standing around every where. Some kids were talking, some were smoking, but oddly enough none had their uniforms on. Was he in the wrong place, was this his school? Eddy was confused and started to panic. It was then he spotted Susan, also out of uniform. He gave his mom a kiss, she started to cry as she pulled away from the school, and Eddy went to see Susan. "Why do you have your uniform on, we don't have to wear them until next week." "What do you mean? No one told me you don't have to wear the uniform until next week" "It was in the bulletin we got silly," Susan said lovingly. "Why couldn't I read any of the bulletins that the school sent me?" Eddy vowed to pay closer attention to the next school bulletin they got. Luckily Eddy was not alone. There seemed to be about three other kids out of about six hundred that also didn't read the memo. They were basically computer geeks and probably wore the uniform on weekends too. They took a lot more ribbing than Eddy had, in fact basically no one had said anything to him. They knew better.

Eddy took his hockey equipment to the athletic storage room and left it there. They had a practice after school and he didn't want to

The Empty Net

drag it around all day, any ways Susan said it stunk and some others confirmed her opinion. Eddy and Susan went to their first class, English. They sat next to one another and waited for the teacher to arrive. The teacher was Mr. Brown, who also happened to be the assistant coach of the hockey team. "Good morning class, I'm Mr. Brown" "Oh! Good morning Eddy, I didn't realize you were in this class, how are you doing?" Eddy was stunned the teacher actually spoke to him like they were buddies. After class, the other kids asked Eddy if he knew Mr. Brown from before or something. Eddy explained the hockey team connection. They couldn't believe it, no grade nine had ever made the hockey team and now one of their own was the first. Word spread quickly and Eddy developed more friends with each passing class. It was as if all the teacher's knew who he was. He didn't know how they did, or even if they actually did, or most importantly, that if they did, was that a good thing?

    Eddy's nerves had settled after the first class started and now he was starting to enjoy the new school. He recognized some kids from his neighborhood, from grade school and some from hockey. He couldn't believe the number of girls and how good looking they were. It was like a fashion show at times, beautiful girls with great bodies, Eddy approved. He couldn't wait until they started wearing their kilts. The high school was so different than elementary school. The hallways were larger, longer and there were more of them. Maps on the walls helped people find their way around. There were lockers everywhere and so many more people, older looking people. It was so exciting for Eddy and his freshman class, all their dreams and opportunities just waiting to be achieved. Eddy particularly liked to stand in front of the huge trophy case and gaze at all the nice hardware. It didn't escape him that most of it was won years ago, but the enduring luster was impressive all the same. He vowed that he would help fill the trophy case and that some of the trophies in there would have his name on them before he graduated. In grade school he had won a lot of events and competitions but the prizes were usually ribbons or certificates, pretty chintzy next to these huge masterpieces of wood and silver.

The Empty Net

    Susan and Eddy strolled into the biggest lunch room they had ever seen, next to the one at the mill, that was, for their first lunch in high school. As they took the first bite of their sandwich Eddy noticed a grape flying past his head. He took another bite as a banana flew by. Eddy and Susan looked up from their lunch and were both quite surprised to see fruit, bags, sandwiches and a lot of other unidentified objects go flying across the room. They were caught in the cross fire of their first food fight. Eddy thought it was great and starting throwing whatever he could find on the table. Even as it left his hand, Eddy regretted throwing the unopened can of pop wildly. Luckily, it just smashed the wall, exploded, and soaked a few kids nearby. After about ten minutes there was nothing left to throw and so people steadily made their way on to other things and out of the lunch room. As they left the battlefield the couple were in awe of how much of a mess had been created. Susan thought about the poor staff that would have to clean the room. Eddy heard later that a food fight seemed to break out every year on the first day of the new school year. It was a tradition that had been going on forever. Eddy was just happy that he didn't get his uniform hit with any of the incoming food projectiles. It was bad enough to wear it when he didn't have to, but to get it dirty would have been too much.

    After lunch Eddy and Susan said good bye to one another, promising to meet up after school. The two classes they had in the afternoon were not together. Susan wondered how they would get through them, Eddy was looking forward to the break. As Eddy walked into his English class he looked around to see if he recognized anyone. He wanted to grab a seat at the back, or as far away from the teacher as he could. In the other classes Susan had carefully selected their seats and so they were generally at the front of the class. Susan was an active participant in the class and liked to give the answer the teacher wanted when no one else had a clue. Teachers loved her for her good behaviour and the adoring respect she showed them.

Susan had always wanted to be a teacher and thought that sucking up now would help her later. Of course, she never considered that it was sucking up, it had become so second nature with her. Her family wanted her to follow her father into the career of Law but she was insistent that she would be a teacher. The family would often have discussions about the future and what would have to be completed to ensure their goals were achieved. Eddy thought that was so cool. In his house they had never really talked about college, University or of achieving goals. He had no idea, other than of being a hockey player, of what he wanted to be when he grew up. If he couldn't be a hockey player then maybe he wouldn't grow up. Shannon had never really spoken about what he wanted to do either. He seemed to have various interests but they tended to change based on the situation.

As he threw his bag down on the last desk in the back row, Eddy saw her. In the seat next to him was Joanne Kennedy, the most beautiful girl he had ever seen. She had black hair, big breasts and the most appealing smile he had ever come across. It took him twenty minutes to build up enough nerve to pass Joanne a note telling her that his name was Eddy and he thought this class was going to be a drag. She smiled at him as she passed the note back to him informing him of her name and promising to help him with his studies if he needed any. Eddy couldn't believe it. This gorgeous angel would help him, could his luck get any better. He was so enthralled with her charm that he wrote her another note asking if he could talk to her after school. When she replied in the positive he thought he was in love. He spent the rest of that class staring at Joanne, daydreaming and praying he wouldn't be asked to stand up. It was only when the bell went for the end of class that he remembered Susan. Before his last class he ran through the hall's to find Susan. He grabbed her just as she was about to go into her class, the last one of the day. He quickly explained to her that he had to meet the coach after school and would call her tonight. Susan understood, after all Eddy was her special guy and was a member of the hockey team. Duty called and she would be the doting hockey wife. Nothing was going on so why inflict her with the truth. She would just be hurt and not understand.

    Eddy was so excited waiting for that final bell to go. He was salivating like Pavlov's dog. After an eternity, listening to the teacher talk about what they were going to learn in Science or Math or whatever, Eddy wasn't exactly sure what class it was, the time of truth arrived. He bolted for the door and ran to the designated rendevous site. He waited and waited but no Joanne. He gave up after about twenty five minutes and took the bus home. The phone rang after dinner with the voice of a young woman on the other end, asking to speak to Edward. That was odd, the only person that had ever called him Edward was his father, and only when he had done something very, very wrong. He took the call in the basement so he could have some privacy. Although the basement was absent any other life forms, no one had bothered to hang up the phone in the kitchen and so his family enjoyed the conversation as much as Eddy did. Joanne apologized for not being able to meet him after class, something left unexplained, had come up. They talked for about an hour. Joanne had gone to a public grade school but decided to go to the Catholic high school. Her parents had pushed her in that direction because they thought it might be good for her. The conversation eventually turned to hockey and Eddy was excited to learn that Joanne had an Uncle who was a trainer for a "Jr. A" hockey team. Eddy asked if maybe she could introduce him to her Uncle some time. She thought that would be great, but didn't know when it could happen. The closest Junior league team was about three hundred miles away from them so he didn't get to visit too much during the season. Joanne and Eddy promised to get together after school the next day and said good night to each other. Just after he hung up, the phone rang again. "Joanne" said Eddy, "No silly" said Susan. "Shit," Eddy thought he was busted. "Are you trying to make me jealous?" "I was just being goofy, Susan, how are you doing?" They talked for about twenty minutes, but the conversation was more like one between two old friends. There was no passion, no desire and eventually they said good night and spoke of

The Empty Net

seeing each tomorrow. Eddy wanted sex from Susan and her seeming lack of interest frustrated Eddy in more ways than one. It was becoming the focal point of every conversation they had. Eddy would tell Susan that he loved and respected her and simply wanted to take their relationship to a new level, a deeper level. Susan's retort would never change, "if you really love me then you will wait until I am ready". Eddy couldn't understand what the hell she had to get ready. They had almost gone "all the way" on several occasions, so what was the big deal in going a little further. It didn't help that everyone on the hockey team had a girlfriend, or two, or three, and were having sex with all of them. Eddy felt ashamed, like he was a freak for not being able to have sex with Susan. He started to wonder if he should be looking in a different direction. He loved Susan, he thought, but wanted to experience all there was to experience. He decided that if the opportunity to have sex with someone else came up that he would take advantage of it. He wouldn't tell Susan because she didn't have to know. Besides, how could she argue with him getting something somewhere else when she wasn't prepared to give it to him. She should be thankful that his needs were being met and they could go on with their relationship without the sex thing hanging over it. The more he thought about it and rationalized it, the more sense it made. Why hadn't he thought of that earlier? Eddy didn't think Joanne could look any better than she did that first day of school, but when she started to wear the white blouse, unbuttoned to the third button, short kilt and high socks, Eddy was floored. He could hardly contain himself around her. He somehow thought she was different, she was special, you didn't screw up twice with a woman like Joanne. He would talk to her five times a week on the phone, see her during and after school and also wrote her the odd letter. They were just friends and Eddy never suggested or initiated romance, it would just complicate things. Joanne knew that Eddy had a girlfriend, although she made a point of not getting to know Susan. Eddy would talk to Joanne about the problems that he and Susan were having. Joanne explained to him that the act of intercourse was a very special act for a girl. It signified that she was

The Empty Net

now a woman and also that her relationship with the guy was a deep and permanent one. She told Eddy that some girls would "give it up" easily, but that most didn't. She heard the rumours around the school but assured Eddy that most girls weren't having intercourse, rather the guys were just making it up. That made Eddy feel a little better, but not much. Although Joanne sounded convincing, there were about fifteen girls from school either pregnant or off having the baby, so he had his doubts. The fact that he could have gotten Susan pregnant and become a father himself hadn't really crossed his mind. He knew that Susan would take the necessary precautions. That was the job of the girl, not his, so if they did get pregnant then it was their own fault. She should have known better.

With the first hockey game still some three weeks away the Crusaders would have lots of time to practice and work on their systems. Eddy loved the new challenge but hated the time involved. The Crusaders practiced four mornings per week at the rink just down the street from the school. That meant getting up at about 5:30 a.m., dragging his equipment the half mile to the bus stop, and waiting in the cold dark morning for the first bus of the day. There weren't many cars on the road at that hour or many people out on the street. It seemed like the perfect time to be sleeping. Some of the older players that had cars would drive by and honk at Eddy as he waited for the bus. They would have given him a ride but their cars were already full. Eddy hoped that he would be able to arrange a ride with someone or that the times of the practice would be changed. He did not relish four years of bus hell. When the bus would finally arrive there would be only a few of his teammates and a couple of other people that you couldn't tell if they were just getting up and going somewhere, or shutting it down on their way home from somewhere. Eddy didn't care, it was warm and he could sit down.

Some guys loved practices, some guys hated them and some guys just didn't seem to care one way or the other. A lot had to do with the coach and how creative the drills were. In his last couple of years before high school Eddy had come to hate the practices. They were mindless repetitions of skating drills. Over and back, blue line to blueline and some other imaginative drills like skating a figure eight. Eddy always liked that one because inevitably in a figure eight you are going to cross over at some point. It was fun to run into other players crossing over the other way at the same time. Some coaches would have a deviant side to them and would have the team do intense skating drills until someone started to throw up. Eddy was a quick enough skater that he could keep up and be mid pack without much effort. He sure felt sorry for some of the much heavier guys on the team that weren't in the best of shape. Practice was almost a death sentence to some of them. Crusaders practices were different and Eddy didn't mind them too much. They would generally be broken down into a warm up, skating for fitness, puck handling, systems work, shooting, skating for agility and then maybe time permitting a ten minute scrimmage. Knowing the pain that was waiting for them made it easier for them to get through it. The practice would start at 6:30 a.m. sharp and last until 8:00 a.m.

Some mornings they would spend the whole practice working on implementing a new system, for break outs, power plays, penalty killing or some other important facet of the game that couldn't be left up to a players skill and ingenuity. Those days were fun because there wasn't much skating. The day the coach taught every one how to block shots was an interesting one as well. He started with tennis balls and ended with pucks. The player had to rush the point and then either slide sideways, stay standing up or drop to his knees. It all depended on where in the shot motion the point man was. If you misjudged the shooter you could get hurt, bad. Drop to your knees after the shot has been made and its lights out. Go down too early and you look bad as the guy skates around you closer to the net. The real fun started when they switched from the tennis balls to the real pucks. It sure focused the players decision about how to block it, and when to go down. Over the course of the year, the Crusaders became the best shot blocking team in the league. Eddy enjoyed the drills, it was good for timing and would help him later. He also knew that it was mostly the forwards

The Empty Net

that blocked shots in the game and so he wouldn't get to use his new found skills too much. Some guys actually got hurt in the shot blocking drill, but that only reinforced their desire to learn how to do it properly.

After practice ended at eight, the boys would have fifteen minutes to get changed, showered and walk to school for their 8:15 a.m. first class of the day. There was always a sprint to the showers and here seniority didn't count for anything. You snooze, you loose. No one ever made it on time, but the teachers understood and never hassled any of the players.

From time to time a couple of keener's would snicker or make an ugly face when one of the hockey players would stroll into class twenty minutes late, without their books. On one occasion the teacher saw what was happening and immediately switched into a lecture on dedication and perseverance. He explained that there was no short cut to success, and that to achieve greatness, whether it be in sports, academics, business, music or any other endeavor, it required a totally focused effort that would be all consuming. He then used the hockey team as example, explaining to the class that they practiced every morning, except game days, at 6:30 a.m., and on game days at 7:30 a.m.. That meant most players would be up at 5:30 a.m. in order to get to the rink. He spoke of the fact that every day after school most of the team would work out with the weights and then go for a run, eventually getting home around 7:00 p.m. They then had to eat and do their home work before the cycle started again in a few hours.

Some in the class were genuinely surprised by the amount of time and energy it took to be on the team. Most students just thought of the glory and perks that went along with being on the team, without ever stopping to look at the effort that made it all possible.

Eddy was pleased that the teacher had said what he did and now he understood a little more where they were coming from. No one ever snickered in class again when Eddy would stroll in twenty minutes late with his hair soaking wet.

The Empty Net

With all the practices under their belt, systems in place, chalk talks and meetings over, finally, it was time for the first game. At about 1:00 p.m. the entire school was called into the gym for the first pep rally of the year. The Principal, a couple of Priests, and other people Eddy didn't know gave some great speeches. The gym had an electricity in it that Eddy had never felt before. There were lots of signs on the walls and kids waving banners. None of the signs had Eddy's name on them, but his time would come. The pep rally culminated with the introduction of the hockey team. "The first grade nine to ever make the team, he is a tough nosed, fast skating defenceman, number four Eddy Walsh". The gym went crazy with applause, Eddy could not believe it, he didn't know what to do, so he finally just started waiving at the crowd and walked over to where the other players that had already been introduced were standing. Eddy knew people were happy for him because he represented the under dog. Those in grade nine or ten could relate to him and were happy for one of their own, even if they didn't know him. The rally took another twenty minutes as the team was introduced. Eddy had a lot of time to look at the crowd and make eye contact with many people. He was pleased that a lot of girls had given him eye contact and although there was some distance, he thought a few had even winked at him or blown him a kiss. The first game was on the road. While it was always tougher to play on the road, it was seen as an advantage this year. The team would have been too nervous with the first game at home. Since most teams want to win most of their home games and half of their road games, it was better to let the butterflies go on the road.

As the bus pulled up in front of the school Eddy was surprised and pleased to see that it was a huge bus, not a regular school bus. The driver opened the luggage bays underneath the bus and the players threw their equipment in. Four yellow school buses pulled up behind the team bus to transport the fans.

The seats were so comfortable and there were several televisions mounted on the ceiling of the bus. Eddy thought he was

The Empty Net

playing in the N.H.L. He knew they had about a fifty minute drive so he decided to go to sleep. It was difficult but he did get a few minutes rest and felt better for it. When they got off the bus there were already a lot of students hanging around the front of the rink. He smiled at a couple who responded with a "fuck you", obviously the fan bus hadn't beaten them to the rink. People were down right hostile to his team. He had never seen anything like that before. He turned to a team mate to ask about it and before he could say anything the team mate told him "don't even look at them, they are just losers that have to pay to get in and watch us, they don't know jack shit about hockey, or much else". That was comforting. It was a bit of a hassle to get into the rink but soon Eddy was in the dressing room getting changed. As he did, he thought he was going to get sick and felt worse with every piece of equipment he put on. The Eagles were a big rival of the Crusaders and had beaten them the last ten times they had played. The coach reminded the players of that during his pre-game talk and of how much he would like to change that right now. They hit the ice first and there was an immediate response. It was hard to tell if most of the crowd was booing or cheering, it was just noise. The band was playing behind the net and Eddy couldn't believe how many people were at the game. Young people, old people, students, parents, girlfriends, neighbours and people just looking to see a good hockey game. As the Eagles came out the noise was deafening. Eddy hoped the crowd would settle down, he couldn't even hear the whistle as the referee tried to get the game started. Eddy couldn't believe it as the Eagles came out onto the ice. They were so big, they looked like a football team on skates. Eddy just hoped that he could handle the physical part of the game.

  The coach had told Eddy as they went out on the ice that he would be starting on defence. Eddy thought he was going to be sick for sure. The Crusaders lost the opening face off and the play developed very quickly. Two forwards came down Eddy's side and he made a move to take the guy with the puck, as he did the puck carrier dropped it for the trailer. Eddy got confused and sort of stumbled, too far from the puck carrier and out of position now to hit the guy that had just made the pass. Eddy turned to the net as the puck went in the top corner. Thirty seconds into his high school hockey career and Eddy had been made to look like a chump.

The coach told Eddy to get comfortable and watch how the play developed. It seemed so much easier, so much slower from the bench. After sitting the rest of the first period Eddy realized that he had been benched. Eddy sat with a couple of forwards who also weren't seeing much ice. Eddy had never been benched in his life. It was a strange feeling, one he didn't like. He was angry and vowed to himself that he would not screw up again, if he was given the chance.

In the second period the coach gave Eddy the nod. His legs felt heavy and he had no feel for the game, but he was glad to be back on the ice. He had about five uneventful shifts and was feeling better. In the third period he felt good and actually got an assist on the tying goal. The game ended in a one all tie and the coach was pleased to get a point on the road. Everything considered it was a good start for the team and for Eddy. It was only as he came off the ice at the end of the game that Eddy could see Susan standing next to his father. He knew Susan would be at the game but hadn't seen her all game. He was surprised, but very happy to see the father there. He didn't know the father was going to be there, Eddy thought he was supposed to be at work.

The bus ride back to the school was a quiet one. A couple of guys told Eddy he had played a good game, a couple of guys told him it wasn't his fault and that he would get better. Eddy wanted the respect of his team mates, but knew he would have to earn it. The coach spoke to him as the bus pulled into the school. He told him that he was pleased with his first outing and would get more ice time the next game. He told Eddy to keep his head up and forget about the game just played because it was history and couldn't be changed no matter how much you went over it in your head. The coach explained

The Empty Net

that he had sat Eddy down early in the game just so he could focus and get a feel for the speed of the game.

Every body in the school knew who he was and would say hello to him. Kids in school would buy him lunch, carry his equipment and hang around him just to see if they could do anything for him. It was nice but was also very strange. It was strange because it wasn't just the students that had caught "Eddy fever", but also many of the teachers. They would tell him how good he played and that he had made good plays and was fun to watch. Eddy knew that the admiration was reflected in his marks, so he didn't mind too much. Even his father seemed to treat him differently. It was as if the father was seeing his son through the eyes of others. His son was becoming a star and that pleased the father. His mom didn't treat him any differently, but maybe that was because she hadn't seen him play and so she hadn't seen how others had taken to him. His mom always got nervous about Eddy and didn't have the nerves to watch him in a game. She had problems even watching a practice and had to rely on the comments of others to know what kind of a player Eddy was. Not that she really cared what kind of a player he was. She loved him as her son and only cared about him playing hockey because he seemed to enjoy it so much. Given her druthers she would have been just as proud of him if he had joined the debating club. Mrs. Walsh was afraid one her boys would get hurt and thought playing a physical sport would just enhance their chances. Ever since the Bobby Gage incident, her nerve to watch had gone. Eddy would have liked her to be at the games to see him play, but understood. The reality was that he was focused during a game and the crowd was usually fairly large, that he wasn't able to recognize anyone in the crowd any way. Often with the noise and the movement, the crowd was just a blur or a weird sort of montage of faceless people.

The first home game was a big thing around the school. The school was decorated, people were talking and some amateurs with video cameras were trying to do interviews with all the players to save for posterity. It was exciting but tiresome as well. On game day Eddy liked to focus and think about the battle ahead. He would be quiet and seem aloof, but really wasn't trying to be. He was just much more comfortable around the rink than around people. People seemed to want something from him and that made him nervous. Instead of the lavish pep rally, the school had a mass. It wasn't the usual mass that Eddy was used to. The Priests spoke and prayed and asked "God to deliver their boys to victory, keeping them safe, while inflicting some pain on the Marauders who deserved such a fate." It was nice to have some quiet, control and decorum. Eddy had thought that the pep rally had gotten the team too high and they peaked emotionally way too early. They weren't going to make that mistake twice. The feeling in the dressing was subdued but positive. Many of the veterans spoke quietly of the Marauders running the score up in a late season game the previous year. That was not going to be forgotten today.

    The game wasn't two minutes old when Chris Armstrong grabbed the captain of the Marauders spun him around and started hitting him. Their captain fought back but was obviously a stranger to pugilistic success on the ice. It was a clear cut decision that seemed to inspire the Crusaders and deflate the Marauders. A minute later the Crusaders were up 2-0 and would never look back. Coach Reilly didn't want to run up the score on them because these things seemed to come back to haunt you, so he used a lot of the third and fourth line and double shifted Eddy on defence. Eddy scored two goals in five minutes and the slaughter was on. Before the end of the second period Eddy had his first hat trick of the season. The crowd went nuts and his team mates all had nice to things to say. He was named first star of the game and received some movie passes. Maybe he would take Joanne.

    The team played about thirteen more games before Christmas. The season was working out better than Eddy could have ever imagined. The physical part of it was becoming a grind and with all the nagging aches and pains he had, Eddy was looking forward to the Christmas break.

The Empty Net

As the season wore on Eddy got much more comfortable and started to live up to the potential he had shown the coach in the summer. By Christmas he was fifth in team points with five goals and fifteen assists. No defenceman had more points than Eddy, so he was pleased.

Chapter Six

Despite her vastly superior beauty, Joanne was not as sophisticated and refined as Susan was. Joanne was not rich, her dad worked at the mill, in management and her mom worked in a modern clothes boutique, just part time of course. They had a nice house but it wasn't homey like the Walsh home. The parents were not around very much and the kids got to do what they wanted and were forced to raise themselves. Joanne had one brother, Bud. Bud was a year younger than Joanne, and like Eddy, played hockey. His dream was to play pro someday, but the reality was that he just wasn't that good. He had a great work ethic that helped him overcome a little of what he lacked in skills.

  The parents didn't seem to have much to do with the kids and seemed more concerned with their own lives. Eddy had only met the parents a couple of times but he sensed that not all was as it appeared. The mother was very attractive, but starting to show signs of aging. She must have been a sun worshiper in her younger days and it was catching up to her. She was like an aging movie star that was having a difficult time with the graceful part of it. If Eddy hadn't known better he would have sworn the mother was hitting on him during their brief encounters.

  The father was a man that was strong, charming and pathetic. His only goal in life was to lease a corvette or back pack through Europe. He had been an athlete at one time in his life, but any athletic prowess he may have had was long gone. He was a man that was pleased his daughter was now a beautiful teenager because now he could hang around with her friends.

  It was clear that he liked young women and there was serious trouble in his relationship with his Wife. Eddy mentioned his observations to Joanne who couldn't believe how foolish Eddy was. She was so mad she didn't talk to Eddy for a week. Eddy never mentioned it again.

Joanne was very close to her parents, individually, and could not take hearing anything negative about them. What she forgot to tell Eddy was that her parents had been separated a few years ago for six months because her dad had an affair with some young women. It was after that the mother had decided to return to work and get in the fashion supply business. Whatever Eddy had sensed scared Joanne.

Eddy got to know Joanne's parents better the more he hung around their house. Her father reminded him a little bit of Bones, the same sort of mentality. Mr. Kennedy was really interested in the fact Eddy had a Harley and would always ask him about it. Eddy got the impression that Mr. Kennedy would like him to bring the bike over to their house and let him take it for a spin. The more he talked about the motorcycle, the less he spoke of the Corvette. Eddy tried to explain to him that the bike was put away in the shed and wouldn't be used until he was older.

Eddy started to devote more time to his homework studying with Joanne much to the chagrin of Susan. He loved Susan but the sex thing was starting to get in the way. Susan thought everything was perfect and loved wearing Eddy's hockey jacket during games. It was only during games that he let her wear it, the rest of the time he proudly wore it. Joanne and Eddy could talk about anything without the threat of sex getting in their way. Both understood that they were not developing a sexual relationship, although Eddy wanted nothing more than to have a long term relationship with her that included sex. He wouldn't push her or frighten her off, the right time would come. He just didn't know when, or if, he would recognize it. Susan had invited Eddy to spend Christmas with her, whatever that meant. They arranged that he would come over Christmas Eve Day and spend the day with the Green's. He was kind of excited about it because knowing their financial situation he anticipated an interesting and expensive present.

Eddy decided to use some of his assault money on the Green's. He went to the main drag and sifted through the shops hoping to have something strike his fancy. He found Mr. Green a nice pewter statue of

The Empty Net

the scales of justice. He thought it would be perfect for his office. Eddy stumbled backwards as the clerk said "very nice choice sir, $245.00 please, would you like that wrapped? Thank God Bones had thrown the beating into him or Mr. Green would be getting a can of mixed nuts. Mrs. Green posed the bigger problem. He wanted to get her something nice but not something too personal. He knew she liked expensive stuff and probably wouldn't settle for something like chintzy crafts. He finally decided on a table top book for her and headed to the bookstore. He looked around for a few minutes and then stumbled across the mother lode. There was stack upon stack of oversized, discounted coffee table books. He found a nice book on castles and decided it fit the bill. Who knows, maybe one of their ancestral homes was in the book. It was perfect.

Eddy would get Susan her present later. On the appointed day at the appointed time Eddy showed up gifts in hand. He even brought a bottle of wine and flowers. Susan kind of chuckled when she met him a the door. "You silly guy, you shouldn't have." Susan almost sounded like he really, really shouldn't have. She took him down the three steps into the sunken living room where her parents were sitting by the fireplace listening to classical music an d sipping champagne.

"Eddy, my boy, top of the season to you, would you like something to drink?" Mr. Green was in fine spirits, and it was only 11:00 a.m. "Ah ! yah sure, that would be great." said Eddy. Mrs. Green asked what Eddy had in his hand. He forgot and said "here the flowers are for you Mrs. Green and the wine is for you sir." "Oh, that is so thoughtful, Eddy." Mrs. Green was very impressed and Susan beamed with pride.

"What else have you got there?" Mr. Green inquired. Eddy was pleased to advise that the other packages were presents for them, but they could deal with them later when they opened presents. The Green's all laughed together, like they knew something that Eddy didn't. He had experienced that feeling before and didn't like it. "Didn't Susan tell you Eddy?" "Tell me what Mr. Green?" "We don't exchange presents Eddy, we simply make a donation to the charity that we all decide on. By giving money to those that really need it, we feel better than exchanging trinkets that none of us will use." "That sounds great Mr. Green," Eddy said unconvincingly.

"It was very nice of you to think of us Eddy, why don't you bring them over and we can open them." For a big philanthropist, Mr. Green was pretty anxious to dive into the gifts. The Green's seemed to really like their presents. Mr. Green said "this will occupy a special place in my office, downstairs." Eddy had been built up and beaten down all in one sentence. It would have been nice if the law bastard had said he would take the stupid thing to the office, the real office. Then every time someone saw it and asked about it, he would have to tell them who gave it to them. But no, it would be relegated to the basement office where no one would even see it.

Eddy choked down the Christmas meal that Mrs. Green had made. He was anxious to get out of the house, and besides the dinner tasted like crap. It was obvious that Mrs. Green didn't spend every waking moment in the kitchen. Her cooking was barely passable. The mashed potatoes were lumpy, the gravy runny, the turkey pink and the corn cold. Every one took their turn telling her how wonderful the dinner was. She didn't even suspect they were simply being polite, or, maybe they were being sincere, it was hard to tell, as they had been eating this crap for a long time. At dinner Eddy told them all about his plans for the holidays. He was using some of the two week vacation to have a skating assessment done. The rest of the time he would work out and just relax for a couple of days. The Crusaders weren't scheduled to be on the ice during the school break, although informally, some players were going to get together to practice. Eddy wasn't sure if he would join them or just work out on his own. Mr. Green seemed to nod at the right times, but Eddy could swear he wasn't even listening to him. Mercifully it was getting late and Eddy said good night. The Green's didn't thank him for the presents, he didn't thank them for dinner.

The Empty Net

    Susan called the next morning to tell Eddy that she had a nice time and liked having him over to her house for dinner with her parents. Eddy said they should do it more often and Susan responded by blowing kisses into the phone. They wished each other a Merry Christmas again and agreed to meet later that night. Eddy's family was going to go out somewhere and Eddy had told them he would remain at home. His parents agreed and Eddy looked forward to the peace and quiet of an empty house.

    Eddy's family left about 4:00 p.m. and Susan arrived at 4:30 p.m. They sat on the dilapidated couch and watched the television. Susan thought it was great to watch the old movies in black and white. Eddy reminded her that the television was black and white and so every show had that same charm. She thought that was neat. The two started to get to know each other better. Maybe it was the Christmas show on the television, maybe it was the freedom of being alone, maybe it was the eggnog, whatever it was Eddy didn't care. Things really heated up and before long the only thing that Susan was wearing was her friendship ring and a smile. Eddy had nothing on either and whispered to her that they should "do it". Susan told him not to ruin it and to be patient. He got on top of her and they started to push. They rocked back and forth to the jingles playing on the television. Before they "connected" Eddy had exploded on Susan's leg in frustration. She ran into the bathroom to clean up, Eddy rolled over to think of other things. It was impossible, she drove him crazy. How could they just lie there naked and not have anything happen? They both got dressed and finished watching the movie. There was no conversation for two hours until Susan finally announced she had to go home. "See yah!" Eddy said sarcastically. He didn't know if they would talk or see each other again. At that moment he didn't really care. Every girl he knew in school would go to bed with him, but his own girlfriend wouldn't. It did not make sense to him and he could not continue the relationship on her terms.

Chapter Seven

Eddy went to the rink to meet the team of instructors that would put him through his paces over the next two days. Eddy didn't even catch the guys name as he handed almost four hundreds dollars over to him. It was Russian or Polish or something. Eddy didn't care, this guy worked for him now and he was just there to help his skating. They made Eddy skate around the rink and then had him do some drills. Everything was video taped and watched carefully by the three experts. After two hours he was done. They told Eddy to be back at the rink the same time the next day. When he arrived the next morning they were already waiting for him. They took him into a dressing room where a small television was set up. They sat him down and reviewed the tape with him. They showed him how he skated now, his tendencies and weaknesses and told him how he could improve. Eddy thought it was great and asked them some questions. They taught him some drills that he could do to improve his skating and gave him a manual to keep along with the tape. They taped up his legs and changed the rocker on his skate blades. When Eddy got out on the ice he immediately noticed the difference. It felt more natural and he thought he was able to go faster with less effort. He said good bye to his new skating pals and thanked them for their help.

    On the way home Eddy purchased a V.C.R., explaining to his parents that it was a gift from the Green family. Mr. Walsh mused that it was too bad they had not bought him a nice colour television to go along with it.

    Eddy watched the tape over and over, read the manual and practiced the drills religiously. He felt great, but his new technique had not been tested. When he did get together with some of his team mates for an optional skate, he noticed how much better he was skating. Even his team mates noticed and commented on it to him. He confessed that he had taken the expensive training and assessment over the holidays. They were jealous and convinced him to teach them the techniques.

The Empty Net

Eddy agreed and spent the next few days coaching them. It was difficult without the video and Eddy didn't know much about skate blades, rocker or how to sharpen them differently. The players mentioned it to the coach who was curious and met with Eddy to discuss it. Coach Reilly thought it was a great idea, but knew the team could not afford such a programme. He thought about it long and hard and decided to stop by and see a figure skater coach he knew. It was agreed that she would come out to the Crusaders practice once a week and teach the boys some of the finer points of skating. In exchange her figure skating class would get an hour of the Crusaders ice team every two weeks. It seemed like a good deal for everybody.

Ms. Taylor was dressed in leotards, a short skirt and a sweater when she glided out to centre ice. The boys were skeptical about what they may learn, but not skeptical about the teacher. They knew she was a great skater and was obviously in great shape. The players had trouble focusing on her instructions. She was distracting. Perhaps the next time she could wear a full track suit. They gathered at centre ice and she gave them instructions. They started prancing around the ice doing skating drills they had never seen before. She taught the fundamentals of movement and how to get the most ice out of the least effort. It was clear after a few minutes that some players attention was wandering. She decided to get their attention back in a hurry. "Who is the fastest player on the team", she asked. Everybody responded that it was John Jett. He was a puny forward that could fly. Being that small if he couldn't fly, he would have been dead. "Okay Mr. Jett, we are going to have a race, would you like once around the rink, twice, or some other distance?" "Twice around would be fine" he said confidently. He took his shoulder pads and elbow pads off, just to lighten the load a little. The players were amazed with the start she got. John Jett didn't have a hope. By the time she had completed the first lap, he was just circling behind the net. When he completed his first lap, she was at the other side of the centre ice line, half a lap ahead. John Jett knowing it was hopeless pulled the shoot and stopped

The Empty Net

skating. It didn't matter, the team got the message loud and clear. When she stopped, she asked them if there any questions. No one dared speak. Coach Reilly having seen this before kept a straight face. He knew that figure skaters could fly around the ice. He was just glad that Ms. Taylor hadn't used him for the demonstration. As the sessions progressed the players all realized they were becoming much better skaters. They started to look forward to the figure skating practice and asked the coach if it could be increased to twice per week.

Hockey, school, love and life started to pass by quickly, too quickly. The first semester final exams had come and gone. Eddy had done well on every subject, particularly typing. He hated typing, but knew he would get through it. The night before the exam was cold, very cold. Eddy had forgotten his hockey equipment in the portable they used for the typing class. Being a local celebrity, Eddy had no problem getting the janitor to open the classroom for him. Eddy got his equipment, and as he left flicked the power switch for the portable off.

The typing teacher didn't know what to make of it, the icicles hanging from the ceiling and the arctic like temperature inside, there was no way the portable would be usable for a couple of days. The typing exam would have to be canceled, with little chance of it being rescheduled. Students were given a spare and no one complained, Eddy was pleased. The teacher spoke to the Principal and it was decided that the test could not be postponed and it could not be conducted under those conditions. They agreed that everyone in the class would be given a mark of seventy five, subject to review if a student deemed they would have done better. Some of the keeners appealed and were granted a higher mark, Eddy was happy with his seventy five. Not being one to brag, Eddy kept his latest prank to himself. He was sad that more of his classes were not held in portables.

Eddy and Susan were still together, but were not burning up the phone lines like in the past. Eddy was more chummy with Joanne but had found out that she had a boyfriend from her neighborhood. She wouldn't talk about him other than to say it wasn't serious. Eddy didn't like it but there was nothing he could do about it. Sometimes Eddy would tell Joanne that he saw a girl at school that he thought was hot and ask if she knew anything about her. Joanne would tell him what she knew, nonchalantly. That bothered Eddy, he hoped that Joanne would get a little bit jealous but she never did. As the hockey team prepared for an out of town tournament over the March break, and the regular students got ready for a one week rest, the rich kids prepared for assorted out of town vacations. Susan told Eddy that her family was going to Florida for the March break to hang out at one of those fancy theme parks. Susan told Eddy that her parents said Eddy could come with them and that he wouldn't even have to pay anything for the trip. Susan was so excited, "I can't" Eddy explained. "We have the biggest tournament of the year during the March break and I can't miss it." Susan was crushed, "don't you love me Eddy Walsh, don't you want to go to Florida with me?" Eddy hated when she started with this love crap. Whenever he could not do something she pulled the love card out. Whenever he tried to use the love card, like when she wouldn't have sex with him, he was being childish and petty. Eddy's parents thought he was crazy not to go to Florida. He had never been on an air plane before, he had never been any where before, his big chance and he was not going to take advantage of it. Mr. Walsh was more impressed with the fact that the trip was free, he didn't particularly care where it was.

    Eddy didn't understand the big deal. Why would anyone want to go to the south during hockey tournament time. His friends agreed with him, although a few of his buddies reminded him of the scantily clad babes that would be lounging around the pools, just looking for interesting guys like him. Maybe there was more to this decision than he first thought, maybe haste was not the best policy here. The more he thought about it the more confused Eddy got. The only problem, was now it was not so much a battle between playing hockey or being with Susan, it was playing hockey or being close to all those southern babes. In the end hockey won out, as it always had. Eddy was pissed off, why had Susan put him through this, she knew he couldn't go and so she should not have even asked him to go. Eddy thought the whole situation was more selfishness on her part.

Susan phoned Eddy three times the first day they arrived. "I hate it here in Florida, there is nothing to do, I wish you were here, blah, blah, blah." Eddy wanted to hang up on her each time, but didn't. They had not been getting along all that well before she left and this wouldn't help. Susan constantly complained to Eddy that he was looking at other girls, especially the slutty looking ones. Eddy tried to reassure her that it was not true, but it actually was true, so he wasn't all that convincing. Maybe it was time they moved on and started seeing other people. Susan only called twice more during the week and Eddy sensed something was up.

Susan was not a great flyer, even though she had flown to Europe, Mexico and many other exotic locations. She failed to mention to Eddy that on the way to Florida she was sick all the way. She was throwing up from the time they said welcome aboard until they announced they had landed.

The smell of jet fuel, the hydraulics, closed air circulation, that smell of bad food and sweaty people was too much. Either that or she had a burning desire to test the capacity of the air sickness bags. In any event it was not pretty. Her family teased her about it for the whole trip and as they boarded the plane to return home they even stepped it up a notch. That seemed strange to her. She would have thought that the last thing her parents would want to do is rekindle her fear and induce flash backs to those ill feelings. Even before she got on the plane she felt the pain in her stomach, the queazy feel and the excess saliva in her mouth.

Her prayer to St. Patrick must have worked because she was fine all the way back. She got so confident that she had the in flight meal and some extra peanuts. Susan had a good discussion with her father on the flight home. They spoke about her future and choices, particularly choices in partners. The more Eddy had told Mr. Green he was going to be a hockey player, the more Mr. Green tried to turn

The Empty Net

Susan off the relationship. At first it only served to solidify her love for Eddy, but the constant pounding was starting to take it's toll and erode the love she felt for Eddy. Mr. Green continued to be polite and friendly to Eddy but he was just being two faced. He probably couldn't help it, it was probably an occupational hazard.

They cleared customs and waited for their luggage at the carousel. Time seemed to stand still as flight after flight landed and the passengers came and retrieved their belongings. Mr. Green got tired of waiting and told Susan to go up stairs to the concourse area and wait while he and Mrs. Green went to the baggage department to see what happened to their precious valuables and stuffed toys. There weren't many people on the concourse level, just a few business people and some religious people in interesting costumes handing out flowers and telling people they loved them. "How curious," Susan thought.

"Hi sister, I love you and God loves you." Susan wondered why some guy with a shaved head, toga, tambourine and flowers would love her. Susan didn't really attend Church even though she was Catholic and so religion of any kind was a little foreign to her. She was intrigued and wanted to know more. The man introduced himself as Rahib, although he easily admitted that his name was previously Randy. He was a sports jock in high school, but now played on God's team. He wanted to help her find peace and eternal happiness. Susan thought that sounded good, real good. Eventually, the Greens found their luggage and met up with Susan. Susan gave Rahib her phone number and asked him to call. He put a flower on her ear and promised he would.

The Green's telephone was ringing when they got home. Susan rushed for the phone thinking it might be Eddy, she was surprised to find it was actually Rahib. She asked her mom to hang up and took the call in her bedroom. They spoke about peace, happiness and music for about four hours. When they said goodbye she was exhausted. It was now so late that she could not call Eddy, she knew he would be mad, but she didn't care. Other thoughts now consumed her. Rahib and Susan spoke on the phone for hours at a time, day after day, for a couple of months. Susan loved the fact that he was a gentle man doing God's work and not rough and tumble like Eddy was. Everything about him was different. He was in a sense the anti-Eddy. Susan learned that to move to that next spiritual level, she would have to get rid of Eddy.

Susan and Eddy did not speak to each other the rest of the week. They were happy to see each other that Monday morning and did not speak about why they hadn't seen each other sooner. They met at lunch and Susan told Eddy all about the trip down south. She bragged about how smart her dad was because he was able to write their trip off. Apparently he registered for a legal convention dealing with Corporate Law. He went the first morning to pick up his materials and never went to another session. Because he was at a business conference, all his expenses were tax deductible. Eddy thought that was a great system that would let someone write off a four thousand dollar vacation simply because they went to a hundred dollar meeting.

Eddy told her about the hockey tournament they were in out of town. They lost in the finals to a team from the big city, but Eddy had be e n named to the first all star team. He told her that they had fun on the road and the guys got to know each other better. He didn't tell her that a chandelier in the lobby got broken, the windows on the main floor overlooking the parking lot were broken during a ball hockey game, that the locks to some of the rooms were locked securely with crazy glue, or that most of the guys, including Eddy had spent most of the week with a local girl. What went on the road stayed on the road, besides what difference did it make. She didn't seem all that interested in the details and Eddy wasn't exactly enthusiastic about volunteering them.

Eddy told her that a lot of scouts from the junior hockey leagues were there and that several had even spoken to him. A couple of scouts even took him out to lunch one day. They told him he could play junior and if he kept developing would probably be good enough to play in the N.H.L. some day. That pleased Eddy a great deal, but he was most pleased that they had played St. Michael's and a certain

The Empty Net

Bobby Gage was not on the team. When they played St. Michael's, Eddy asked one of the other players if he knew Bobby Gage. The player said he did and explained that he was cut from the team during try outs and he wasn't sure where he was playing now. It meant everything to Eddy that he had made his high school team and that Bobby had not made his. Eddy didn't even care that the Crusaders had won the game three to nothing to advance to the finals. His victory was more personal.

    Susan was happy for Eddy, but the care and the spark didn't seem to be there anymore. Susan would call less, and Eddy would ask for sex less. Their relationship was fizzling. Eddy spoke to Joanne about it and she advised him to let it go, part as friends while there was still time. Eddy would regret not taking her advice. The big high school dance was scheduled for late March and Susan and Eddy had already agreed to go together. Eddy got his mom to drive them to the dance. Susan was very quiet on the way there, only politely responding to the inquiries of Mrs. Walsh. They went inside and chatted with others. As usual people came over to say hello to Eddy and tell him how well he was doing. In the past Susan loved that part of their relationship, but now she detested it. She told Eddy they were all losers that should get a life and seek some real purpose. Eddy was defensive and thought Susan had a screw lose. He asked her if her head hurt, or if it was just that time of the month. Susan started yelling at Eddy, saying he was a fraud, a lousy person, a lousy boyfriend, a lousy everything. She took off his jacket and threw it on the floor, she took off his ring and threw it at him. It got lost in the dark and disappeared. Eddy was very embarrassed, picked up his coat and went outside.

    Within no time he was being consoled by a couple of girls in grade twelve that had seen the break up. They were both friendly to him and invited him back to their house. Marcia and Kim were cousins, who were very close and lived in Marcia's mothers house. The mother was out most of the time and so they had the place to themselves most of the time. Marcia put some music on and Kim went

The Empty Net

and got them some drinks. They sat together on a small couch and started to talk. They asked him about hockey and were obviously fans. As he spoke they started to undress him. Before he knew it they had him down to his underwear. He complained that it wasn't fair, that they were still dressed. They agreed and started to undress one another. Eddy was amazed but sensed that they had done this before. Totally naked the three went up to Marcia's bedroom where they spent the next four hours. Eddy was totally spent mentally and physically. It had been the best and worst evening of his life. Marcia and Kim were really good looking and to have sex with both of them, and to go all the way, with both of them, was something he would never forget. It certainly erased any memory of Susan. Good riddance to her. At school Monday, Eddy felt like a new man. He saw Kim during a spare, she dragged him into the girls change room and teased him. She said they all should get together again, soon. She explained that they weren't looking for a boyfriend, just a special sort of friend. Eddy knew he could be that special sort of friend.

During that day Eddy was given seven phone numbers from various girls all telling him to call them, so they could talk. This was so easy, Eddy thought, why didn't he get single earlier. The girls seemed to love him and he thought it was his duty to allow them the opportunity to get to know him. Other than the odd time in class, Eddy never saw or spoke to Susan again. Susan's interests had changed. It bothered her when she saw Eddy with other girls, but she knew it was right to move on. She wished they had broken up some other way because now everyone considered her to be the bad guy. That just cemented her feelings that there was more out there for her.

Rahib was now her new best friend. Rahib explained to Susan that his name use to be Randy Winter and he grew up in a lower class, economically challenged neighbourhood in the big city. His father, an alcoholic had left the family when Randy was four years old. The father was a member of a bike gang for awhile, sold drugs, drank a lot, and fought whenever he could. When he didn't get enough fighting out in the street he would come home and beat his wife and the kids. He was rumoured to have been killed about a year after leaving them, but Randy had never tried to confirm it. He didn't care, the guy was out of his life and that was all that mattered.

Randy was closer to his mother because she had always tried to protect him from the abuses of the father. His mother was a professional woman that worked mostly evenings and weekends. She didn't have a pimp and was therefore able to set her own hours and work when she had to. The father would force her back out on the street if she came home too early or without enough money. She was arrested on a regular basis and Randy and his little brother would be put in a foster home by the Children's Aid. The routine was predictable and didn't seem to matter to the young children. When Randy was eight years old, his mother went out one night, never to return again. The Children's Aid put him and his brother in separate foster homes, they never saw each other again. Randy found out later that his mother had been found dead in an alley, all beaten up, with no money on her. The police never solved the case and probably didn't care to. It was another hooker killing that had no priority. None except to Randy.

If Randy and his brother had been from a middle class home and their parents had been murdered, they probably would have been adopted very quickly by someone in the saddened community. No such luck for poor kids with no voice. Not only did they not get adopted, they weren't even kept together. Randy missed his brother even though he remembered little about him. He still hoped someday they would meet up again.

As they spoke, Susan had a hard time concealing her sobs. She was so upset by his life and what as a small child he had to endure. Randy never cried, his tears had dried up long ago. To him it was like reviewing a sterile movie, he was void of emotions. The little boy he spoke of was not him, it was someone else, long gone and almost forgotten. He was now Rahib. Susan was curious and asked him how he turned it around and found God. He explained that he ran away

The Empty Net

from his last foster home at age fourteen because of the rules. He lived on the streets for a few years, selling drugs, stealing and selling himself when he had to. One winter it was very cold and he needed a place to stay. All of the regular shelters were full. There were no parking garages, bus shelters or vacant buildings available either. He thought he was going to die and accepted his fate. He crashed beside a convenience store with no blanket, pillow, heater, card board or anything else to protect him from the cold. He awoke to find an angelic looking woman holding him with a blanket wrapped around him. She helped him up, put him in her van and drove him to where she was living. When they arrived there were about twenty other people there as well. It was a converted factory with lots of beds and tables and warmth. There were older people and some younger people about his age. They gave him some soup and coffee and a bed to sleep in. And sleep he did, not waking for two days. When he did, they helped him to the shower, fed him and gave him new clothes to wear.

Randy learned that they were a religious organization dedicated to spreading the message that God loved everybody. They mostly did that at the airport, but would also go to other places as well. They taught him about parts of the Bible and provided him with other information from their own teaching manuals.

After a few weeks he was committed to them, baptized and took the name Rahib. He had been with them now for three years and loved his life's work. Susan was fascinated and jealous that his life had so much meaning to it. She was interested in obtaining that level of peace and contentment. Rahib explained to her that it was possible but she would have to change her lifestyle, denounce her present life and give her worldly assets to the church. If she did she would be a new person and be always looked after by the church. It was almost too good to be true. It was everything that Susan had always wanted. It was better than teaching or going to the peace corp. It was a chance to help real people in a real way. She could even help street people and others who needed her. It was perfect. The two spoke nightly conspiring as to how they could make it happen.

The Empty Net

    It felt good for Susan to turn the four thousand dollars that was in her bank account over to Yogi Bill, the leader of their congregation. It was like a great weight had been lifted from her. The chains that kept her bound in that despicable Green lifestyle were gone. Susan moved her clothes and other personal goodies into the congregation over a period of a few weeks. She knew she would have to confront her parents eventually, but wanted to get through the school year first. There were only a few more weeks and she knew she could hang on until then. If nothing else, Susan was disciplined. She figured her parents would have some reservations, but would probably be as happy as she was. At the end of the school year Susan decided to make the move with Rahib and was compelled to tell her parents the truth about her plans for the future. Mr. Green took a two month leave of absence from the firm, Mrs. Green remained in treatment for three months and is still drinking more than one person should. Susan had hoped it would have gone better, but her mind was made up so it didn't really matter how they reacted. Rahib had warned her in advance that they would have a hang up about it.

Chapter Eight

The Crusaders were really hungry for the up coming game with the Eagles. First place would be secured with at least a point and they could taste the win. The mass that day took on a special feel with destiny just hours away. They had never ended up in first place and didn't want to blow it now. The Crusaders had done all that was expected of them and more. They had each prepared for this day. They had each looked in the mirror for a long time and knew what had to be done. They had eaten, slept, practiced, focused, met, done everything necessary. There was only one more thing to do, win.

    The crowd went crazy as the Crusaders came out onto the ice. The band was playing, the Fire Marshall had stopped counting bodies. Eddy saw a couple of guys sitting in the rafters above the stands. He was glad he was on the ice because it would have been hard to get a seat for this one. He hoped his father and Shannon were able to get a good seat. He hated to think that Shannon would skip school, with permission, and then not be able to see the game. Eddy was pleased to start the game on defence, but he had earned it with his play all year. He was the best defence man on the team and one of the best in the league. The game started fast and physical. It was a nothing game for the Eagles, they were going to end up in fourth place no matter what happened in the last three games of the year. The Crusaders could end up first or second, but controlled their own destiny.

    There were two fights within the first two minutes of the game. The Crusaders did not want a physical game, but would not back down if challenged. The coach had told them to stay away from the stupid stuff, play their game and get the two points.

    Going into the second period it was three nothing for the Crusaders and they felt good. The score was not really indicative of the play, it should have been about five to nothing, but the Eagles goalie was hot. Eddy opened up the second period with a great rush from his own blue line. He skated across the crease and snapped the puck into the top corner as he went by. Within five minutes it was six

The Empty Net

to nothing and the rout was on. The Eagles were getting frustrated and stupid. They knew fourth place was not going to get them anything, they just weren't good enough to go very far in the play offs. Many of their players were older and this was the third or fourth last game of their high school hockey careers. Other than some that would go on playing in men's league many of these guys would never play competitively again. By the start of the third period there had been seven separate fights, a few misconducts and a lot of cheap shots dished out. Eddy was carrying the puck out of his own end and put a couple of excellent moves on an Eagle's forward to get to their blueline, just as he did, one of his forwards moved to o quick and the linesman blew the whistle for the off side. Eddy dropped the puck and turned to go to the bench. Just as he turned to go to his bench an Eagle player flew towards him and checked him low. It was a stupid play and the ref blew the whistle for another penalty. Eddy didn't care about the penalty, his right knee had never quite felt like it did at that moment. It was like pins and needles, pressure and daggers all at once. He couldn't move it and laid on the ice. The trainer came down on the ice to help him and so did the coach. After about five minutes his father made his way down to the ice as well. Eddy could see that the cheap shot had set off a major brawl as every one on the ice was paired up. He didn't know which guy had taken him out, but was confident that a team mate had seen it and sought some revenge. Eddy was hopeful that no one would fall on top of him, that was all he needed. After what seemed like an eternity the ambulance crew was on the ice trying to make him more comfortable before they took him away by ambulance. They strapped him in and took him towards the end of the rink. As he looked up he could see that his father had grabbed some guy on the Eagles and was physically involved with him. Eddy couldn't believe it but was in too much pain to care.

His mom met them at the hospital. She was very upset and crying. Eddy comforted her as best he could. She was too upset to drive, not that she had a car anyway, so she had asked one of the neighbours to drive her to the hospital, so the neighbour came in to emergency as well. His mom hated asking any one for anything, so Eddy knew how important it was for her to be there with him. The nurse tried to help calm everyone down by saying how Eddy would be up and walking again in no time. The neighbour mused that it was probably just a bad sprain and would probably respond to a brace and be fine in no time. The orthopedic surgeon entered Eddy's room and put all that crap to rest. He matter of factly told them that Eddy had extensive damage to the knee and they would operate the day after tomorrow when some of the swelling had gone down. The mood of the room instantly reverted back to that of being upset again. Eddy tried to comfort his mom all over again.

    The coach and all his Crusader team mates came to the hospital to see him the next afternoon and early evening. They told him that his father had grabbed the kid that had hurt him, and beaten him up pretty bad. The father then got jumped by the Eagles coach and a couple of their players. That is when things got a little nasty, the benches emptied, the stands scattered with fans ending up on the ice, and eventually the police came and settled things down. The game was called by the ref and the score was registered as a seven to nothing win. The Crusaders would end the season in first place, but it was slight consolation. Without Eddy they were going no where. The police laid a lot of charges, particularly against those fans found on the ice, Mr. Walsh was one of those charged. He was mad at the police for charging him, but got over it quickly. He was not hurt at all and that was the main thing. He hadn't started out to make a point, but certainly ended up making one. Although, what the point was, was unclear.

    The nurse came in early the next morning and gave Eddy a pill to make him relax. He had never had surgery before, just a lot of fractures, stitches, that sort of thing. He did not know what to expect, and for that he was glad. Eddy didn't mind new experiences but didn't like to do something twice if he didn't like it the first time. They wheeled him into the operating room , or theater as they called it, at 8:00 a.m. He was surprised by how small it seemed, how bright it was and how sterile it felt. He was freezing and started to shake so the

The Empty Net

Nurse gave him a nice heated blanket. It felt better but he wished it was over. They put a needle in his arm and started to pump fluids into him. The doctor told him they were going to give him something to fall asleep and asked him to count to ten. By the time he got to five he was out. For the surgeons, it was game time. The surgeons took almost three hours to repair the torn anterior cruciate ligament, torn medial collateral ligament and the other damage done to his tendons. The knee was bad but not the worst that they had ever seen. It was rare to see such an injury in a young person unless they were involved in some sort of motor vehicle accident. It took a lot of force, well directed, to cause the trauma that Eddy had suffered. Usually with a sports injury, there would be damage to the "a.c.l." or the "m.c.l." but not both. Eddy had just been unlucky.

It was like a dream. Eddy didn't know where he was. "Had the surgery ended?" "Where was he?" He didn't know where he was, but he knew he didn't feel very good. His knee didn't hurt, but he felt weird. His arms felt tight, his legs felt like he had been running and his head felt like he had been beaten up again. Within minutes of arriving in the recovery room, he was throwing up. Obviously the anesthetic was not to his liking. The nurse ran to his stretcher to help him. She brought him a bucket and put a nice cool wet towel to his mouth. He must have thrown up for an hour. The nurse told him that it was good, he was getting rid of the anesthetic which would actually make him feel better, sooner. Eddy didn't care, he didn't want to hear the medical bullshit. He felt like crap and wanted to die. Eventually, his stomach settled down and he was moved from recovery to his room. His room was nice, which helped because he would be in it for the next two weeks. The doctor met with Eddy and his family about twenty four hours after the surgery. The doctor assured them that it was a success and that Eddy should have a normal recovery. He would stay in hospital for two weeks, go home to rest for another four, and would be able to put weight on the leg after about six weeks. The huge, stiff, white cast that dominated the room, would remain on his leg for three months. It would then be taken off and a smaller walking cast would be put on for another four months. Seven months in a cast and then three months of rehabilitation. Eddy could not fathom the numbers. "Are you saying I won't be able to skate again for nine months?" "No Eddy, you won't be able to skate until your rehabilitation is complete, it could be another month or two if you don't respond to the treatment as quickly as we think you will." The doctors warned him that if he tried to work the joint too soon that he could cause permanent and irreversible damage to the knee that would end his hockey career. Eddy asked everyone to leave. He wanted to cry by himself. He couldn't believe that he would lose a whole season just because of one cheap shot.

Mr. Walsh had been taken to the police station and charged with assault and trespassing. He presented no risk to leave the jurisdiction, was co-operative with the police and had his own home. As a result the police did not keep him in overnight, they allowed him to sign a Promise to Appear Notice and sent him home. Some of the people arrested with him were not as lucky and
spent a night or two in jail.

When he finally arrived home late, smelling and with ripped clothes, Mrs. Walsh and Shannon went into the kitchen to see him. Mrs. Walsh was furious with her husband. "What were you thinking, you , you, meatball", "I know Eddy was hurt, but beating up another kid, right on the ice." The father also grew angry, "I was standing up for Eddy, and besides the kid is twenty and I didn't beat him up right in the middle of the ice, I beat him up closer to his own bench." "If I had have beat him up at center ice then I wouldn't have been jumped by his coaches and other players so easily." Mrs. Walsh had heard enough, she went to her room. She was upset and concerned about what Eddy would think of it, what Shannon would think of it, and what the community would think of it. It didn't help any when the next day the picture on the front page of the newspaper was Mr. Walsh grabbing some kid as others grabbed him. Inside they listed the names of all those arrested including the street they lived on. "Just great, what kind of nut is going to come by looking for some revenge, she thought. The more she thought about it the sicker it made her feel.

It was about a week before the father and Eddy discussed the incident. Eddy was proud of his old man and thought he had a lot of balls to do what he had done. He thought most dad's in the same situation would have chosen to do nothing. He was pleased because it wasn't planned, it just happened. He thanked his dad and they spoke of other things. His dad never spoke again of his motivations or the why's, just about how he could beat the rap and get back to their normal life. His dad mentioned about five times that they had gotten him a television for his hospital room, and inquired several times if Eddy liked it. Eddy didn't know if his dad was more pleased with beating the kid up on the ice or springing for the television. Mr. Walsh left the mill early so he could meet with Mr. Green, the only real lawyer he knew. Mr. Green was friendly to him, expressed his sadness to hear of Eddy's injury, but maintained a strict business demeanor. Mr. Walsh thanked him for his concern and told him that Eddy had been home for a few weeks and was feeling better. Mr. Green did not ask any questions about Eddy, he was not there to listen to the sad stories. It was the business of Law that he was concerned with, with the emphasis on business. The ten foot wide board room table that they were sitting across from each other at reinforced that this was not a social call. Mr. Green did not practice a lot of Criminal Law anymore but thought he could keep him out of jail. It would cost him two thousand dollars and he would need one thousand up front, the rest could be paid in six installments. They talked in generalities and Mr. Walsh thanked Mr. Green for his time. "Those greedy bastards." Mr. Walsh suddenly hated the legal system and all those involved in it. He had no idea how he would scrape up $ 500.00 let alone two thousand. It just wasn't possible, they did not have that kind of money, nor could they get it. At dinner that night the topic came up. The parents were both genuinely upset and afraid that Mr. Walsh, the sole bread winner was going to go to jail. Eddy said he would look in to it that there were lots of lawyers at the gym that he could speak to. He did not want his dad to go to jail, nor did he want him to have a stroke because of the money. After dinner Eddy got one of his team mates to drive him to see his old friend Bones. Luckily he was home. Bones inquired about the cast and Eddy explained what had happened to him. Bones had seen the picture in the newspaper and was impressed by Eddy's old man. Eddy didn't really need Bones help, he only wanted the name of a good lawyer that would get his dad off. Bones didn't really follow sports but knew Eddy was a gifted hockey player and wanted to help him out.

    Bones seemed disappointed. He offered to have the kid that hurt Eddy disappear, or any one else for that matter. He could make it look like an accident or he could make it look like a statement, it didn't matter to Bones. Eddy explained that he wanted a lawyer not the St. Valentines Day Massacre. Bones recovered from that zone he would get in when talking about violence, long enough to give Eddy a name. Eddy thanked Bones and started to leave. As he did Bones suggested that when Eddy got his leg better that they could go for a ride. Eddy told him how good that sounded and promised to be in touch.

    The office of Jake Miller was sparse but interesting. It occupied the last section of a strip mall near the downtown. On his walls there were pictures of mobsters, bikers and other degenerates that apparently were former clients. This was not an office that Mr. Green would be comfortable in. He probably didn't even know Jake Miller, nor would he want to know him. Jake Miller's receptionist was hot, with a real sexy voice. She was wearing a barely there mini skirt, and a tight fluffy sweater that was missing some material below the neck. Her face was beautiful, the kind you could stare at for a long, long time. There was no computer, typewriter or paper on her desk, or even near her desk. It was evident that she wasn't there to take notes. There was another secretary hidden in the back of the long office, but the clients never really dealt with her. Eddy surmised that she probably did all the work, and probably made half of what the receptionist made. Jake's office was like a meeting place, a real bee hive of activity. In the hour that Eddy had waited for Mr. Miller there must have been thirty people come and go. Some people picked things up, some people dropped things off, but all shared a couple of minutes with Roxy the receptionist. Eddy got the impression that some of the visitors were just there to see what Roxy was wearing that day. It was obvious that some had no business to transact at all. Jake Miller walked into his office and every one turned to look at him. He was a short man with a huge belly, unkept hair, tacky clothes and a raspy voice. His lizard skin cowboy boots were very impressive and added a couple of inches to his height. He was perfect for what Eddy needed. Roxy got Jake's attention, which wasn't difficult, and reminded him that Eddy Walsh was there to see him. "Hi, Mr. Miller, I'm Eddy Walsh." "I'm sure you are kid, good for you, good for you." They went back into the war room as Jake called it. In reality it was a big room, dimly lit, with a wet bar, couches and a television. It could have been someone's basement. Eddy thought it was interesting and said so. "Law is a tough racket, kid, you got to be loose and comfortable, or they will fucking kill you." Eddy hadn't thought of the law as a racket, but Jake knew best, he did it every day. Eddy was somewhat surprised to know it could kill you, but again, Jake was the expert. "Can I get you a drink, kid?" Eddy couldn't believe it, but thought it would be a good idea. "Yah sure Mr. Miller, how about a beer?" "Who the fuck is Mr. Miller, is my grandfather here, c'mon kid, call me Jake." The two shared a couple of beers, which went down smooth and made a good breakfast. The more Jake had to drink, the more sense he seemed to make. Maybe that was the secret, get him loaded before you needed him to perform. Eddy wondered how Jake would do in court but he had been highly recommended. Eddy told Jake that Bones had highly recommended him. "That crazy fucker, where did you meet him, in the bucket?" "No, he beat the shit out of me at a fitness centre and then we became friends", Eddy explained. "Got to love that Bones", Jake said over and over. Eddy started to understand why they got along. Eddy explained the problem that his dad had gotten himself into and he wanted Jake to fix it for him. Jake said it was possible but would cost

The Empty Net

two grand. Eddy didn't have two grand left, but was willing to part with what he had left. "I will give you fourteen hundred cash, on the condition that you never tell my old man I paid for it, and you don't charge him anything." "What the fuck kid, you trying to shake me down, I don't give a shit if your old man goes to the bucket or not, I just want to get paid." How could Eddy deal with a guy that sucked people in every day of his life. It was of no use. "Okay, I hear you Jake." "Look this is important to me and to Bones, how about if I give you the fourteen hundred cash and you charge my dad two hundred?" Eddy begged. "Okay kid, sure, it's a deal, get your old man in here." Eddy gave him the fourteen hundred and got a receipt. Other than the nine hundred that had been put in the bank by his parents, the assault money was all gone. Easy come, easy go. Maybe he would get assaulted again and earn some more money. He hated to part with it but couldn't stand by as his dad's health got worse and worse because of the stress. It was a good cause and well worth the expense.

    Eddy told his parents at dinner that night that he had found a great lawyer for his dad at the gym and that he was only going to charge him two hundred bucks. Mr. Walsh was ecstatic, he had worried about remortgaging the house, taking out a loan, or maybe going to jail. Two hundred was affordable and just about what he had put aside already. Immediately he started to feel better, the stress was gone. Sure he still had to go to trial, but at least now he would be going with a top notch criminal lawyer.

    A couple of weeks before the trial, Eddy and his dad went to meet with Jake. As they walked into the office, Mr. Walsh got a sick feeling in his stomach. His mind drifted to thoughts of another place. A place with bars and guards and bad food. A place were people didn't know your name and didn't care, they gave you a new name. Maybe Eddy was playing a joke on him. If he was, it was a good one. "Hello Mr. Walsh", Roxy purred as they entered. Mr. Walsh thought she was talking to him, but she was talking to Eddy. "No silly, the cute one, but hello to you too". Eddy couldn't help but notice that his dad had his radar locked on Roxy. Whenever she moved, his radar moved as well.

The Empty Net

It was almost embarrassing, but Eddy knew his dad was nervous and cut him some slack. Jake explained to Mr. Walsh what would happen, who would be there and how long it would take. Jake went over the questions he would ask him and warned him about coming off as hot head. He taught him how to answer the questions and the things the Judge would be looking for. It was obvious that Jake had been in the trenches before. Jake told them that the Crown owed him a favour and so probably the trespassing charge would be dropped before the trial got started. "How can you do that", the dad asked curiously. "You know Gerry, lets have one of those special relationships, you know, you don't ask and I don't tell, things will be so much better that way." Jake did not want to have to explain the legal system to them, he wasn't getting paid for that, just for results. Gerry Walsh had read the newspapers for enough years that he knew about the deals and plea bargains and all the other crap that went on in the justice system. He had nothing but contempt for it anyway and nothing Jake Miller would say could change that. Mr. Walsh felt better when he left Jake's office than when he arrived. He said goodbye to Roxy and told her to have a nice day. "Like she could have anything but a nice day," Eddy thought. The night before the trial Eddy heard his dad throw up in the bathroom several times. When he wasn't being sick, he would pace around the house, occasionally attempting to sit down, were he would lose himself in fidgeting. It is unlikely that he slept much that night. Jake Miller got more sleep than his client, but it was alcohol induced. There had been some sort of professional association meeting the night before that deteriorated into a drunk fest. Jake led the charge and was a total mess by the time the Hotel security asked every body to leave. Eddy wasn't concerned, he knew Jake would peak at the right time.

    When they arrived in the court room they were all amazed by the majesty of it. The room was huge, had twenty rows of pews for people to watch, a jury box with three rows of chairs was to the side, chairs along the walls for the lawyers and a large elevated area for the Judge, clerk and security officer. There were pictures of the Queen and coats of arms with a lot of Latin phrases that no one knew. The Walsh

The Empty Net

family took a seat and watched as the court room slowly filled up. The Judge, the Crown and Jake all wore flowing black robes with a vest and white shirt and tabs. They looked sharp, and every one was impressed. There was a certain majesty and civility about the court room. Eddy thought the impressive court robes went well with Jake's lizard skin cowboy boots. After some preliminary matters the clerk called the case. "The Queen versus Gerry Walsh" he bellowed out. Jake and the accused went up to the counsel table. The Crown Attorney stood first and advised the court that they were prepared to drop the charge of trespassing and would only proceed on the count of assault. The Judge accepted the Crown's request and just like that half of the charges were dismissed. Jake turned around and gave Eddy that knowing wink.

    The crown called two or three witnesses that had been at the game and seen what had happened. Two thousand people at the game and the Crown could only find these three clowns. The witnesses were horrible, they couldn't remember what day it was, what the score was, when in the game it had occurred, one witness didn't remember when it happened at all. The testimony they gave was useless and probably helped Mr. Walsh. Jake was so confident that he didn't even cross examine the witnesses. That is a gamble but also sends a large message to the Judge that their evidence didn't even hurt the accused at all. The only witness the Crown had left was the player that Mr. Walsh beat up. Gord Davey was a tall, well built guy, now twenty one years old. He was finished high school, unemployed and had no plans. He was cocky and did not impress the Judge. The C rown led him thro ugh the events of the game and the historic rivalry of the two teams. He acknowledged that he knew Eddy Walsh because he was the best player that the Crusaders had. When asked how old he thought Eddy was at the time of the incident, Gord Davey responded with eighteen or nineteen, he had no idea that Eddy was just fourteen at the time. He indicated that the hit was accidental and that it happened during the play before the whistle. He had that sly smile that screamed out that he was lying. He described the aftermath but said he never saw who actually jumped him and beat him up. He said he wished he had seen the guy because then things would have been different, he would have taken care of business. The Crown finished his examination in chief and now it was time for Jake Miller to cross exame him. Jake started off quick getting the witness to confirm that he had never seen who had jumped him and then allegedly hit him. He diminished Gord Davey's injuries by reminding him of previous injuries that he had. He convinced the witness that a big tough guy like him could not get hurt by just anyone. Obviously Jake knew something no one else knew. He got the guy to confess to being in a gang and being beaten up or beating someone else up on a regular basis. The crown tried to object, but it was futile, the Judge wanted to hear about this guy.

Jake pulled out a drawing of a hockey rink with little magnets on it representing the players. He had the witness place the magnets in the same spot the players were in at the time of the incident. Gord was no genius, he had two players heading to the bench and one already at the bench. Jake tore into him. "Is it usual for players to casually skate off the ice towards their bench when the play is still on and in your own end.?" "The whistle had gone, you knew it, your team mates certainly heard it, but you didn't care." "Eddy Walsh had hurt your team all year by his play and you were sick of it, you only had a couple of games left in your high school career and decided that was as good a time as any to take him out. "The only real question Sir, is did you plan to cause as much damage to his leg as you did?" Jake was the snake charmer. The witness started to cry and apologize profusely, almost to the point of embarrassment. Jake had turned things around so that it seemed his dad was no longer on trial, this chump was. Even though there was no jury, it was very effective and the Judge was moved. Jake stood up and asked that given no witnesses were able to identify the accused that the charge be dismissed. The Crown looked down and shuffled his notes as though he was looking for something significant. Finally he looked up and told the Judge that the Crown could live with that.

The Empty Net

The Judge cleared his throat and said, "In a free and just society there is no room or tolerance for those that inflict pain and suffering on others, or hold others in fear by their potential violence. Public places such as hockey rinks are shrines that should also be regarded by those in the community as places of safety. I understand it is difficult when a parent sees their child hurt, all the nurturing and protection mechanisms flood to the surface to look after that child. It is unclear if Mr. Walsh reacted to seeing his son hurt or if someone else did, but obviously there was a reaction by someone." "A just society also holds that it is better to have nine guilty men go free than have one innocent man go to prison. The evidence has to be reasonable, unequivocal and compelling, and must show that the accused is guilty beyond a reasonable doubt. If there is that reasonable doubt then the accused should leave the court a free man. In this case the evidence is very weak against the accused. There is reasonable doubt in several areas of the evidence presented by the Crown, however I will not address them individually. For all of the above reasons I find the accused Gerry Walsh not guilty, you are free to go Sir." The Walsh family was ecstatic and started hugging and joking even before the Judge had fully left the court room. Gord had come over to apologize to Eddy and his family. He never meant to cause any injury, just to send a message and maybe get him out of that game. Eddy accepted his apology as they left the court.

Jake invited everyone back to his office for a little celebration. The Walsh family was so excited they couldn't say no.

The mother hadn't seen the office before and was quite shocked. Having gotten off with the charges, Mr. Walsh didn't care what it looked like, Eddy loved it. They went back to the war room and had a seat. Jake threw Eddy a beer and asked what his parents would like. Eddy threw the beer back and laughed it off as a mistake. The parents asked for ginger ale. He said no problem and called Roxy in. "Honey can you go down the way here and get these fine folks some ginger ale." "Sure Boss," Roxy purred back at him. Roxy was so hot that day. It looked as if her skin tight outfit had been painted on. Eddy thought to himself that one day she would be his and set about dreaming how he could make it happen. With the ginger ales in hand, the new pals made a couple of toasts, listened to Jake's stories and congratulated one another. They finally wrapped it up and were still thanking Jake as they left. Eddy dropped his name and phone number on a piece of paper for Roxy. He told her he was going to play in the N.H.L. and that she should call him sometime. She flashed him a huge smile and said good bye, have a nice day. Eddy took it as a positive sign. Eddy would never let his dad know that he had paid the bulk of his legal fee's for him. Mr. Walsh was a proud man and would not like the thought that his son was carrying his load. He always believed that Jake did them a favour by only charging him $ 200.00. As if Jake some how cared if this mill worker nobody went to jail or not.

Chapter Nine

Eddy received his grades in July and had passed everything. He hadn't just passed, he excelled with a 76% average. It was the best that he had ever done. His dad told Eddy that he had done well and that he was proud of him for his effort. It was a rare compliment from the father and one to be savoured. Mrs. Walsh was very proud as well and told Eddy that he was more than just an athlete. Even Shannon thought Eddy had done well. He knew his brother was smart, but now it seemed that he had actually put out some effort and gotten a result. Eddy was pleased and thought to himself that he would like to maintain that kind of average, especially since it hadn't seemed to have taken all that much effort. Besides next year he would have much more time to do homework since he wouldn't be on the ice.

The summer was pretty much consumed with rehab. There really wasn't much else to do. He spoke to Joanne on the phone regularly and she encouraged him. In August he got a package from Joanne's Uncle Jimy. It was a letter telling him to get better, that many of his players over the years had gone through the same injury and had come back to play just as good as ever. It was very encouraging. There was also a picture of the Niagra Falls Flyers that was signed by the team. Eddy thought that was really cool and thanked Joanne for arranging it.

The first day of grade ten was odd, as there were some kids that were not there any more, including Susan. He didn't know where she was and he didn't care to know. The first thirty kids that asked Eddy how his leg was feeling were flattering, the next two hundred were just annoying. Eddy got sick of the stupid questions like "does it hurt?", and "will you be playing soon?" Luckily, by the second day most had figured out that he would not be a part of the hockey team for his grade 10 year and was really looking towards coming back in grade 11. His school mates slowly started to realize how serious an injury he had sustained. There were no shortage of female helpers to help carry his books from class to class. Eddy had decided that if he couldn't play hockey this year, he would play the field.

Every day after school Eddy would get on the bus and head downtown to the physiotherapy place. They would sign him in, he would get changed into shorts and climb into the huge tub. It sort of looked like a laundry machine, and operated just about the same. The water contraption would heat up his muscles and then the jets would massage them. After twenty minutes he was ready for the next form of torture. One of the nurses would get him to lie down on the table, then they would take his leg and start stretching it and turning it. Eddy would usually scream during this part as the pain was excruciating. For five minutes four times a week, Eddy wanted to die. They would then have him bend the knee up and down for about five minutes. Next would come the electronic machine. The nurses would strap electrical leads onto various parts of his leg and start the machine. It sent electrical currents deep into the muscle to stimulate growth and strength. It didn't hurt, so Eddy didn't care how long it took. He would then go back into the water machine for about fifteen minutes. The last thing he had to do was lie on the table with his knee wrapped in ice. He would lie still for fifteen minutes counting the small holes in the tiles on the ceiling. After about an hour and a half, Eddy would get changed and wait for the nurses. For the first few months of rehab, they would put a walking cast back on, after that they would simply tape it up and put a brace on it for stability. It was a routine he came to know well and hate intensely. Eddy thought his knee was never going to get any better. It still hurt all the time and any sudden movement felt like someone had stabbed him. Walking through the snow would cause terrible pain and in his condition was quite dangerous. He hated to go anywhere in the winter because of the perils inherent in the snow and the ice.

There were many nights he cried himself to sleep either because of the pain or feeling sorry for himself. His parents would hear him and it tore them up. To comfort him would be embarrassing and of no benefit, so they ignored his cries. They cursed the game that caused their son so much pain. They wondered how it could be worth it and why they allowed him to play, like they had some choice in the matter.

The first semester had come and gone pretty quick. Eddy had worked hard in class and been rewarded with a 79% average. He was even more pleased than the year before, because these marks were obtained without the benefit of being a Crusader hockey player. Eddy liked to read and had found much more time to do that without the onerous practice schedule of the previous year. The Crusaders were not doing as well as last year, but Eddy didn't know what the problem was because he hadn't seen any games. It was funny when a player was injured, especially with a serious injury. Even though he was a key part of the team and would be again, guys shied away from him. It was as if he was hurt and they didn't want that bad luck or whatever to rub off on them. At the same time Eddy really didn't want anything to do with them. He didn't want any pity because they thought he was damaged goods. He would go back to the rink when he was well, when he could contribute. The coach understood, told him he was welcome any time, but would understand if he didn't see him again at the rink until he was on skates. Some class mates would bug him to come to the game with him, but he always declined. They didn't understand, they weren't athletes.

After Christmas his knee started to feel a little better. He no longer screamed when the nurse manipulated the joint and he no longer had to wear the walking cast. He sensed there would be an end to his personal hell soon, even if soon was several months away. At the physiotherapy he met a girl named Anna MacDonald. She looked familiar and they started to talk to each other during their rehab visits. Anna was a track star who had damaged her achillies tendon the year before. She had two operations and was still in rehab. She understood that her track career was over, she just wanted to be able to walk properly without the pain. She was in grade 12 and had no illusions that she would be going to a college in the States on a track scholarship, despite the fact that she had seven offers the previous year. Eddy was interested in how she had dealt with the mental part of it and gotten to the place were she was at peace with it. She explained that track wasn't her life just something she did. While others may have defined her by it, she never had. The scholarship would have been a means to obtain an education, nothing else. There was no real professional end for what she did. She could not make a career out of it like Eddy could, and besides who really cared about track athletes any way. Eddy told her that wasn't true, but when she asked him to name three track athletes from the last Olympic Games he couldn't name any. Good point, he thought. Anna was smaller than Joanne, taller than Susan and fitter than both of them. She had great looking, strong legs, a tight rear end and a well proportioned top. She was pretty with flowing auburn hair and that determined champions look in her eyes. Eddy liked her a great deal and she liked him. They started to call each other regularly and help each other out with their rehab.

    Anna had a maturity about her that was appealing and refreshing, she could put things into the proper perspective. She was goal oriented but also liked to live life to its fullest. She still had that fierce determination that had propelled her to the top of the high school track world, but now track had been replaced by school. Her goal was to be number one in her class and try and get an academic scholarship. She wanted to be a doctor and seven years in school was expensive for any one, even a rich kid, which she was not. Sometimes the two would study together, even though they were in different years. Eddy was amazed by her dedication and focus. Nothing could get her off track when she had committed to learn something. The relationship was growing deeper every day and soon became a sexual one. She loved having sex with Eddy, but not during study time. She wanted to learn the material inside and out and had a schedule as to how she would do it. She would learn it inside and out. Anna did background reading and looked for information in other sources, not just the assigned text books. Eddy wasn't surprised when she ended up with a 98% average and secured a scholarship to a college in the

The Empty Net

States. Grade ten was a transition year for Eddy in many ways. Because he wasn't hanging out with the hockey team or other jocks, he started to hang around with a tough bunch. Most of his new pals were from the bad neighbourhood and from broken homes, whatever that meant. They drank, fought, stole and got in to trouble. They were the type that if they lived, would end up with a dead end job, or at the mill, if they were lucky. Eddy was like a project to them. He wasn't quite one of them, but could certainly act like one of them at times. They knew he had a motorcycle and that was cool, they knew he had a lawyer and that was cool. The difference was that Eddy came from a loving home, one with security and values. He didn't need to steal, to act like a jerk, he had no excuse. The boys loved getting together at one of their houses in the evening to listen to music and drink. They would either steal enough money to get booze or they would steal the booze from whatever house they were in that night. If there was an adult home, they didn't seem to care. A couple of the guys lived with their old man. Sometimes the old man would come down and party with the kids. They would even provide the booze, which Eddy found both sad and perverse. These weren't what parents should be, setting an example for their kids. They were over grown hippies that were self centered and had never grown up. They wanted to be their kids buddy and not their parent. Unfortunately, these kids needed parents, not buddies. Eddy liked the booze but not hanging around with the parents, because he considered them nothing more than losers. They had no lives, no ambitions and no history. It was as if they had always been in the state they were then in. Eddy saw how the generations would repeat themselves quickly and it scared him. He had been drinking way to o much, way too often. It was effecting his grades, his health, his relations, and his chances of ever making it to the N.H.L. He had convinced himself a hundred times that he should stop, but didn't. Shannon knew what was going on and tried to talk to him about it. Eddy didn't need to be given any advise from his young punk brother. Shannon was concerned about his older brother but could not reach him. He didn't know what to do, but had to do something. He didn't wanted to talk to the father about it for fear it would end up like the smoking scenario. It didn't help that Shannon's friends would come to the house and tell Eddy how cool he was. Eddy knew better than to bring any of his new buddies over to his house. That would be rude.

There was a big blow out planned for the weekend. Basically, the blowout was just an expression that meant lots of booze, no girls, and a few guys that weren't in the circle, just so there was someone to beat up at the end of the night, in case the feeling struck, which it usually did. Eddy thought it was somehow barbaric that guys would be invited to a party just so they could be beaten up later. He wondered if they ever had an inkling of what was going on, but then he thought it would be pretty odd for someone to come to a party if they knew they were going to get beaten up. But lots of guys wanted to break in to that dangerous circle, so who could know for sure. When Eddy got to the party, he was surprised to see the whistler, Danny Goren already in attendance. They really hadn't spoken to each other since they exchanged pleasantries on the ice the previous year. Danny still hadn't learned to shut his mouth at the right time and bugged Eddy for most of the night. Eddy mentioned to hi s buddy Terry that he was getting sick of this Danny clown and perhaps it was time he went home. Terry raised a glass to Eddy and said "right on". Eddy continued with his drink trying to find something decent to play on the stereo. He heard the commotion upstairs but paid it no attention. When he finally did get up to go upstairs to use the facilities, he could see Danny hunched over on the drive way puking his brains out. "You okay man" Eddy asked him. "Yikes, what the fuck happened to you?" Danny was twice the mess that Eddy had made of him on the ice. He was seriously hurt and looked like he was having trouble breathing. A couple of the guys came out to laugh at him and pour beer on his head. One of the guys told Eddy that Terry had come to talk to Danny and Danny had slipped or something. That was how Danny had gotten hurt. Eddy knew better and went inside the house to call an ambulance. No one but Eddy knew the ambulance was coming. When it arrived, they took Danny to

The Empty Net

the hospital. Within minutes three police cruisers were at the house. The cops smashed down the front door and started throwing guys against the wall. They yelled that everyone was under arrest. Some guys tried to take off out the back door but the cops nailed them before they got any where. Eddy went out a side window and vanished into the night. His years of sleeping out in the back yard and then wandering the neighborhood at night had prepared him well for this night. He easily got himself out of the area and back to his house without any one noticing.

The next day Eddy found out that eight of his buddies had been arrested. The charges ran the gambit from drinking in public to attempted murder. Terry Barker had beaten up Danny Goren pretty bad. There was a time overnight that they thought that Danny would not make it. Everyone except Terry was out on bail. Terry would remain in custody pending his trial.

Eddy had long talks with Joanne and Anna over the next few days. How could he be involved with these idiots. Where was his life going and did he want it to end in jail. He was scared, again. The two girls whom he most admired, loved and respected told him to get as far away from those guys as he could. The advice they gave was solid, but Eddy still had to find out some things for himself.

The jail was not a nice place. It was large, dark and smelt like animals were being housed there, which arguably they were. Eddy had to sign in and wait while they did a back ground check on him. He was then led into a small room with glass in the middle and seats on both sides. Eddy was claustrophobic and had trouble breathing as the heavy double door closed and locked securely behind him. There was no way for any one to get out of that place quickly, no matter what their status, no matter what the emergency. Eddy wanted to run from that place and never return. He waited another five minutes until Terry strolled through the double steel door system and entered the small room. They were on opposite sides of the glass and were monitored by guards sitting on both sides of the glass. So much for privacy. These weren't two pals meeting at the local coffee shop for a coffee and a donut. This was jail, a rough place for rough people. It was easy to determine that these inmates weren't there on scholarships.

Terry was in a fairly up beat mood, he had just been told that the charge had been reduced to aggravated assault, which meant a world of difference in terms of the possible sentence, if convicted. He was now looking at about eighteen months, out in twelve, possibly less. Not the best way to spend grade twelve, but better than life in prison. Terry was also playing the role of the cool guy. If he let his guard down in his new home, he could wake up dead. Although all of the inmates were scared to some extent, any external sign of it was seen as weakness, and this culture had no tolerance for weakness. Terry relished his new found celebrity and was going to get maximum exposure from it. Even though he was in jail, he was a somebody and being talked about. He laughed with Eddy, said he should have finished the loser off. Eddy laughed a nervous laugh but thought that it was disgusting. At that point Eddy wanted to be anywhere but there. He said goodbye to Terry and privately hoped he would never have to see him again.

Sometimes people make mistakes that can be corrected, sometimes they cannot. The bad mistakes inspire that sick feeling, that feeling that if there was a hole to climb in, you would do it. If only things could be changed. Eddy did not want to get dragged into the life of hell that he knew his new friends were destined for. He was determined to stay away from these people, he owed his mom as much. Booze was starting to change his life. He was getting heavy, mouthy and kept a micky of Rye in his locker just in case the urge for a sip was too great during the day. He had lost the respect of others that he had spent the previous two years building up.

Eddy avoided the tough guy crowd as best as he could. He would say hi to them in school but did not go out drinking with them any more. Anna was relieved as she had pretty much given Eddy an ultimatum. He would have to choose between the booze and those friends, or her. She would not stand by while he squandered his life

The Empty Net

like an idiot. He had too many things going for him to allow that to happen. His good friends loved him and would not let him unravel. Joanne was at Eddy's house almost everyday. She loved spending time with Mrs. Walsh and would show up and stay there even if Eddy wasn't home. Eddy loved coming home to find Joanne there. She was so beautiful and so nice to have around, even if they weren't involved. Anna knew Joanne and had no problem with her relationship with Eddy, in fact she encouraged it.

Chapter Ten

Before Eddy swore off booze, during one of his drunken escapades Eddy had met up with a girl named Cheryl something from his school. He thought she was a year ahead of him or a year behind him, but he didn't bother himself to confirm any details about her. Eddy had seen her at a party, but had left by himself. She had followed him out and caught up to him at the park near his house. "Eddy, Eddy wait up for me." "Sure baby, what's going on," Eddy replied cooly. "How would you like to party some more, just you and me?" "Yah, that sounds good, where do you want to go?" "Right here", she said, "why go any where else?" Eddy thought she had a good point and they found some privacy in amongst the bushes. The girl was prepared as she opened a bottle of rum and passed it to Eddy. He drank it like it was water. Before too long he started to get that spinning feeling, which inevitably always signaled the end of his night. As he was starting to pass out, the girl was busy making her move. She took his clothes off and then started to take her own off. Ordinarily, this would have been a great ending to the night, but on this night there was no chance. His amorous tendencies had been dulled by the booze. The last thing Eddy remembered before he passed out was the vision of the girls perfect breasts heading down towards his face. When he woke up in the park the next afternoon, his pants were missing and there were young kids playing on the swings near by. He didn't think they had taken them, but couldn't remember who might have. As the oxygen started to refill his head, he started to have vague flash backs of the previous night. Eventually, he even remembered the girl and thought they had great sex. Eddy found a sweater in the bushes and wrapped it around his waste. He ran home and snuck in the back door. A couple of hours later his dad banged on the door, told him it was 4:00 p.m. and time to get up, and that there was a girl on the phone. Eddy dragged himself to the phone and said hello. "Hi!, its Cheryl, remember me from last night?" "Oh yah, Cheryl, how could I forget, you were great." "Thanks Eddy, you were great too." "I can't believe that we had sex that long

The Empty Net

with you so drunk." They talked for a couple of more minutes and said they would catch up to one another in a few weeks when school was over. Both knew it was not going to be a lasting relationship, Eddy could hardly remember what she looked like. He thought he had passed her in the halls of the school a few times but couldn't be sure. A short time later she called again, this time not as friendly and sounding a little scared, "hi Eddy, I'm late, I haven't had my period, I think you got me pregnant." Eddy could not believe his ears and didn't say anything for several minutes. "How do you know, have you had a test, could it be any one else?" "It's you Eddy, don't be a bastard, I need some help." Cheryl got so upset she couldn't talk and hung up. Eddy ran to the bathroom and threw up. He couldn't fathom being a father, especially when he didn't even know what the mother looked like. He didn't know what to do. The next few days he went around like a zombi. He was surprised that Thursday night to see Cheryl sitting in his living room with his parents and Joanne. His mom was crying and obviously they had all been talking. Eddy played it cool pretending not to know what was going on. "Cheryl here says the two of you are having a baby, is that true boy?" The father was in no mood for bull shit. "I don't know, I was drinking one night and she followed me home after a party and I don't remember any more." It was pretty much the truth, but didn't seem to help the situation. Cheryl started to cry and ran from the house. Joanne flashed Eddy that look of disappointment and left the house as well. Eddy wanted to dig a hole in the middle of the living room floor and escape. He would prefer more surgery to this. His parents talked at him for about three hours before they got tired and went to bed. Eddy went to his room and stared at the ceiling for a few hours before falling asleep. In one night his parents found out he smoked, drank, had sex, lots of sex, and came home late, often. What a night. The hell ended a few weeks later when Cheryl Goren phoned to say she was not pregnant. It was a quick conversation with no promises of see you later. The name sounded awfully familiar to Eddy. He read some of his old year books and looked at the pictures. Sure enough, Cheryl was the older sister of one

Danny Goren, the same Danny Goren that Eddy had beaten up and that Terry had nearly killed. Eddy called Joanne who was speaking to him again and they concluded that she had set Eddy up, that she was likely never pregnant and that they had likely never had sex. Eddy wasn't so sure about that part. Eddy tried to explain it to his parents but it fell on deaf ears, their only reaction was relief that they weren't going to be grand parents. Eddy swore to himself that he would never get himself in a vulnerable situation like that again.

Two weeks after the blow out party the school was rocked by the death of Terry Barker. He had been out on bail for a couple of days, got all liquored up, stole a car and tried to out run the police. He had little driving experience and didn't know the roads. The alcohol, adrenalin and high speeds were fatal. Terry wrapped the stolen car around a tree and then was thrown through the window about a hundred feet landing into a ditch. He was killed instantly. The funeral was a difficult one, no one that young, even a dangerous alcoholic, should die at that age. The girls in the school were upset and crying. They were upset and crying for a lot of reasons. Very few of them knew him, or probably even liked him. But he was one of their own, he was their age, with their dreams, their problems, their aspirations, and now they were all snuffed out. They related to him and it scared them. How could any one their age die? They were invincible and weren't supposed to get hurt at all. Life was ahead of them , not behind.

The tough guys that Terry and Eddy hung around with were quiet, there was a certain sobering quality about having one of your friends killed. They were reflective and confused. Was this the start or the end? Who would be next? Most of them had the same questions Eddy had. They wanted to change, at least they didn't want to die. The real question was could they change. The sad reality was most couldn't. Eddy remembered the times that Terry would show up at his house in a car. Every time he came he was in a different car, a different stolen car. Eddy didn't care where the car came from and most of the time he didn't ask. Ignorance was bliss. Eddy would blindly get in, sometimes being relegated to the already crowded back seat. He never thought of the danger then, but now it made him sick. Why did he allow himself to get stuck in the back seat of a stolen car, driven by a drunk driver, with four drunk passengers egging him on. Why would anyone take those risks? Eddy vowed to never again get in the car driven by someone impaired, or into a car that was stolen, or into the back seat of a crowded car, even if no one was drinking. He could walk and at least arrive alive.

    The worst year of Eddy's life finally came to a close in June. His second semester average had fallen to 58%. His parents were horrified with how far he had regressed. They didn't suspect for a minute that their son was having the problems with alcohol and getting into the trouble that he had. They knew, compliments of Cheryl, some of his bad habits, but didn't know the extent of those bad habits and how much damage they had done. Eddy didn't care because he knew why his marks were so low and he knew that he could build them back up again.

Chapter Eleven

Eddy was finished with physiotherapy and could start to run, work out and skate again. It was a very exciting time, but one wrought with fear. He was concerned that he would not be able to skate again, and if he did, that he wouldn't be able to skate full out, and if he did it would hurt. Eddy put the test off for a couple of more weeks and focused on running and pumping iron. He slowly started to feel strong and confident enough to tackle the ice. The day of truth finally came. Eddy put on his knee brace that he would wear for as long as he played, tightened up his skates and hit the empty ice. It felt so good to be back on skates. There was something about the feeling of flying around a rink, spraying snow and ice in your wake and creating your own wind pattern. The grace, speed, control and exhilaration was the essence of life itself, his life any way. If you ask any hockey player they will tell you that they feel best on the ice, skating around, doing their own thing. Even the pro's love to get back to their roots and play a little shinny on an outdoor rink when they can. They recapture the magic of the game, and forget the demons of the business. Why do men in their late eighties and nineties insist on tying up the skates once or twice a week and hitting the ice? It is their shrine and they are at peace paying homage to it. Eddy hoped he would always be able to skate, even if he could never play again, he couldn't stand the thought of not being able to skate again. He wanted to teach his kids, if he had any, how to skate, he wanted to coach kids to skate, if that was his role. So far so good. He skated hard for about thirty minutes and then decided to shut it down. It was a good first test and he didn't want to over do it. The last thing he needed was a relapse or the return of the pain. He took his skates off, and then the brace. He walked on it and did his cool down stretches. The knee had passed with flying colours. There were no problems and he would test it more each day. It was only early July and he had lots of time to get in game shape. He didn't want to peak two months before training camp and so timing and a proper programme were important. Through the help of Joanne, Jiggs Smith was able to talk to Eddy on the phone and then able to set up a programme for him. It was a combination of on ice and off ice activities that featured flexibility, strength and fitness. Skating was mechanical and did not have to be done every day at this point. Eddy felt confident that he had recovered and would be one hundred per cent for the start of the season. He planned his skating schedule carefully so he would be in top shape but not burnt out before the season. He started to play weekly with some of his Crusader team mates, a couple of junior "A" players and some college guys. Eddy was much better than his high school team mates and almost as good as the college and Junior "A" players. Those players were a little stronger, a little faster and a little smarter than Eddy was, but they were three to seven years older than he was. He felt good about his progress and how he compared to others.

Anna decided to stay in town for one more year and work before attending college in the States. Eddy was pleased that they would be able to continue their relationship. It seemed to be perfect. She was beautiful, athletic, intelligent and enjoyed having sex. Not a bad combination and certainly a long way off from the constant head games that Susan would pull on him. Joanne and Anna got to know each other very well because they were at the Walsh residence more than Eddy was. Mrs. Walsh enjoyed their company and Mr. Walsh had no complaints. Shannon would try to chat them up at every opportunity which they found to be cute.

Shannon was ready to go to high school but was conflicted in where he would go. He wanted to go to high school with Eddy because of the convenience and other positives, but didn't want to be lost in his shadow. The public school was in walking distance and most of his friends were going to be going there.

Shannon didn't care about the sports programme and was mostly interested in the academic part of it. The local school had a computer lab that was unique in town. Shannon was interested in computers, even though he had never really worked with them. He figured they were the future and he was interested in planning his future properly. The worst fear that Shannon had was that he would end up in some mindless job at the mill all his life. He was bound and determined that would not happen to him. He didn't have lofty goals or a burning ambition, but he knew he didn't want to be subjected to the control that his dad had faced all of his working life. He knew there must be a different, better way. Shannon decided to meet with a guidance counselor from both of the schools before he made any final decision.

    Eddy took Shannon on the bus to his school and introduced him to Ms. Clarke. She was a pleasant serious woman, who had probably been attractive thirty years ago. She was a bit of a contradiction, what with her nice smile, appropriate make up and support hose partially hidden under an ankle length dress. She spoke about the school , the teachers and the various programmes. Shannon asked about computers but she confessed they hadn't really given any thought to creating a computer programme or even in acquiring any so that the students could learn how they work. They thought that was a business issue and should be best dealt with by business not by the school system. Shannon wondered how any one would get the job in the first place if it was up to business to teach people how to use a computer, but he didn't press the point with her. Ms. Clarke spoke more about the athletics than about the academics. Shannon told her that he was not interested in athletics, but she only laughed and kept talking, as though he was joking. He told her again, "I don't care about athletics, I don't play any sports." Ms. Clarke turned red and apologized, "I"m sorry, I just thought that because you were Eddy's little brother, naturally you would be involved in sports as well."

    Shannon walked around the school looking for Eddy. He got lost and asked a couple of guys if they knew where the cafeteria was. They flashed him a grin and started to hassle him. "So are you a minor niner, punk?" They kept bugging him until one of their friends came along. Shannon thought this was trouble because now there were three

The Empty Net

of them. He wanted to run down the hall screaming but knew that wouldn't be cool. The new kid seemed to have more sense. "Hey guys what are you doing with Eddy Walsh's brother?" "What do you mean", one kid said nervously. The kids apologized for joking around and took Shannon down to the cafeteria. The other kid gave him four quarters to get a pop, just in case he didn't have any change and was thirsty. Shannon met up with Eddy, they toured the school a little bit and then headed home. All the way home Eddy told Shannon how great the school was and how much he would love it. He also talked about all the things they could do together. Shannon could not see Eddy letting him hang around with him or his friends, but it sounded good.

  The next day Shannon went to the local high school to meet with a guidance counselor and a couple of teachers. The local high school was bigger and older than Eddy's school. It had a lot more hallways but had an institutional smell about it. There was a big gym but not a lot of banners and trophies on display. They had more wood shops and auto shop s than Eddy's school had. It looked like a great school for someone in a mechanical programme. There were probably a lot of graduates employed at the mill. Shannon met the guidance counselor. Mr. Sharpe, who seemed any thing but. His name was a misnomer as he hardly knew what day it was. If he had said anything remarkable Shannon may have thought that he was the absent minded professor type, but he didn't. He was nice enough though and got Shannon the information that he needed. The next stop was to meet some of the teachers and some of the senior students. The students were very frank with him. The school was not an athletic one and mostly appealed to geeks. Shannon wasn't sure if that was true, or, if the only senior students that would sign up to help with the orientation were geeks. Whatever was true the bunch that Shannon met were definitely geeks and proud of it. He found that rather refreshing and looked forward to just studying without all the jock stuff in the background. Shannon heard enough sports stories at home, he didn't have the need to live them out at school as well. The geeks took him for a tour and showed him the computer lab. It looked great. He thought it was the future and also his ticket to a decent job. There were several computers that had been donated by the big companies, there were broken down computers that the students could take apart and see how they worked, there was every thing Shannon could ask for.

    At dinner that night Shannon surprised the family by telling them he would be attending Memorial High School and not the Catholic School with Eddy. His parents were surprised because they didn't even know he was thinking of attending the local school. They were pleased and not surprised that he had attended both and checked out the various programmes and gotten a feel for both of the schools. Eddy was simply pissed off and didn't say much. After discussing it a little more the parents were quite pleased with the decision that Shannon had made and knew it was the best one for him. They were a little concerned about Shannon following in Eddy's footsteps and getting into trouble with Eddy and his friends. They thought it best if Shannon made his own friends, friends his own age. They also knew it would be rough on Shannon trying to be Eddy's little brother in a school dominated by athletics and not being even slightly interested in them. Eddy and Shannon spoke about it that night, but Eddy never did understand his decision. He wanted to look after his brother and impress his brother and he couldn't do that with Shannon going to another school.

    In preparing for the new school year, Eddy realized he would be turning sixteen early in the year and it would be nice to have wheels. He had his motorcycle but didn't think it would be too good for driving to school in the winter or for dragging his hockey equipment around. He placed an ad for it in the local newspapers and put up a few flyers at the bike shops. Almost immediately he had lots of response. Many people of various sorts came over to the house to see the bike. Eddy had met a cop, a dentist, a drug dealer, a hooker and several other professionals before the day was out. They all loved the bike but had differing opinions on what it was worth. Eddy would not settle for less than ten thousand and no one was prepared to bite at that

The Empty Net

price. He did have a standing offer of nine thousand dollars from a pimp, and that made him feel good. He said he would decide tomorrow and let the guy know. That night, low and behold, Jake Miller showed up on the back of some bike driven by some mean looking out law type. Jake renewed acquaintances with Eddy and offered him ten thousand for the bike. Eddy didn't want to get into the haggling game with Jake again and said sure. Jake pulled out ten thousand in cash, got Eddy to sign over the ownership and said goodbye. Eddy didn't believe it. Jake couldn't believe he got Bones back his bike for only ten thousand. Every body was happy that night. Eddy took the ten thousand into the house and gave it to his dad to put away for him. His parents couldn't believe his good fortune in selling it for the price he did. Eddy was happy about the price but sorry to see it go. He had never ridden it and could only imagine how much fun it would have been and how cool he would have been on it. He always figured he could buy one in the future if he wanted but for now he was happy to save his money and buy a car before the next summer. People had always told him not to buy a car in the winter for some reason and he had believed it. He could wait. A lot of people had told Eddy that he could use their car if he needed to, so he was in no rush.

Chapter Twelve

The first day of high school was very exciting for Shannon. Not only could he wake up an hour and a half later than Eddy could, he could also walk to school and come home for lunch if he wanted. Shannon could not believe his luck in the time table he got. He was able to take English, Math, Science and Computer Sciences in the same semester. He was really excited about the challenge ahead. Eddy stayed away from the tougher courses, Shannon welcomed them. Shannon was there to get an education, to give himself a future, he could tough out the work involved. Many of his classmates were not motivated and wanted to be any where but at school. Shannon couldn't believe their attitude, why wouldn't they embrace the challenge and take advantage of what was being offered to them. Shannon knew there was no short cut to success and he wasn't looking for one. Shannon couldn't wait to get home at night so that he could do his homework and start on the next days work. He was always a little bit ahead of his class, he sat in the front row of every class and was an active participant. The teachers genuinely liked Shannon.

    The second week of school, Memorial had a club day. It was an opportunity for all the clubs and various groups to set up displays and try and recruit new members. Shannon was excited and set about to tour all of the different displays. He didn't have any sort of club in mind, but knew he wanted to get involved in a couple of things. He studied what they all had to offer and decided to join the camera club and the computer club. He figured these were important things to know and would help him in the future. The camera club met on a weekly basis in a classroom. The members were told that they would be in the classroom for the first few months, they would then learn how to work in a dark room and after Christmas they would start having trips in town to take pictures. Over the next month Shannon learned all about f-stops, film speed, shutter speed, lenses and the mechanics of taking a picture. They had some old camera's in the club that had been donated and so each member was able to use one to work with. Shannon learned how the camera worked, how to take them apart, how to clean them and replace parts, really everything there was to know about camera's.

Shannon loved photography and thought he might have a gift for it. He decided to invest in a camera of his own. He asked his parents for three hundred dollars to purchase it, but they politely turned him down, but encouraged him to pursue his new hobby. Shannon decided to spend some of the money that he had earned over the years. He had worked hard shoveling snow, cutting grass, doing odd jobs and delivering tons of newspapers. He had about two thousand dollars in the bank and had spent very little of it on himself over the years. His parents thought that was a good idea and were relieved that he wouldn't have to hound them for the money. One Saturday Shannon and his friend and camera club mate Cameron went to the camera store in the Mall. There were many different types of camera's and Shannon and Cameron inspected every one of them. They wanted to know the technical specifications, things most customers didn't care about. It was clear that the two camera buffs knew more about the various models than the store clerk did. They didn't care, they knew what they were doing and didn't need help. Two hours after they arrived, Shannon had decided on a package. He bought a camera, two lenses, a flash, a speed winder and metal case. The metal case was great. It looked like an oversized silver briefcase with foam padding inside. He had to cut out the foam pieces so his equipment would fit tightly. That way the stuff didn't move and was well protected. Shannon spent almost seven hundred dollars on his new hobby and didn't want to spend that much on camera equipment again any time soon. The hard metal case would protect his equipment perfectly.

As soon as he got home he showed his parents what he had purchased and headed down the street. Despite it being late in the flower season, the tulips of Miss Dunn had held up remarkably well and were looking exquisite. He used up two rolls of film on the tulips and then headed to the school to develop the films. He developed the two rolls and had a lot of great shots of tulips. He chose the two nicest ones and blew them up so they were eighteen by twenty four inches large. On the way home from the school he went to a store and bought two frames for the pictures. At dinner that night Shannon told his family all about the camera equipment he had purchased and what he could do with it. Eddy had a couple ideas of what he could do with it, but they weren't very constructive. After dinner Shannon went down the street to see Miss Dunn. She was pleased to see him and went into the kitchen to make them some tea. When she came back into the living room she saw the two beautiful pictures resting against the wall. She couldn't believe it. Shannon told her that he had gotten a new camera earlier in the day and could think of nothing more perfect than Miss Dunn's tulips to take the first pictures of. The pictures were for her and he would hang them any where she wanted. She told him that it was the nicest gift any one had ever given her and she started to cry. She gave Shannon a big hug and thanked him about a hundred times. She didn't know where to hang them and said they could stay where they were until she found the perfect spot for them. She stared at the pictures for about fifteen minutes before Shannon announced it was time for him to go home.

When Shannon got home his mom gave him a big hug and told him how proud she was of him. Miss Dunn had just gotten off the phone with her and told his mom what he had done. Even the father gave him a nod and told him what he did was pretty nice. Shannon was pleased with their obvious joy but hadn't done it to receive any thanks. He did it because it made sense and was a nice thing to do. That is what guided Shannon, not the spot light that guided Eddy. The parents mused to themselves that it was too bad that Eddy didn't have more of those qualities of compassion and decency that Shannon had. They knew they didn't have to worry about Shannon in the same way they worried about Eddy. Of course they always worried about Shannon being bullied or taken advantage of. Perhaps the brothers could look after each other and utilize both of their strengths and minimize their weaknesses.

    Shannon took as many pictures as he could. He didn't just take pictures, he kept notes about the lightning, flash speeds, lens settings and any thing else that effected the picture. After the pictures were developed he would study them and refer to the notes he had made. As a result he learned very quickly what combinations were the best in a given situation. The school had a newspaper that came out every three weeks. The editor in charge asked Shannon if he would be their official photographer. The teacher that was involved in the camera club had recommended him. Shannon agreed on the condition that he didn't have to take pictures of the sporting events. There weren't that many sporting events in any case and so the paper agreed with his request, and they had their new staff photographer. Shannon wanted to raise the profile of the clubs and other activities in the school at the expense of the few jocks they had. His pictures captured feelings that struck a nerve with the students. They enjoyed his photographs and looked forward to seeing the five or six he had in every issue. His reputation was growing by the week. Before Christmas the local town newspaper called Shannon and asked him to come and see them, he readily agreed. The town newspaper had seen his work and wanted him to be their freelance photographer. Shannon knew they were taking advantage of his age and the fact that he was a student, but he didn't care. Shannon was told he could take pictures of anything he wanted, anything that was, that was of interest locally. If the paper used his work he would be paid per picture. The part that grabbed Shannon was that he would be given an unlimited amount of film and use of the newspapers dark room. All the photographers met on a monthly basis and he would be able to learn from the pro's. Shannon happily agreed and left the building loaded up with film and a press pass. His parents were very excited and couldn't believe it. Shannon started to take lots of pictures. Joanne and Anna were at the Walsh house all the time and became regular models for him. He took glamour shots of them, portraits, action shots and even some bikini shots. At first the girls were shy and very modest but Shannon acted like a professional and was able to get them to relax and act naturally. He was sure they would have posed in the nude for him if he asked, but he never got up the nerve to impose on them. It was a regret that he would have for a long time.

One of the pictures he took of the two girls frolicking in the snow made it to the front page of the newspaper. He was paid two hundred dollars for it and given two copies of the original framed. He gave one to Joanne and kept the other one hung up in his room. The school also got a copy of the cover page picture and hung it near the trophy display case. They attached a plaque to it with his name and the date boldly engraved on it. The camera club geeks were jealous of him but pleased that he was getting free film which sometimes found it's way to their camera's.

Eddy tried to convince Shannon that he should be taking sports photographs. He told him that there were a lot more opportunities and he could make money at it. Shannon didn't care. He was happy marching to his own drummer and was reluctant to get sucked into his brother's world. He did not like the jocks or what they got away with. Shannon thought the world had screwed up values by putting athletes and movie actors on a pedestal while diminishing the value attributed to doctor's, nurse's and teacher's. The occupations that were of most value to society were not given there appropriate due, while drug popping, drunk, criminal actors were earning millions of dollars per picture and athletes were earning millions to play a sport. From Shannon's perspective the athletes were mostly total jerks that had no sense of reality. He liked reading stories of retired jocks who suddenly had to fend for themselves in the real world. Most of the stories were pathetic tales of hopelessness that was encountered by the previously famous. A retired athlete and a competing athlete were like night and day. No one really cared about yesterday's news, other than as a curiosity. Most of Shannon's experience was from watching people hang off his brother and from what he read in the newspaper and

The Empty Net

watched on the television, but he was convinced of his position and rejected Eddy's suggestion.

The Crusaders had their first try out and it was an eye opener for Eddy, the coach, the players and any one else that bothered to watch. This was not the championship team of two years ago. This team was smaller, slower, younger and no where near as good as that team was. They were going to have a long season and most around the team sensed it. There were thirty five players trying out and only about five really should have been playing at the high school level. The coach decided to take his lumps and go with a younger team. He hoped that the experience they gained would help them next year. At the teams first meeting the coach announced who had made the team, the schedule and named Eddy Walsh as the captain. Eddy was thrilled but not exactly surprised. He was clearly the best player on the team. Eddy reviewed the schedule and was pleased to see that they opened the season against the Eagles. He was anxious to get that game under his belt and move on with the rest of the season.

The day of the first game the school held a huge pep rally. It was exciting to be on the stage with the whole school in the gym below, but it lacked the energy of the first pep rally Eddy had experienced. That one was special and would not be repeated. There wasn't much to talk about and the coach didn't want the team built up just to disappoint later. As a result the coach spoke mostly about working hard and competing. He also spoke of Eddy and how he expected him to win the scoring title that year. Eddy was flattered but didn't need the pressure. He hadn't even thought of the scoring title, he was a defenceman and wanted to focus on his defensive skills and skating abilities.

When the bus arrived at the Eagles arena Eddy was surprised to see so few people outside. There were no hecklers, no fans, no one swearing at the Crusaders as they entered the building, how disappointing. Eddy was nervous in the dressing room but remained focused. He tried to put the thought of an injury into the deep recesses of his brain but it was hard. He didn't want to think about the possibility of getting hurt because it could change the way a player played the game. He was relieved when the buzzer sounded and they were able to go on the ice. He looked over at the Eagles and didn't recognize a single player. He did recognize the coach who sort of gave him a funny look. Eddy was not impressed and mouthed a couple of pleasantries to the coach, but wasn't sure if he heard him. The coach gave Eddy the finger which caught Eddy by surprise. Eddy thought a coach should have a little more control and should lead by example. The coach was just a jerk and was probably responsible for Eddy's injury. The puck was dropped and immediately came back to Eddy. He charged up the right side just over the red line and fired a snap shot into the Eagles bench. The puck bounced off the glass and hit the coach in the back of the head. He was cut in the back of the head but had managed not to pass out. The game was delayed as the coach was helped to his dressing room so he could get some help. The ref skated over to Eddy, bent over next to him, and asked him what was up with that? Eddy explained to him that it was just one that got away and shouldn't happen again. The ref flashed him a smile and skated to the corner to await the face off. Eddy looked into the crowd and saw his dad. He gave him a wink and his dad knew that shot was for him. The game started again without the Eagles coach. A couple of the Eagle players said something to Eddy but no one challenged him seriously. Eddy was the best player on the ice and no one could stand up to him physically. The game continued but there was no flow to it. The Eagles were just as lousy as the Crusaders were and were also in for a long season. Eddy scored the first goal of the game late in the third period and the Crusaders went on to win their first game of the season one to nothing. The game was not a classic but a win was a win and they would take it. Eddy felt good after the game and as the games went on he thought less and less about his knee injury or about getting hurt again. The Crusaders struggled during the early part of the season, losing more times than they won. Eddy dominated the league even more than he had in his first year. He scored at will and physically out powered all his opponents. Eddy ended up leading the league in scoring, but it was not rewarding. He was not challenged by the games and was bored in the practices. He was more concerned about his long term development than he was about the immediate glory at the high school level. He thought about quitting and joining a men's league but that would mean letting his team mates down and he could not do that. He would tough out the season and consider his options over the summer. This was his junior draft year and so maybe he could play junior next year instead of high school. As much as Eddy like the lime light that individual success brought, he also liked to be part of something important, a team that was going places. Losing was no fun for a pure competitor like Eddy. As bad as the season was going school was the opposite. Eddy had worked hard and also received every break possible from the teachers, as a result he had raised his average to the 75% mark. His parents were thrilled that it once again looked like their oldest boy had a chance of finishing high school.

    Eddy's relationship with Anna was solid and they greatly enjoyed each others company. It was sometimes tough with her working as much as she did but at least there was lots of money to go out and do things with. It was also exciting for Eddy to be dating a sophisticated older woman. Anna had really matured and did not look like the girls back at high school. Joanne continued to visit and be a regular guest at the Walsh house, although now she was more like family than a guest. Mr. Walsh and Eddy bugged her every chance they got about her status as a beautiful, single young woman. They couldn't believe that she did not have a boyfriend and both had offered to set her up on many occasions. She always turned them down, but was probably a little interested in who exactly Mr. Walsh would set her up with. It was probably himself, but the issue was never discussed. He was very found of her and would sit and talk with her for hours. Things at home for Joanne were not the best and so she stayed away from the place as much as possible. It was too much for her to have to listen to her parents fighting and putting each other down. Both saw her as an ally and would try and enlist her help in their dispute. She hated that and didn't want to have anything to do with either one of them. She was glad she was getting older as that meant she would soon have options and choices to make about where she wanted to live. She hoped her parents would stay together long enough for her to finish high school. Joanne loved the fact that the Walsh home was a calm home. There was no real fighting or arguing and the parents treated each other with respect and dignity. She never had any hint that they had a bad marriage or were not content with one another. She would talk to both of the Walsh parents about that and got the same response. Basically, they enjoyed each other's company, knew their roles, didn't have wild expectations of one another and were at peace with where they were in life. Restlessness in marriage was for the young and foolish, not them. They had also both committed themselves to doing all they could for their children often at their own expense. They just knew that was what a parent should do and so they did it. Eddy and Shannon never really thought about their parents marriage except when Joanne would raise it. When they did think about it they were pleased that with all the rest of the things happening in their lives they didn't have to worry about whether or not their parents would be together or not. It just wasn't an issue at all.

Eddy's sixteenth birthday was on a Tuesday but the family decided to celebrate on the Saturday before. The whole family, including Anna and Joanne went out to a fancy Chinese restaurant for dinner before returning to the Walsh house for gifts. They spent three hours in the restaurant telling jokes and stories and just generally enjoying each other's company. Mrs. Walsh so wished that she had been blessed with girls to go along with her two boys, but knew she would have to wait until the boys got married and gave her granddaughters. It was far too late to think about having more kids now, she had completed menopause ten years earlier. She was so thankful for Anna and Joanne and never hesitated to tell them that. Although they weren't her daughters, she loved them like they were her own.

The Empty Net

The day after Eddy turned sixteen and got his learners permit he was out in the school parking lot putting Dylan's mother's car through its paces. The odd grinding sound and that certain stench, not quite brake fluid, not quite rubber, permeated the air of the school area. Dylan's mom didn't know why she went through two clutches in three months. She thought that it was that shitty Yugo technology. The truth wouldn't help her to feel any better and besides she traded the old Yugo with the faulty clutch for a new Honda. Dylan wanted her to get a sporty car. Eddy didn't care as long as it had a back seat and gas in the tank. Dylan was the only real friend Eddy had on the hockey team. He liked the other guys and they all liked him , but the only guy he hung around with from the team was Dylan. It probably didn't hurt that Dylan had use of a car and would always let Eddy do the driving.

Grade eleven was such a breeze for Eddy. As long as he played hockey and played it well, his teachers, particularly the priests were happy to accommodate him by taking liberties with his grades. How many times had he been asked, almost sheepishly by a teacher, if he had been afforded an opportunity to look at any of his homework. How the non-athlete students hated that reverence reserved only for the Crusaders. So what if they played hockey, we are here to go to school and learn for the future they would argue. How silly, how myopic. The good priests knew better, they knew what life was all about, and in small town Canada, it was about playing hockey.

The only thing Eddy liked as much as hockey and girls was driving. He loved to go fast and take chances. He enjoyed speeding along and then hit the brakes for no reason, just to see how long it took for the car to stop. He didn't get to use the family car too much because it was always in use, but that didn't matter as it seemed everyone was lined up to lend him theirs. It was such fun to drive, the mobility and freedom, the ability to nail puck bunnies somewhere other than a bus shelter or school yard. It didn't even seem to matter to Eddy that he didn't have his own car. Being the local hockey star, in a hockey crazed town meant that someone was available to lend that helping hand and part with their car any time his need arose. And arise it did, on a regular basis. The fact Eddy was a lousy driver and smashed more than one of his hockey crazed fans cars didn't seem to bother anyone, least of all Eddy. Eddy could buy a car if he wanted to, but why bother. It was like he had his own car, but he didn't have to pay for anything. He would keep his money in the bank, earn some interest, and continue to test drive the cars of others until he found one he really liked.

    Eddy loved the young ladies and they loved him. Eddy lacked discretion, taste and quality always played second fiddle to quantity. Unfortunately, when it came to satisfying the local girls, Eddy didn't discriminate, as long as they were over fourteen, he didn't care that the only beauty contest they might be able to enter, let alone win, would be a wet t-shirt contest in a dark, stink filled, red neck bar. Drinking less and less meant he was losing his excuses. It was nice to make special friends in different cities and Eddy fancied himself as a goodwill ambassador, a Diplomat. He loved when his hockey team was out of town on a trip as it afforded him an opportunity to reach out and make new acquaintances. When it came to extra-curriculars with the ladies, Eddy only had one rule, don't say anything to Joanne Kennedy or Anna. If anyone broke that rule, they were out, no more school parties, no more hockey parties, no more fun anywhere. Joanne was his ultimate woman. He loved that statuesque, athletic, Irish girl with the long dark hair, five feet of leg, and delicious emerald eyes. She was the reason that cave men learned to draw on walls and went to war. The other girls were a mere attempt to forget and medicate himself because she wouldn't go out with him. Not that he had ever really asked her, but he knew she was special and didn't want to blow it with bad timing. Besides , other than having sex with her, he was with her almost every day and could call her up whenever he wanted to. Eddy also secretly worried that maybe Joanne's brother Bud had let on about Eddy's prowess with other girls. No, that couldn't be, other than Bud's odd habit of wearing pantyhose under his hockey equipment, he was for the most part a stand up, normal guy. Besides what goes on the road, stays on the road. No hockey player, even for

The Empty Net

his sister's honour, would break a hockey tradition like that. Eddy remembered a few years ago in the N.H.L. when a certain defenceman started being intimate with the wife of one of the wingers on his team. The tryst became public, however, the winger was able to forgive his team mate for the indiscretion. After the winger found out that his team mate had also used his car, and left it stained and with a heel mark on the roof, he went crazy and demanded a trade which was granted shortly after. Eddy sensed from the reports of the affair that the player was more concerned with someone using his car than taking liberties with his wife.

Chapter Thirteen

Eddy was in grade eleven when he turned sixteen years old. No big deal for most people, but for hockey players this meant it was his draft year. In June of each year the three Major Junior Hockey leagues in Canada drafted the best sixteen year olds in the world. While most of the talent still came from Canada, there were lots of players from the states, Russia, the Czech Republic and other European countries.

In the weeks leading up to the draft, Eddy had done the obligatory fitness testing and interviews with various teams. They all seemed to like him, but most of the G.M.'s had a kind of bull shit quality about them, that he both loathed and admired. They were Eddy's kind of people. They cared about their own teams and maintaining their own job and didn't really give a shit about the pieces of meat that wore the skates. Eddy had a great year in high school. His crusaders had lost in the first round of the playoffs to St. Michael's, the big Toronto power-house in a bitter five game series, losing 4 games to 1. Eddy didn't care so much about the loss as he did about looking bad, especially against his old best friend and newest nemesis Bobby Gage. In the series with St. Mikes, Bobby was the leading scorer and Most Valuable Player. He taunted Eddy every chance he got and given the score Eddy could not fight back.

It was weird to see Mr. and Mrs. Gage in the stands cheering against him. Despite all that had gone on, they were still like his second family and he missed them. Eddy's real concern was that Bobby would be drafted ahead of him in the June Draft, or worse, that they may end up on the same team.

It was a warm day that June in Toronto, what with the heat, smog and number of people, it seemed like it was 90 degrees. Inside the venerable Maple Leaf Gardens it seemed even hotter. As Eddy, Anna, Joanne and his family walked in to the Gardens two things struck them, how big and beautiful the building seemed and how many people there were inside, all Eddy's age. You could sense the tension and smell the clearisil in the air.

The Empty Net

The Oshawa Generals are pleased to select from the Royal York Royals, six foot three left winger Dave Smith. With that the draft was under way. Players drafted in the first round had their pictures taken with the coach and General Manager in the teams sweater. It took about fifteen minutes to draft a player in the first round. In the rounds 3 through 12 it would take about five minutes between picks.

Eddy and Bobby were both slated to be picked in the second round. If you weren't drafted in the first four rounds you probably wouldn't have a shot at making the team. The first two picks were pretty much locks for a spot. Even if the player turned into a bust over the summer, the team would not admit their scouting was so bad that a second round pick could not play, and so the team would play the player anyway. Despite the frivolity and ass kissing and group hugs, the first round seemed to fly. There were twenty teams in the league and they were on number nineteen.

Eddy was looking around the cavernous Gardens at all the clowns that would either be drafted behind him or not at all. Some of the sixteen year olds looked like little kids in grade eight graduation suits, some looked like monsters. He didn't care. He knew the big ugly kids couldn't skate. He knew some of the other players from reading about them or playing against them. Many he didn't know because they were from the big city. He thought it was funny that these pretenders would come from all over the province and the States hoping to hear their name called. He knew many of them would sit there all day with their families and never hear their name. Too bad.

"The Peterborough Petes are pleased to select from St. Michael's, centerman Bobby Gage". What the hell did he say? Eddy suddenly woke from what was like a trance when he heard the name. Bobby picked in the first round by the defending league champions. Screw him! Eddy didn't want to see Bobby on stage getting what should have been his, so he went to the washroom.

The Empty Net

The Gardens was an old building and that was no more evident than in the washroom. It looked like they hadn't been up graded since 1933 when they were installed. There weren't individual stalls, just a long trough to piss in. It was more designed for cattle then for budding young hockey stars, something that wasn't lost on Eddy. There must have been a lot of people with the same concerns as Eddy because the place was packed. There were at least two kids puking in the shitter, there probably would have been more, but they would have to wait as there were only two shitters in that washroom. Eddy stood in the middle of the piss trough and tried to relieve himself. He must have had stage fright because nothing happened. Eddy and all young men hated that moment of truth. A busy washroom, a line up and stage fright. It was bad enough in a regular washroom, but here everyone could see what was happening or as in Eddy's case what wasn't happening. If you wait too long, the other guys start to think you're gay or something, just there for the view. Eddy turned to the guy next to him and said "hey, what's up". It even sounded somewhat odd as he said it. The guy was obviously in his own, undrafted world. He seemed confused as he turned to Eddy to reply. Before he said anything Eddy heard that funny noise.

Comforting if in the forest or by a pond, but not so comforting when standing at a packed urinal trough. His new friend, in his haste to reply had pissed all over Eddy's leg. "Shit man, what are you doing." Sorry about that man, I really didn't mean to."

Not that there was a time limit or anything, but after five minutes of simply standing there and getting pissed on, it was time to leave the washroom. As he got back to his seat Eddy's mom asked what happened to his
pants. It wasn't that easy to hide a piss stain on tan coloured pants. He told his mom not to worry about, it would dry.

A bead of sweat appeared on Eddy's forehead as they started with the third round selections. He couldn't believe that he was still available. All those G.M.'s that told him he wouldn't last into the second round, where were they?

In the third round, the Niagra Falls Flyers are pleased to select from the Crusaders, defenceman Eddy Walsh. Finally, and to Niagra Falls where he had a decent shot of playing. As he walked up to the stage he heard the snickers. He didn't appreciate that they were directed at him. When he got on the stage, the coach shook his hand and asked if he had pissed himself. Shit, Eddy had momentarily forgotten about his new friend leaving his scent on Eddy's pants. If he ever found that kid he would kill him. His first official meeting with his new coach, Jiggs Smith, the legend, and the conversation is about Eddy being pissed on. No doubt it happened to Jiggs, probably many times, but he wouldn't let the kid forget it.

Eddy went to the Niagra falls table and met all of the scouts, coaches, trainers, current players, some past players and players just drafted. It was amazing how many people were involved with a team. If there was any doubt about the professionalism of Junior hockey, it was gone now.

Eddy met with Dr. Aaron Rife, the team nutritionist. During the forty minute meeting the good doctor provided Eddy with computer charts indicating fitness targets, meal plans and other tips for getting in peak shape and staying that way throughout the season. There was a fitness evaluation in July and another one in August. As Eddy would soon find out, hockey fitness in high school hockey was not the same as hockey fitness in Junior hockey. After his meeting with the fitness doctor, Eddy had to meet the educational consultant, John Thompson. John explained that he was a former teacher and semi pro hockey player and was now in charge of co-ordinating school schedules for the players and checking the attendance. John took his job very seriously. He cared more about the student athlete than about the athlete student. You miss a class, you miss a game. You fail an assignment and you become a sustaining member of the after hours study club. John would also ensure that when ready Eddy was enrolled in the local University to start working towards a degree.

The Empty Net

Eddy was not there to get a degree, he was there to play in the N.H.L. He had no difficulty explaining that to Mr. Thompson. Mr. Thompson smiled and summoned the coach Jiggs Smith and the General Manager Stan Jones over to their table. Mr. Thompson explained to them that Eddy wanted to play pro and thought that attending at school might slow him down. The three men looked at each other and then at Eddy and laughed. Stan Jones, who was developed through the business side and not through the hockey side, spoke first. He was generally very mild mannered, political and complacent, but certain topics certainly aroused a passion in him. "Mr. Walsh, in my 25 years in professional hockey I have had 31 players move on to the N.H.L., about ten of those had decent careers. Another 50 or so have played in various minor leagues or in Europe. Sounds glamorous, $300.00 per week, 5 games per week, bus travel, cheap hotels, lots of fighting and guaranteed trades almost every year. Perfect for a 22 year old, hell for a married man. You my friend are a third round pick. I don't give a rat's ass who told you how good you are, they were wrong. You have some potential, but, and this is a big but, you are slow, don't see the ice well, have an average shot, and have a bad attitude. You can agree now to attend school, do what the coach tells you, do what the trainer tells you, do what your captain tells you, or you can get on the next bus to polookaville and play industrial league hockey for the rest of your life." Eddy didn't know whether to cry, tell him to fuck off, or get on the bus. He did know it wasn't a great start to his career. "Would I be able to take Political Science courses at the University?" The chorus was in unison as they sung songs of rejoicing. "Oh yes Eddy, you can do it, we will set it up, you'll do fine."

Eddy felt sick and wanted to go home. He asked to take a break before his next meeting and went to find his parents. They were in their own meeting with other parents, billets and the away-from-home co-ordinator. This team had everything. He got his parents attention and met them over by the boards.

The Empty Net

Eddy told them that the team told him he had to go University. His mom was concerned as to how he would get in with his marks, and his father was concerned with who would pay for it.

Eddy's father Gerry was a practical man of limited insight. He had enormous skills as an athlete and young scholar, but early on developed a chip on his shoulder that prevented him from realizing that potential. After a couple of minor league try-outs he packed in hockey for almost ten years. Until Eddy came along, he didn't even remember where he had put his skates or even if he still had any. He had quit University because of the Politics and the cost. No one ever really knew what that meant, other than it meant no degree and no prestigious job. A job at the mill beckoned and with two kids, Gerry didn't have many options. He worked 35 years there, maybe enjoying 30 days in total. Every day was a struggle, but God bless him he did it. Eddy always thought that all those poor bastards that hated their jobs but did them day in and day out for many years, they were heroes. Any one can have a great job they love and do it easily, but when the job absolutely bites and you still do it , that is something. Either the dedication and perseverence of a hero, or the stupidity of a loser that never tried. The jury was still out.

The Walsh family decided to have a conversation with Mr. Jones. "My boy is not that bright, besides I have another child and really can't afford to pay for University" "You don't pay for University here, the team pays for it. We pay your tuition, books, incidentals, and any thing else you need for school" Gerry couldn't believe it. " Its part of the education that we have for all the players. Once you sign a contract , then you are entitled to four years of University tuition, books, and room and board, if necessary." "If you are of University age now, then we make you attend. Once your career is over, if you haven't completed your degree, we will continue to pay your costs."

Gerry couldn't believe it, he almost soiled himself on the spot. No one knew if he was more excited that his boy might actually have a shot of becoming the first one in the history of the family to complete

University, or if it was because they were getting something for free. Whatever reservations the Walsh family may have had about Junior Hockey had now vanished. This was better than their wildest dreams. "Why couldn't your brother play hockey?," the father thought.

With the schooling issue cleared up, it was off to see Jimy about skates, equipment, and other stuff. Joanne introduced Eddy to her Uncle Jimy. Eddy knew he would like Jimy and Jimy didn't disappoint. As soon as Eddy said hello, Jimy handed him a cheque for $750.00. "What's this for" "Your summer training expenses and some gas money, there will be more later." Eddy thought things were starting to come together. Eddy thanked him again for the help he had given him with his knee.

Jimy explained to Eddy that he needed to set up a bank account so that the team could automatically deposit his weekly pay. All the players received $75.00 per week plus gas money. If they didn't have a car then they were supposed to give the gas money to the player that would be their driver for the year. Eddy did not have a car, so he would be giving his gas money away. He tried to figure out how much money he would get if he drove guys around but quickly the math became overwhelming. He would think about buying his own car later.

Jimy sized Eddy for skates and equipment and told him it would be sent by courier to him in the next few weeks. He was to use it in the summer but was not to wreck the gloves or pants, they were for the season. The skates were just one of three pairs he would get during the year.

Some of the new guys were going out to celebrate and invited Eddy to come along. Eddy declined. He was exhausted and besides his parents wanted to drive home. It had been a long stressful, rewarding day. He wanted to go to sleep, but knew it would take a long time to fall asleep that night. He didn't want to get off on the wrong foot with the guys and hoped they wouldn't hold it against him.

Chapter Fourteen

The Crusaders end of the year banquet was a difficult one for Eddy. He was the only bright spot on the team and he won most of the awards. The coach talked about building the team around Eddy the next season and how much better they would be. Eddy wanted to be part of it but knew he had to move on. He had achieved everything he could at that level and was not learning or developing as fast as he wanted to. If he did not make the junior league then he had already decided to play in the mens league. The hockey was not any better but he would be challenged by men not boys. It was hard listening to the speeches knowing that he had already made his mind up about the future. He decided that this was the night for the team and he would not ruin it by disclosing his plans. There would be better opportunities to break the news to the coach and then his team mates.

  The final exams that year were particularly easy. Eddy didn't know if it was because he had studied for them or because they were such bird courses. He didn't care, he would take the 77% average with grade eleven now in the bank. One more year and he would graduate. He thought how odd that was. The time had gone very fast, even the time when he was injured.

  Eddy got his equipment the second week of July and he was thrilled. As much to get the equipment as he was to get it by courier. There weren't many courier deliveries in town, other than to the mill, and so the locals would be talking about it. He immediately got his mom to drive him to the local rink where he knew some guys were playing shinny. He couldn't wait to show off his new duds. How envious everyone else would be. The local jocks didn't disappoint. They were all eager to see Eddy's new equipment and talk to him about the draft and his new team.

  Eddy worked very hard in the summer to stay in shape and improve on his game. He worked in the gym every day with Anna at his side. She was in great shape and her achilles tendon problem had corrected. She would not pursue track but was glad she could walk without the slight limp. She had decided to go to a small college in Niagra Falls, New York, but live on the Canadian side of the border for the next three years. Eddy was so happy and it gave him more incentive to work hard so he could make the team. How great it would be to live in a new city with your girlfriend nearby. It would certainly ease the transition from the small town to the bigger city. The two talked about it often and were both very excited about the prospects. Eddy was surprised that she was going to Niagra Falls, she hadn't even mentioned it and then all of the sudden it was a done deal. A couple of days after Anna's announcement, Joanne told Eddy that her parents were getting a divorce. They were going to sell their house and the father was going to go to the states to live. She wasn't sure what her mother was going to do but knew she didn't want to stay and be a part of it. Her plan was to move to Niagra Falls and live with her Uncle Jimy so she could complete her last year of high school. Eddy was beside himself, his two favourite girls were going to be with him in the big city. Away from home for the first time in his life and he would be able to explore a new city with Anna and Joanne. He wondered though if they would both be going to the Falls if he weren't going to be there. Just the though t boosted his already healthy confidence. Joanne would move down in mid July, Anna in mid August and Eddy the end of August.

    The off-season had been a good one to Eddy. He managed to add twenty pounds of muscle to his 180 pound frame of last year and added three inches to his previously large six foot body. He was bigger than a lot of guys that he had been playing against last year and he knew it. This year it would be different. The players were older, smarter and bigger, some much bigger. He couldn't wait to test himself against these guys. He had worked the heavy bag all summer in the hopes of not getting his ass kicked. He had heard that there was a lot of fighting in junior hockey and wanted to be prepared. This year there was no way to lose. If he won the fights, he got the girls, if he lost the

The Empty Net

fights, the girls felt sorry for him and waited in line to console him. After all he was a rookie and not much was expected of him.

Chapter Fifteen

Training camp was scheduled to start the last week of August. There had been a rookie and free agent camp in early August, but Eddy had not been required to attend. From the rookie camp the team brain trust selected ten players to attend the main camp. Thirty six players would compete for twenty three spots. The team dressed twenty players for each game, but generally carried the extra players who would practice but not dress for games. The extra players were handy in the event of injury but were mostly for the coach to be able to point them and remind every body it could be them. It wasn't always the same three players that sat out. If you didn't have a good game you could find yourself in the press box very quickly. The team also had a junior"B" affiliation where they could send players back and forth.

      The team had two meetings before the camp started to go over rules and what was expected. It was driven into the guys heads that they were not there to have fun, they were there to win. Anything less was unacceptable. Between the first meeting and the second meeting the team had swung a three player trade. The younger players were shaken up but the veterans dismissed it as part of the business.

      When Eddy walked into the dressing room for the first time he couldn't believe it. The place was huge and in sections. The main section was fully carpeted and had stalls for the players. Their equipment hung up above them. Eventually, once the team was picked, the players names would be placed above their stalls. There was a shower room that had change facilities and washrooms. Behind it was the weight room and all the exercise bikes. Off to the other side was the trainers area where they had a whirlpool tub, a table, and a small medical room. Around the corner from that, the coaches rooms. There were pictures of previous teams hung proudly on the walls and speakers every where. The loud music seemed to be always playing. Eddy liked it a little quieter but would have to make the adjustment. Once you were in the dressing room you could make your way to the weights, study area, coaches rooms or trainers area without ever going

The Empty Net

outside. It was very professional and made him think like a professional. The team repeated that a lot to the players, that they should act like professionals, play like professionals and look like professionals. Even in training camp they were not allowed to wear sweat suits to the rink, it was a shirt and tie, but thankfully no jacket. Eddy had a stall next to Andre Fiset, Zak McDougall and John Swinson, three other rookies who he was also sharing a hotel room with.

The first day on the ice was simply drills and some conditioning exercises. There were two fights during a skating drill. Eddy was concerned and made sure he was always aware of what was happening on the ice. Eddy had heard that the physical part of the game was important, but fights during skating drills, that was crazy. The first day went well and Eddy was full of confidence. For the first time in his career, Eddy was able to wear a helmet with just a small, clear visor. In previous seasons it was mandatory that he wore a helmet with a full cage on it. The cage was heavy and made it hard to see the puck when it was in your skates. The new lighter visor was great. Eddy figured it would help his game because he would be able to see the puck that much better. He just had to remember that he didn't have any protection around his face any more. Eddy was exhausted and glad to get back to his hotel room. His new buddies felt the same as they all fell asleep before dinner time. Most of the new guys had never experienced any thing like this training camp before. It was very hard on them physically but also mentally. Just when it looked like the drill was over, the coach would have them go through it again. Not knowing when something was going to end was very difficult. It was hard sleeping that night in the hotel room with three other guys but eventually Eddy fell asleep. Andre, Zak and John were all good guys, but he didn't know them that well. Eddy was accustomed to his own room and didn't like other people sleeping in the same room with him. His sleep was shattered by the sound of something breaking on the floor beside him. He had a canvass bag put over his head before he could do anything. His hands were tied behind his back and he was told to be quiet. He was scared and didn't know what was happening. He heard the commotion with his roommates but couldn't see it. One of the other rookies started screaming as if in pain. Eddy smelt a different smell, sort of a lemony, girly type smell. He could not tell through the bag that it was a woman's hair removal product. After about ten minutes his hands came free and he heard the door slam beside him. He took off the bag just as his room mates were doing the same thing. One of them turned the lights on so they could see what had happened. The room was a mess and one of their fellow rookies was whimpering in the corner of the room. His hands were still tied and he was naked. They couldn't remember what he had looked like when he had gone to sleep, but they were darn sure that he had body hair. John Swinson a small, fast forward from Toronto now had no eyebrows, no chest hair, no hair on his legs or underarms and no pubic hair. It appeared that young John had either not yet hit puberty or had been the first victim of a hazing by the veterans. The other players felt sorry for him because they knew it could have been one of them. John made his way to the bathroom to wash off what remained of the burning hair remover. The four put some furniture against the door and tried to get back to sleep. The next day in the dressing room, as John began to change, the veterans started to laugh uncontrollably. Eddy thought they were jerks and vowed not to be like them when he was a veteran. John lasted one more practice before packing it in and returning home. Eddy bought a special door lock on the way back from practice, there would be no more over night surprises for him. At the daily team meeting the coach said he did not want any hazing incidents and that everyone was equal on the team. It had a hollow ring to it and every one sensed there was more to come, even though no one spoke about it. Eddy figured the coach looked upon it as team building, but it was really nothing more than intimidating, hurtful acts of bullies. It did nothing to help the veteran and rookie players bond. The third day saw the first of two a day scrimmages. The players had been divided into three teams. There were only three defence man per

The Empty Net

team, so there was lots of ice time for every body. Eddy felt comfortable but was amazed at the speed of the game, the reaction time required and the skill of the players. At that level every body could handle the puck well, very well. Eddy hung in and had not been beaten one on one during the scrimmages. He wished the coach would talk to him, but quickly discovered that these guys were not big on two way communications. If there was something they wanted you to know, you would know it. They were not concerned about your input and did not have time to listen to it anyway. Eddy would sit on the bench between shifts and look up into the seats high up in the arena. The coaches, scouts and other team personnel sat there together, talking and making notes. Sometimes he would see them collectively shaking their heads when a player screwed up on the ice. Too many mistakes and a player was gone.

The first exhibition game was a week after training camp had opened. The list went up at the dressing room the day before the game and Eddy's name was not on it. He was devastated and could not understand why. He met with Jimy who told him not to worry about it. A lot of times they didn't dress a lot of rookies the first game. Some coaches wanted to win, even in exhibition games that meant nothing in the standings. It was always Jigg's way to try and win the first game and then play the rookies in the other games to see what he had. It was no consolation and Eddy was pissed off. He went out to a bar and didn't even bother going to the game. When he arrived the next morning he was advised that he had been fined $ 75.00 for not showing up and if it happened again then he would be sent home. This was not high school, the players didn't dictate what would happen and what wouldn't. He didn't know that if a player wasn't dressed for a game that they still had to attend at the rink and ride the exercise bike during the game. Eddy would not forget.

The next exhibition game was against Peterborough in Peterborough. The list went up and sure enough Eddy's name was on it. He was relieved and frightened at the same time. This was a test that would show him and the coaches if he belonged and if he could compete at the Junior "A" level. Eddy wondered how it would be to play against Bobby Gage again and if his parents would be there.

    The bus ride to Peterborough was about three hours long and most of the players slept. There was not much talk on the bus at all. Eddy didn't know if that is how it always was or if that was peculiar to the day. The bus arrived about two and a half hours before game time. The players got off and made their way to the dressing room. Eddy started to get dressed when one of the veterans told him they didn't generally get dressed until about an hour before the game. Eddy was embarrassed but thanked the guy. He went out to the hall way where most of his team mates where hanging out. Some were playing mini stick hockey and some were throwing a football around. In the corner there were four guys bouncing a soccer ball around. It was explained to Eddy that every one had a different way to unwind and get ready for the game. He should find something that works for him. He got in the middle of the football game and enjoyed that. For the rest of the season that is what he did to loosen up and get ready for the game. Depending on the rink, they could run around and run plays, in the smaller buildings they just had enough room to throw it back and forth. It really took Eddy's mind off of the stress of the impending game and got him loose and warmed up at the same time. The pre-game timing was the same all year. The teams were on the ice forty minutes prior to game time for a twenty minute warm up. Then off the ice and back to the dressing room while the Zamboni did it's job. The buzzer went two minutes before the game and that was the signal to go back out on the ice. The coach didn't care when you started to get ready but you had to be ready at least five minutes before the start of the warm up, that is when he would give a pre- game talk, if he hadn't said anything on the bus ride down. Some players could get dressed in five minutes. Some took thirty minutes. Every one seemed to have their own little ritual. Which piece of equipment went on in which order, which skate got tied first, how the tape was put on, these were all important things and were not changed during the year. To change a ritual would bring bad luck. Most hockey players had at least one or two superstitions, but most wouldn't admit to them. Sticks were another source of distraction. Guys could spend hours getting their stick just right. They would start with the length, then work on the blade making sure it had the correct warp and was the perfect dimensions. The tape job was the coup de grace. Some would tape half of the blade, some would tape it twice, some liked white tape while others preferred black tape, and some would use baby powder on their sticks. Players never bugged other players about their sticks, that was sacred. The guys started to drift into the dressing room and Eddy knew that the time had come. He got dressed and was focusing on the game. He knew none of his family were going to be at the game so there wasn't any added pressure. The coach didn't say much before the game other than Peterborough had kicked their ass all season last year and perhaps it was time for that to change. Eddy had a good warm up and wondered how some guys did it. The warm up was just as draining as some of his practices were in high school. He still had a game to play. After the warm up some guys got changed, some switched to another pair of their skates and some just sat and starred at the floor. The two minute buzzer went and it was show time. Skating out onto the ice Eddy could not help but look into the stands and marvel at how many people were at the game. There were more people at this exhibition game than he had ever played in front of before. They were also very vocal. The announcer announced the scratches and Bobby Gage was one of them. Eddy didn't know if he was hurt or it was a numbers thing or something else. Eddy wanted to talk to Bobby about it but knew that was impossible. With the National Anthem over it was game time.

  Eddy got his first shift about three minutes into the game. It was uneventful and lasted about thirty seconds. Eddy didn't want to come off, but understood you did what you were told. He got back on about four minutes later for a forty five second shift. At least they were getting longer. In his third and last shift of the period Eddy made a nice check on the boards and sprung a forward with a nice pass, if the guy had better hands it would have been a goal. Eddy didn't know why he was sat after his best shift of the period. He asked one of the veterans on the bench what the deal was and the guy just smiled at him and said "once you get used to the mental bullshit and the head games they play, it's not too bad." Eddy didn't like it but understood. He had heard that he would have to be patient, everyone had told him that as he prepared to go to camp. The coaches could be funny about how they would use a player. One game the guy would be the star and get forty minutes of ice time, the next night he might get five shifts all game. No explanation would ever be given.

Eddy got more ice time in the second period and felt more comfortable. He made some good hits and didn't get scored on. It was hard to take chances to make something happen for fear of making a mistake. It was a delicate balance that every player had to learn for themselves. The third period was worse than a wrestling match. The rule in the pre-season was that if you fought, it was a game misconduct and you were out of the game. As a result guys would wait until the third period to show how tough they were. There was a scrum in front of the Niagra Falls net after a good save. Eddy saw the first guy come in drop his gloves and grab the rookie winger, but Eddy didn't see the second guy that had lined him up as his target. The guy grabbed Eddy and swung at the same time. Eddy had no chance as the guys fist smashed his nose. The pain was immediate. Eddy couldn't see and bent over. The guy hit him a few more times but none of them connected. The linesman could see that Eddy was hurt and got in between. He helped Eddy to the bench so that the trainer could take him to the dressing room. Jimy said he would need a couple of stitches and that the nose was probably broken. Eddy felt sick, not because of the pain from the injury, but from the fact that maybe this goof he had never seen coming just took away his chance to make the team. Jimy took Eddy to the local hospital where Eddy received four stitches and had his broken nose set. They got back to the rink just as the bus was leaving. Often if the player was hurt and going to be in the hospital for any longer than an hour, the team bus would leave and the player would make his way back to town later, either by getting a ride from

The Empty Net

some one or by taking the bus. Eddy found his seat and Jimy went to talk to the coach.

    Eddy found out that the guy that had sucker punched him had gotten a game misconduct and match penalty for intent to injure. He would be suspended and wouldn't start the season for his team. Eddy found out his name was Kevin Gleason and he fancied himself a tough guy, even though most of the players in the league fancied him a cheap shot weasal. Eddy was a scratch for the next home game and thought he might be on the way back to his home town. Luckily he didn't know if the coaches had seen enough of him to keep around. He didn't have to wait long. Eddy got called into the managers office after the exhibition game that he didn't play. The manager reviewed how he thought Eddy had performed and what the teams expectations were of him for the rest of the season. He had made the team basically as the sixth defence man. Eddy didn't care at that moment how much ice time he would get, he was just glad to be part of the team and one step away from his dream of playing in the N.H.L. Eddy rushed home and called Joanne, Anna and then his parents. They were all very happy for him. Joanne told him she knew he had made the team but was sworn to secrecy. Her inside information may come in handy later so he let it slide.

    The next morning a nice couple met him at the rink. The Brady's were an attractive couple in their early forty's. They had two daughters, a dog and a nice house. They lived close enough to the arena so Eddy could walk if he wanted to. The Brady's would be his billets, his home away from home for the rest of the season. When Eddy got to their car he met fifteen year old Tara and thirteen year old Tina. On the short drive to their home, Tara could not stop looking at Eddy. Eddy had noticed and returned the looks. She was pretty good looking, but would have to be off bounds. Tina asked him why his face was so ugly. Eddy explained that he had a broken nose and a nasty cut, but it would get better. It became obvious very quickly that Tina didn't care much for hockey or hockey players and that her older sister was a would be puck bunny who could easily get herself in trouble. Eddy presumed that it was probably Tara that had convinced her parents to be billets. Eddy was determined to look after her and make sure none of his team mates tried to take any liberties with her, no matter how tempting she made it.

    The Brady's had a nice four bedroom home with all the bedrooms on the second floor. Eddy's bedroom was next to Tara's. It was a big room and had it's own bathroom. Well it was sort of it's own bathroom, there were two doors and so it adjoined with Tara's room. It was handy but made Eddy nervous. Thankfully it didn't have a bath tub or shower in it. Eddy was shown around the house and told the rules. The rules were really the team rules about drinking, having people over and curfew. The house had all the extra's. The big screen television, stereo, air hockey game and video games. It would be a great place to relax when he wasn't on the ice. Daisy the Beagle was the family pet. She was a nice dog, not too big, not too small. She was fun to play with but would leave people alone when she was told to. Tara suggested that Eddy could join her when she went to walk every day after dinner. Eddy said "sure", without thinking.

    Joe Brady was an accountant who worked for a large multinational corporation. He had an important job and made a lot of money. The down side was that he had to travel a lot and was out of town for at least a week every month. Joe was a fit man but certainly would not be mistaken for athletic. He was educated, articulate and a rational thinker. Donna Brady was a good looking home maker who was probably a cheerleader in high school. She did not work out but was able to magically maintain her figure. Donna was smart, interesting and attractive, but she had a sadness about her. She had been in the same course as her husband at University but decided to quit in her second year to pursue other endeavours. Once they were married there was no need for her to provide financially for the family and so she remained at home to do as she pleased. She had two beautiful well behaved daughters but that was not enough.

Eddy was quite pleased with his new family. The team had talked about their billets at practice and it could have been worse. One guy was living with an older woman who had a lock installed on the fridge. Another guy was living with a young family that was going through some matrimonial problems. The wife focused most of her attention on the player. The player had to explain several times to her that he did not want to have sex with her. Apparently his pleas fell on deaf ears and after a couple of weeks the player was discreetly moved to another home.

The rest of the week was comprised of two a day practices and meetings. There were so many meetings that Eddy didn't remember if he was playing hockey or running a business. The police came in to talk to the players about safety. It was not long before Eddy figured out that they were talking about other peoples safety, not his. They should be careful if they go to bars or public places because some nut trying to impress his friends might challenge them because they are hockey players. They should be careful about getting themselves into any potentially vulnerable situations with young woman. They should not take chances by drinking. They shouldn't accept gifts from people they don't know or take rides from strangers. A few players snickered at that one. The next meeting was with a referee who went over all the rules, showed video and answered questions. It was a good session and the players enjoyed it. The ref talked about some of the things that they could get away with and some of the things that they would always get called for. His final piece of advice was that they should never, ever, make the ref look bad. If they did they would be out of the game.

A minister met with the team to talk about spirituality. He didn't talk about any organized religion but that the players should develop their spiritual inner self. He would be around the team during the year and available if any one wanted to talk to him. Eddy laughed to the guy sitting next to him, but was told that every one on the team had spoken to Reverend Dan at least a few times during last season. Eddy was intrigued.

There were meetings that dealt with the team rules, schedule, bus trips, expectations and everything they should know about the team. There were meetings that talked about nutrition, rules in the billet homes and the educational expectations. Mercifully, the week was over and with it the bulk of the team meetings.

Eddy's first day off with no obligations to be at the rink was going to be a busy one. Eddy had talked on the phone with Joanne and Anna all week and they decided to explore their new home. Joanne arrived with Anna in a car they had borrowed from some new friend. Today was going to be the day they took the tour of Niagra Falls and learn more about their new home. Tara got dressed and made her way to the car. She had only met the two older girls once and wanted to be their friend. She asked if they could use a tour guide, but both of the older girls said no, but thanked her. They both thought that Tara was a little tart and dangerous for Eddy. They had heard the whispers and wondered how Eddy would be able to control himself if the little vixen decided to come onto him in the house. Neither girl had much faith that Eddy had the ability to do the right thing. Tara was upset at the girls reaction and went back into the house. She told Eddy that the two "bitches" were waiting for him and he had better hurry. When Eddy got in the car the girls told him what had happened. He thought they were way off base and should have cut Tara some slack and invite her along. Joanne and Anna looked at each other and wondered if their worst thoughts had already come true.

Joanne knew the city fairly well from visiting her Uncle on family trips over the years. Eddy and Anna had never been to the Falls before. They went to the falls and looked at the massive amounts of water powering over the huge incline. They had seen it in pictures and on television, but never close up. They all thought it was amazing, the roaring noise, the spray of water, the perennial rainbow and the thousands of tourists. Eddy felt a great peace and affinity with the falls and it would quickly become one of his favourite places to go. The three made their way up Clifton Hill experiencing the various wax

The Empty Net

museums as they went. They were like three kids that had just found their favourite amusement park. The gangster hall of fame, the oddity museums, mini golf, ice cream and fudge shops were too much. For two blocks there was nothing but glitz, bright lights and people. If anyone needed a cheap t-shirt, tacky Canadian flagged souvenir or plates with pictures of Royalty on them, this was the place to be. Eddy saw more Moose in the stores at the falls than he had ever seen back home in the North. The adventurers made their way over to the Casino but it was too crowded to get in. They didn't care because they weren't really in the mood to lose their money anyway. After walking for hours the trio started to get tired and decided to go for a drive. They drove far away from the tourists area and found a totally different city. There were a lot of people living in the suburbs and they had their own amenities. It was unlikely that many that lived in the "burbs" spent much time in the tourist area, unless they worked there.

    Anna wanted to show Eddy her school, so they headed to the bridge. Joanne had already been there, which was a surprise to Eddy, and knew the way well. They crossed into the States with no problem and within ten minutes were at a big College campus. It was pretty nice and there were lots of intellectual types sitting around reading or thinking, Eddy wasn't sure which. Joanne showed Eddy where most of Anna's classes were held and where the student hall and book store where located. Eddy was impressed with Joanne's knowledge about Anna's school. They decided to have dinner at one of the beef places in the tourist area and headed back to Canada. The dinner was great and very filling. The girls hardly ate anything and gave most of their dinner to Eddy. Eddy bugged them about how skinny they were getting. During dinner Joanne told them that her brother Bud had been named captain of the Crusaders for the coming season. Eddy joked how pathetic the team must now be, Joanne did not laugh. Exhausted, they skipped dessert and made their way back to Eddy's place. He was not allowed to have two visitors, or girls in the house, so the two girls decided to go back to Joanne's. Eddy said good night and they both gave him a big kiss. As they pulled away Eddy wished he could go with them, but he didn't want to mess up with curfew. Tara was at the door, in her pyjamas, to welcome Eddy back. Eddy laughed but thanked her. He apologized that she wasn't able to go with them but that maybe just the two of them could go for a tour some day. Tara smiled and giggled about how nice that would be.

Niagra Falls was a very interesting place for Eddy. It had a blue collar feel to it that was similar to home, but it had more. It was a dynamic place that was inundated with cultures from the far corners of the earth, at least for a short time, any ways. Eddy could walk down to the falls and hear just about any language spoken on earth. The tourists loved the falls. There was also the border aspect that made life more interesting. Eddy was five minutes away from another country, the most powerful nation on earth, at least that is how they billed themselves. He loved to cross the border and go shopping in the States. Even though the Canadian dollar was not worth much compared to the U.S. dollar, the selection and discounts made it worth while. In Canada he would go to a store and find five shirts in his size, in the states he would find fifty. The food was different, the people were different, the roads were different and the feel was different. Eddy couldn't really put his finger on it, but that was it, the states had a different look, feel and smell to it. Eddy was glad he was Canadian.

Eddy's parents regretted that they could not get down to the Falls to watch him play. They promised they would make at least one trip down, after March when the weather started to get nice again. They really wanted to be a part of his new life and know everything he was going through. Even though they received the Niagra Falls newspaper once a week, the summaries and stories did not tell them how their Eddy was doing. The mom asked him to write out a typical game day for her so at least she knew what happened on those days. Eddy sent her a letter with the following schedule attached.

The Empty Net

Game Day

Wake up at 8:00 a.m., have a small bowl of cereal and some juice. Drink a small bottle of water on way to the rink. Arrive at rink 8:30 a.m., get dressed, stretch, fix sticks. 9:00 a.m. until 9:45 a.m. on the ice for light skating drills, work on power play or penalty killing. 9:45 until 10:30 a.m. get changed ,ride the exercise bike, have shower. Home by 11:00 a.m. to have lunch, which is the main meal of the day. After lunch play video games, go for walk with billet and dog, watch a movie, read a book, write letters. 2:30 p.m. until 3:45 p.m. sleep. At 3:45 wake up and have something to eat, fruits and lots of water. Get changed and arrive at rink at 4:45 p.m. Get partially changed, then go out in the hall and play football, walk around, chat with guys.

After the game, if it was at home and there was not a road game the next day, then it would be home to bed, curfew at 11:30 p.m. If there is a game the next day, then generally the team would have a pasta dinner in the dressing room after the game before they went home to get some sleep.

Sometimes the routine changes a little, but not too much. If a player didn't play in the game they would have to ride the exercise bike during the game for about an hour. If the player developed any pain or had an injury during the game then they would line up to be dealt with by the training staff.

The team was on the ice every day. Every couple of weeks they may have a day off and did not have to be at the arena. The players look forward to those days and there was usually great expectations as to what the players would do. Often it turned out to be nothing more than a sleeping day. During the week it is harder because there is school. Most of the guys were in high school but some were in College or University. There was a practice everyday at 3:30 p.m. until 5:00 p.m. every day. If the practice didn't go well or the team was in a slump then sometimes the practices would go a little longer.

The Empty Net

    The on ice commitment was a large change and a big transition for Eddy. His high school league played three fifteen minute periods, had a twenty four game schedule, and practices most days. In junior the teams played three twenty minute periods, had a sixty eight game schedule and could be away from home for four days at a time. Some of the bus rides were twenty hours long which wasn't all that much fun in the dead of winter, being in the middle of nowhere. The team never flew or took the train because of costs. With all the team personal it was expensive feeding, housing, and transporting twenty five people for any extended period of time. Eddy knew that the trips weren't too bad compared to some other leagues. In the Western league there was a team in Manitoba and teams in British Columbia, what a drive that would be. Eddy had developed a passion for cross word puzzles and playing his hand held video game. Shannon had sent him the first cross word puzzle book and challenged him to complete it. He did not get them right, most of the time, but he did enjoy them, was addicted to them and they passed the time away nicely. Shannon would send him a couple of them a week. Eddy thought it was just Shannon's way of staying in touch, but he didn't mind, he missed his brother. After the fourth game of the season there was a party scheduled to be held at the house of the captain, Ron Tait. The rookies were told to bring a case of beer and a change of clothes. Eddy was not looking forward to it and did not want to go. On the Saturday of the party Eddy called Jimy and told him he felt sick. Jimy told him to see the team doctor and report back to him. Eddy ran all the way to the doctors office, holding a hot water bottle to his head. When he met the doctor, Eddy was burning up. The doctor wrote him a prescription and told him to go home and sleep for at least two days. The doctor called Jimy and told him the news, Jimy called the coach and the captain to let them know that Eddy was sick. He would be a definite scratch from the party that night. Eddy was so relieved that he did not have to go. He had dreaded it all week and had a bad feeling about it.
    The goalie Zak McDougall was the first one to call. "It's three in the morning, what's going on Zak?" Zak could hardly speak. Eddy

The Empty Net

thought he sounded a little drunk, but there was something, much more, something was wrong. "Walshy, it's Andre, he's not too good, he wasn't breathing or any thing." Zak was getting more upset and making less sense. "What happened, what's wrong with Andre?" "Just get down to the hospital Walshy, hurry." Joe Brady was away for the week at a convention and not around for Eddy to get to drive him. Eddy went to the bathroom and when he came out Donna was knocking on his door. "Can I come in Eddy?" Donna entered his room in a t-shirt to see if everything was okay, she thought she had heard the phone ring but wasn't sure. "It was a team mate, can you drive me to the hospital, I'm not sure what's happening." "No problem Eddy, I will just get dressed." The two made it to the hospital in about five minutes. When they arrived it was like a team meeting, every one was there, the players, the coaches, Jimy and Mr. Stan Jones. Eddy was the only player that was not at the party and didn't know what was going on. Mr. Stan Jones took Eddy and Mrs. Brady aside and explained. "Apparently at the party Andre was forced to drink a lot of alcohol, he got sick and threw up, but choked on his own vomit. He passed out, but no one immediately noticed it, when they did, he wasn't breathing. Someone called the ambulance and here we are, the doctor hasn't spoken to us yet." Eddy grabbed Mrs. Brady and held onto her. He wanted to cry but not in front of the team, not that any one would have noticed. He thought about it being him. Maybe he would have been forced to drink and he might be in the hospital now himself. It was obviously a rookie initiation party that had gone too far.

    At three thirty in the morning the emergency room doctor came into the lobby and told Mr. Jones and the team that Andre Fiset had died at 3:20 a.m. of alcohol poisoning and asphyxiation. At first there was a hush over the room and then the players started to lose it. They could not believe that one of their own was dead, and that some of their own, if not all of them had somehow killed him. Eddy remembered Terry Barker and how unfair it all seemed. Terry had contributed to his own demise with his lifestyle, Andre did not deserve this. He was an innocent.

The Empty Net

    Mrs. Brady got Eddy back home and made some tea so they could talk. Tara and Tina were waken by their voices and came into the living room to see what was happening. Mrs. Brady explained what she could and the girls started to cry. Eddy was crying and Tara tried to comfort him. The four stayed up the rest of the night, but didn't say another word. As soon it was late enough in the early morning, Eddy phoned home to talk to his mom. His mom was in shock and couldn't believe it. She wanted him to come home, to get away from there. They agreed to talk later.

    The mid day news on television opened with the story of the dead junior hockey player from the Falls. They said while the cause of death is unknown, it is reportedly alcohol related. "Those bastards, why do they say that, they never even knew Andre." It was all over the radio and on the news that night. The newspaper had lots of pictures and lots of speculation. The phone rang off the hook at the Brady residence, but they never answered it. There was no one they wanted to talk to. Jimy showed up with Joanne around 5:00 p.m. to tell him the team had a meeting at the rink at 6:30 p.m. that night. Joanne stayed and tried to comfort Eddy. They spoke of home and how maybe it would be nice to be there right now.

    Their Sunday game and the games for the next week were cancel l ed. Everything about their season would be reviewed and decisions made at the appropriate time. Eddy thought maybe their season would be cancel l ed, but was told it would just be rescheduled. So much for Andre, life would just go on. Eddy felt sick, he thought that the season should be cancel l ed. After Mr. Jones and Jiggs had spoken to the team, Reverend Dan took over. He spoke of life and death, preparation, meanings and a whole bunch of other stuff. It was so much that it became meaningless and confusing. When he finished three police officers entered the meeting room. They would have to meet with the players individually and take statements. Eddy was one of the first and told them he wasn't there. They confirmed his story and asked him to leave. Zak called later that night and told him that the cops were there until about 11:00 p.m. and were going to meet with about ten players the next morning. Zak got the distinct impression that the police wanted to charge one of their team mates with murder or manslaughter. Life was getting too complicated. It was bad enough some one had died, but to affix blame was not quite fair. Eddy thought there was a lot of blame to go around. The manager and coach who knew of the party, the league that did nothing but pay lip service to the whole issue of hazing, the beer companies that aimed their advertising at his age group and society in general for tolerating it all.

The team gathered together at the Church in Toronto where Andre Fiset had been baptized, confirmed and attended all his life. There were a lot of people, old, young, athletes, family and others. Eddy saw the Fiset family and nodded to them. He had never met them and they probably didn't know who he was. He wondered how they felt about all these young men from the Falls standing there in the Church while their son lay in a coffin. He thought that if it was him that he wouldn't want the team there. They would be just a reminder to his parents of their loss, plus one of them may be a killer. He suddenly felt very uncomfortable being there. After the funeral the players met back at the Fiset house to meet the parents. Eddy met the mother and expressed how sorry he was. Mrs. Fiset talked about Andre and how happy he was to be playing with the guys he was. She said that she knew all about him from her son. She recalled the story of that poor boy getting shaved in their hotel room during training camp, but that Eddy had gone to the store and gotten a special lock so it couldn't happen again. Andre had told her that was pretty smart of Eddy and helped them all sleep better. Mrs. Fiset also knew he wasn't at the party. She gave him a hug and told him to always trust his intuitions. He thanked her and went outside. Anna had come to Toronto with them and was there to comfort him. Eddy didn't really know Andre, not really, and he thought that was a shame. If he was going to stay and play, he wanted to change, he wanted to know the people he was going through the battle with.

The Empty Net

It was an emotional week at school and on the ice. All the questions, all the knowing glances were a strain. It was announced on the Thursday that they would resume their schedule on Sunday night, and that the police had decided against laying any charges. As soon as the police announcement was made it set off a domino of events. Three players were traded and one was sent home out right. It was only speculation but Eddy was pretty sure who the police and team blamed for Andre's death. The players that remained met and decided to dedicate the season to Andre. At Sunday's game there was a presentation to Andre's family, a few moments of silence and the retiring of his number 14 and his sweater. The fans were crying and upset, but they had come and wanted to see a game. It was the strangest game of Eddy's life but he got through it. Eddy could not focus on anything he was supposed to do. On one shift he went into the corner to get the puck and could hardly see it because he was crying. The opposing forward gently rubbed Eddy against the boards to get a whistle. Eddy didn't know if the guy was trying to hug him or to hit him. The other team seemed to feel just as bad as the Flyers did. Both teams were just going through the motions. There was virtually no hitting or shots on goal. Eddy knew that there were at least four guys that had played on Andre's teams in the past and he realized that hockey was a fraternity. A death of a player shook all the teams. The game ended one to nothing for the Flyers and every one was glad it was over. The team wore a patch on their sweaters with the number fourteen and A.F. on it for the rest of the season. Like they needed any help remembering Andre. It was mostly for the fans.

Jiggs Smith had been a good, tough minor leaguer for about twenty years. He got smoked so many times in his career that he hardly knew what day it was or where he was. He didn't win many fights but the important thing was that he always showed up for them. He was a good team mate and a loyal player. Team mates loved him and over the many years he had played in the minors he got to know a lot of people and develop life long friendships. Relationships were very important in the game of hockey, and could lead to life long employment. If a player was known as not a stand up guy, then their chances of getting hired as a coach, scout or something else after their playing days were over, was remote. As a coach it was said that he couldn't coach a starving dog out of a blizzard with a t-bone. Every year though Jiggs would do just enough to get the team into the play offs, the team would financially break even and so the owners loved him and kept him around. Once in awhile Jiggs would have a great season and everything would come together. Jiggs was smart and always surrounded himself with good hockey people. The assistant coaches were responsible for the systems and running the practices. The death of Andre had hit him hard. It was not the first player that he had coached that had died, there were others, but they had all died in the off season of car accidents or at their summer jobs. He had never felt as responsible for a death as he did now. Eddy went to the Catholic School in town, the same school that Tara went to. All of the other high school age players on the team went to the local high school just down the street from the arena. Being the only Flyer in his school meant that Eddy had to answer all the questions about Andre's death. After a week he decided to not discuss it any further. Tara tried to shelter him from their school mates. Despite the fact she was two grades below him, she seemed to always be around wherever Eddy was. Eddy would speak to his parents on the phone at least three times a week. They would speak of hockey and the weather and lots of non specific things. It was comforting just to hear each others voice. They would talk about the games, what went right, what went wrong. They would always ask about Anna and Joanne. It was very hard on them. Not only had Eddy moved away but so had their "adoptive" daughters. They got very spoiled seeing them every day and now they were lucky to speak with the girls once a month. They encouraged him to work hard in school as some day it might be important to him. Eddy never wavered from his position that he would finish high school, but it would not help him. He was going to be a pro hockey player and that was his only focus. Everything he did was to further his hockey dream.

The Empty Net

The days became weeks and the weeks became months. Everything was a blur and time just flew by. Eddy was tired all the time and either getting through an injury or just about to get a new one. The games were exciting but tedious. It was a rush to play before five or six thousand people and experience the trappings of celebrity, but even that got tiring at times. There were too many practices, too many games and too many people that wanted a piece of him. If they weren't at the arena the team often had them at a shopping centre or store opening doing promotions. The team did a reading series at the elementary schools during the week and that took more time. Eddy didn't mind going to a school once in awhile and reading to grade two kids, but every week was too much. Most of the kids were so afraid of Eddy they couldn't even hear what he was reading to them. Eddy was six foot three and his face was usually cut. The kids were three feet tall and not accustomed to seeing people that looked like Eddy, people that were over six foot three.

Chapter Sixteen

A week before the Christmas break the team had a Christmas party for the team, the billets, medical personal and others. The President spoke of the team being a family and how every one was important as a person first and a hockey player second. Even in the spirit of the season the guys laughed at that one. Andre was remembered and a prayer was said for a safe holiday and stronger second half of the season. Each player received a team travel bag with their number on it and a suit bag. After the dinner was over word spread quickly that two players had been traded to Kitchener for a goalie and a draft pick. Zak joked to Eddy that he would be next, but the apprehension in Zak's voice made it anything but funny.

There were two more games before the Christmas break, both at home, then the team would get a four day holiday. Even though four days was not a lot of time it seemed like an eternity to the banged and beat up Flyers. The last game before the break was like the first game they had played after Andre's death. It was obvious that the other team was just as anxious to get home and no one was going to do anything to prolong the agony. The teams skated through a three to two sleeper, but at least it was over.

Eddy couldn't wait for the Christmas break. Not that it was a long one, only four days, but mentally it would give him a chance to forget about the first half of the season. Eddy missed his parents, his home town, his room and his innocence. In four months life had worn him out. The mind games, the death of a team mate, the pain, the work, it was too much.

The bus ride home was the most wonderful, relaxing bus ride Eddy had ever taken. Joanne and Anna had decided to stay in the Falls so Eddy was on his own. The trip gave him almost an uninterrupted day to do nothing but think about his future. He wondered if hockey was for him and if he could continue to play in the Falls. After Andre's death a couple of players had packed it in, unable to focus on a game.

The Empty Net

Maybe he could end the season with the Crusaders and learn some skills that would allow him to get a job.

His mom grabbed him hard as soon as he got off the bus. He looked bigger, more mature, but very tired. Her young man was growing up quick, perhaps too quick, but he did not seem happy. They talked in the car, they talked walking up to the house, and they talked in the kitchen until early the next morning. He was pleased that he had his parents to talk with and wished that they were in the Falls with him. He was exhausted yet refreshed when he finally went to sleep at 10:00 in the morning. He was so tired he slept right through the day and evening until 7:00 the following morning. He woke up feeling better than he had in months.

Eddy went for a jog while his family slept. He ran into a few old friends and former team mates. He welcomed their company and enjoyed talking to them. A year ago he could hardly remember their names and wouldn't give them the time of day. The guys told Eddy how lucky he was to be in the Falls playing junior. They asked him all sorts of questions and treated him like a superstar. They didn't ask him about Andre and just focused on the experience of playing junior hockey. They all had the same dreams that Eddy had, but he was achieving them. Eddy wished them good luck in their season and resumed his work out. When he got home Shannon was up and working in his dark room. The two embraced and started sharing stories. Even though they didn't have a lot in common, they were brothers and that gave them an intense commonality that could not be disturbed. They were brothers and loved each other and were proud of each other. Time flew and around 2:00 in the afternoon their mom called them up to have lunch. Christmas Day was nice, but meant that Eddy would soon be on a bus ride back to his new life. The Walsh's reveled in each other's company and were truly thankful for the time they had together. Eddy's dad took him aside and talked to him about his plans. He told Eddy that he was disappointed that he had not taken advantage of opportunities when they had been presented to him.

The Empty Net

Although he enjoyed his life and was thankful for his family, he never was fulfilled because he never truly challenged himself to the ultimate, to the point of failure. He avoided failure by avoiding the challenge. It was something he had to deal with all his life. Many opportunities presented themselves once, in youth, and never again. If they are not taken advantage of, they are lost for ever. Mr. Walsh did not want his son to throw way the opportunity he had now. The opportunity would never present itself again. If Eddy walked away from hockey now he would think of that decision his whole life. Everything he would ever do or ever accomplish would be through the filter of what if. What if he had continued and become a hockey player, how would his life be different. His dad told him if it was easy, every one would do it. Eddy had a chance few other people ever had. It would be a shame for him to give up on his dream now. Eddy was very impressed with the passion with which his dad spoke. They had never spoken about hockey in those terms before and Eddy had never seen hockey in those terms. It was the right talk at the right time.

    The break had recharged him and Eddy was anxious to get back to the Falls to show those bastards what he could do. He would not let opportunity pass him by. His goal was to play in the N.H.L. and he would do whatever it took to get there. He would try to be more like a duck and let the abuse and other nonsense roll off his back. He would nod at the right time and say the right things, but he would not listen to the criticism or the crazed rants of the coach, or anyone else. Eddy almost missed the bus because his mom was reluctant to let him go. She wanted to hold him and protect him forever. She hated to see him away from home, pushing himself too hard and not enjoying the experience. To her it made no sense. It was a game, nothing else. She wanted her boy to be happy and more importantly healthy. She rejoiced every day that Shannon had not followed the dreams of his older brother.

    Shannon had loaded Eddy up with cross word puzzles and pictures of the neighborhood so there was no shortage of things to do on the long bus ride south. There was a small blizzard they went through about a half hour after they left but it hadn't lasted too long. Eddy thought about his brother and how well he was doing in school and with his photography hobby. He was pleased that his brother had developed something that he enjoyed and was obviously very good at. He was sure that Shannon would be able to pursue photography as a career if he wanted to. Eddy also thought a lot about his relationship with Anna. He loved her but the relationship was changing. Instead of the flaming passion they once had it was now just comfortable. They were more like pals than lovers. Anna was busy a lot with school and Eddy was busy with hockey. Their lives were too busy to share it with one another. Eddy was afraid of being alone. He thought maybe if something did happen to their relationship that he could now make the move on Joanne that he had always wanted to. He dismissed that notion quickly, as crazy as he was about her, there were no sparks between them, no electricity. Maybe he was simply destined to be single.

When Eddy got back to the Falls and made his way to the dressing room things seemed different. Certainly the team was much different than the one that had started the season. Some had come back from the break recharged, some looked as bad as they did when they left. Eddy hated that loser attitude and said something to a couple of the guys. It almost came to blows but everyone got his point. They were there to perform, to win. Acting like hard done by jerks would not cut it. If they did not want to be there then there were hundreds of guys lined up to take their place. The first game after the break was on the road in Cornwall. The snow storm and freezing rain made a long trip across the 401 seem that much longer. The team arrived at the rink two hours late and so the whole pre game regimen was thrown off. The weather conditions had forced their diner of choice to close for the day, so the team had not eaten all day. Three thousand faithful had found their way to the rink and so the game would go ahead. Maybe guys blood sugar was low, maybe guys were hungry, maybe guys were angry that the break was over. It didn't really matter what the cause,

The Empty Net

the result was a disaster. Down three nothing two minutes into the game the team decided to play it a different way. Five fights before the game was four minutes old told everyone that this was not a normal game. Eddy felt sorry for any one that was five minutes late. They would have missed five fights, three goals and a botched National Anthem. The first period took an hour and a half to play. Eddy got lots of ice because there were only three defenceman left in the game for the Flyers. Of all nights to be reduced to three defence this was not the night. Eddy and his team mates were hungry and starting to tire out. Eddy went into the corner to get the puck when some guy gave him a stick across the back. The guy didn't have to say "wanna go" twice. Eddy grabbed onto the guy and starting swinging as hard and as fast as he could. If helmets bruised then these guys would have been black and blue. Exhausted the two combatants finally just held onto each other until the linesman broke it up. Eddy thought he was going to throw up and was exhausted, he could hardly skate to the penalty box. The ref went by to tell the scorer the penalties and Eddy went crazy. He verbally attacked the surprised "zebra" until he was rewarded with a ten minute misconduct. Eddy looked at him with disgust. Surely that tirade was worth a game misconduct, not just a measly ten. Eddy made his way to the dressing room to relax. The fighting major combined with the ten minute misconduct would at least get him out of the second period. He made his way into the dressing room and found some things to eat and drink. Jimy had found some place that was opened and delivered. A good trainer was worth their weight in gold. Eddy felt much better and got ready for the third period. The third period started exactly three hours after the first one had. Usually a game would take two to two and a half hours to play, tonight it was any ones guess. The only good thing was that there was lots of room on the players bench. Most rinks had benches that were too small. Often the back up goalie would have to sit in a chair down from the bench. That was not a concern that night in Cornwall, with only eleven Flyers still in the game there was lots of room for every body. The third period was agonizing, two flyers threw up on the bench. The lack of food, dehydration, late arrival and double shifting was taking it's toll on the guys. The other guys hadn't gotten most of the second period off so they still hadn't eaten. Eddy was the only one that looked like he had anything left in the tank, a reality that wasn't lost on the other team. Five minutes into the period a guy grabbed Eddy from behind and spun him around. The guy was already swinging before Eddy dropped his gloves. Eddy made up for it quickly and soon had the guys helmet off. He hit the guy about six times in the head, cutting him with one of them. The linesman got in as soon as they saw the guy was cut and broke it up. As Eddy went to the penalty box his hand began to swell. By the time he got to the penalty box his hand was three times the size it usually was. Eddy knew something was wrong, the time keeper got the linesman's attention, and he skated Eddy to their dressing room. Jimy came in and said the hand was probably broken. The team was going to stay over that night so they decided to take Eddy to the local hospital. Jimy had to stay at the rink to deal with other potential injuries so the assistant trainer joined Eddy in a cab ride to the hospital. The emergency room was not crowded at all, but it was obvious that didn't matter. Eddy would be looked at when the nurse was good and ready to set things in motion. After almost forty minutes Eddy was taken to x-ray. Within an hour he was scheduled for surgery to put pins in his hand and fix the multiple breaks. When Eddy heard surgery he almost threw up, but there was no alternative. He went into surgery at one in the morning and was in recovery by two. When he woke up he felt good, it was not like the last time at all. He thought he could deal with surgery if it was always going to be like that night. He had a big cast on his hand but wasn't really in any pain.

  The team bus pulled out at 11:00 a.m. but Eddy would not be able to leave for another day. It didn't really matter though, now that he was hurt and couldn't contribute it didn't matter when he got out. Mrs. Brady and Tara walked into his hospital room and surprised him. They had been listening to the game on the radio and knew what happened and they had spoken to Jimy when the team got back into town. They didn't think it was right that Eddy take a bus back on his own and so they decided to go for a drive. Tara was on holidays and so it was a good time to get away. Tina was busy with homework and decided to stay behind, Joe Brady was in Mexico or some other hot climate place, they weren't quite sure. The ride back was enjoyable, filled with interesting conversation from two attractive females.

Eddy was out for almost a month. In that time he could not use his hand, but could ride the bike and do some skating, he just had to be careful. His strength was diminishing but his cardio was still good. Finally in early February the cast was taken off and he was able to start physiotherapy. His hand was sore and his arm was weak but he was cleared to play the second week of February. Eddy had learned early that once you were cleared to play, you either played or went home. No player had the luxury of playing 100% healthy.

Eddy could hardly hold his stick properly, but the doctor had approved him to play and so play he would. His first game back he was as nervous as his first game in the league. He was nervous because he knew he couldn't perform physically. He had his hand frozen before the game and taped his stick to his glove. He would be in trouble if his stick broke but he didn't have much choice. He was very tentative on his first few shifts. Every time he got the puck he would get rid of it. Sometimes to his team mates, but sometimes to the other team, which wasn't good. The coach came running over to him on the bench after one such gaffe and tore a strip off him. Eddy let the sarcasm of the coach roll off his back. He was not going to let other people drag him down anymore. After a few more weeks the hand felt a little better and at least Eddy could hold onto his hockey stick. As the hand got better his on ice performance improved dramatically.

It was late in the season and the players were bored, most anxious for the summer and the rest and healing it would bring. Some of the guys had heard about a lesbian bar in town and were eager to check it out. It was not officially a lesbian only bar so guys were permitted. Most of the guys that frequented the bar were gay, but the odd straight person could also be found. Not that anyone could tell who was who anyway. Zak, Eddy and two other guys decided to give it a whirl. None of them were gay and they weren't sure exactly why they were going, but they knew they wanted to be there. Zak talked in the car on the way over to the bar about threesomes and picking up some lesbian chicks. Eddy pointed out that these chicks were gay, which was different than chicks just not wanting to be picked up by guys. Presumably, they didn't like guys, that is why they were gay. The bar was bustling with people, lots of people, drinking and having a good time. The music was a little softer than a regular bar and it seemed like a safe place to be. Other than that, it seemed like a regular bar. It wasn't until you looked closer that you could see that women were dancing with women and men were dancing with men. Most of the guys had never seen that before and for some it made them just a bit uncomfortable. They also realized quickly that they were four guys in a gay bar. No one there would have known if they were gay or straight. No one would have asked if they were just bored hockey players trying to have a laugh. Eddy thought it would be good if they approached some girls and struck up a conversation. It didn't take long to figure out that gay girls could dismiss a guy quicker than a straight girl could. The guys were not there to drink and agreed that their plan was stupid and they should leave. As they started to leave the bar, Zak turned to Eddy and said, "hey man isn't that Anna over there?" Eddy turned and sure enough Anna was standing in the corner talking to a girl with long hair. As the girl turned around Eddy could see that it was Joanne. He wondered what the heck they were doing there. Anna had told Eddy earlier that she had to go to the school to study. Eddy started to walk towards them but was stopped in his tracks half way there. The girls were in a full embrace and kissing. They made their way to the dance floor and slow danced together. Eddy thought he was going to be sick.

    Eddy ran to the front door of the bar hoping to get some fresh air. A million thoughts were running through his head. Should he go back in and confront them, should he start a fight, should he go home and forget about it. He decided to talk to them later and jumped into the car with Zak. None of the guys said a word on the way to Eddy's

The Empty Net

place. Eddy hoped they would be as quiet around their team mates as they were in the car.

Eddy finally got Anna on the phone about midnight. He didn't want to talk about it over the phone and asked her to pick him up. She was more concerned about his curfew than he was, but he explained that the coach had already called and never called twice in one night. Besides Eddy had not broken curfew all year and was not considered a problem in that area by the coaches.

Anna picked up Eddy and they proceeded back to her place. Eddy insisted that they pick up Joanne on the way over. Anna must have sensed something was up by Eddy's insistence. They got to Joanne's and Eddy hid in the back seat, he didn't want Jimy to see him. After about ten minutes the two girls got in the car. There was an eery silence for the rest of the short trip to Anna's place.

Once inside the house Eddy told them where he had been and what he had seen. Anna started to cry, but Joanne was all of the sudden talkative. She told Eddy that she first realized something was different about her in grade six. She had never been attracted to boys and that bothered her. She tried to deny her feelings and forced herself to go out with a couple of boys, it never worked. In grade ten she had an intimate physical relationship with an older women and knew she was a lesbian. She never said anything to Eddy over the years because she didn't know how he would react. She recounted a couple of times when Eddy had spoken of gay people as fags, queers and degenerates, the kind of people that needed a beating. She was reluctant to share her inner most secret if that was his attitude. Strangely, Eddy some how understood and had sympathy for her. He started to cry, he told her how much he loved her and didn't want to lose her. Joanne hugged him and told him how much he meant to her and how much she loved him. She wanted to be his friend always.

Anna was another story. She didn't know if she was straight or gay, but decided that she must be bi-sexual. She loved Eddy and enjoyed being physical with him, but she loved Joanne and enjoyed being physical with her. They talked for hours, not knowing what to make of their relationship. Eddy loved Joanne, Joanne loved Anna and Anna loved them both. It was the perfect foundation for a future of heart break and misery. They agreed they all loved one another but did not figure out what they were going to do about it in practical terms. The girls dropped Eddy at home about five minutes before the coach called to tell him about a special meeting later that morning. The call home that night would prove to be an interesting one. Eddy was caught between his anger and embarrassment and not sure what he should tell his parents. His mom, as only a mom can, sensed a concern in his voice. She knew something was wrong and wanted to help her son through it.

"Mom, Anna and Joanne are gay, lesbians or something." "I know Eddy, but they are still lovely girls and love you dearly." Eddy couldn't believe it, what the hell, how did his mom know? "What do you mean mom, you knew they were lesbians?" "Yes Eddy, I knew a little while ago that they had a secret, they shared it with me and swore me to secrecy." "Joanne has known for a long time that she was a lesbian, it has been very hard for her because of the stigma attached to it and how young people treat people poorly when they are perceived to be different."

"Mom, I don't know what to do. The guys on the team are starting to whisper things, I thought I knew her, I thought I might marry her some day, but all that is changed." "No it's not Eddy. You may not marry her, but both girls love you and care for you deeply, they will always be there for you." They spoke for another couple of hours, until they were interrupted by the coach calling with his curfew call.

The more Eddy thought about it the more okay he was with it. He understood that this was their life and not a decision they had made to impact him or hurt him. They were simply gay, whether Eddy was alive or not. His real concern was the embarrassment, how would every one react to the news that his girlfriend was a lesbian. Anna, Joanne and Eddy got together for dinner the next evening. Eddy told the girls how much he loved them and how he was most afraid of losing them. The girls swore that wouldn't happen, they said they would always be there for him. They started to cry and pretty soon Eddy joined in. It was an odd sight in the restaurant with all three of them crying in the corner booth. The manager stopped by the table and apologetically said he would give them free dessert, he apologized as he went back to the kitchen.

    The three burnt up the telephone lines over the next few weeks working on the details of their new relationship. In reality not much had changed, they still went out together, still kissed and hugged, they just didn't have sex, which wasn't much of a change any way.

Chapter Seventeen

Shannon got home from school early and decided to go down the street and see if there was anything he could do for Ms. Dunn. He knocked on the door but there was no answer. He could hear music playing in the house and figured she just couldn't hear him. He went around to the back and knocked on a couple of windows, still no response. Shannon decided to go home and get the key that Ms. Dunn had given him years before. He had not had the opportunity to use it very often, as she was always home. Shannon opened the door and went inside. He called out her name but got no reply. He walked around the house and finally found her sitting in her big chair in the den. She was holding on to one of the tulip pictures that Shannon had given her. He called her name and she didn't answer. Shannon was scared and didn't know what to do. He got closer and pushed her on the shoulder. Other than the picture sliding out of her hand, there was no response. When it finally dawned on Shannon that his old lady friend was dead, he started shaking like a leaf in a wind storm. He didn't know what to do. He ran to the phone and called his mom. She called the ambulance and before long the house was full of people in uniform. They took her away and Shannon and his mom straightened up her house. Later that evening a lawyer, Mr. Green, called and told Mrs. Walsh that he would be making the arrangements and thanked her for her help. Mrs. Walsh thought the lawyer must be a distant relative or friend or something, although neither her nor Shannon had ever seen him at her house before, the name sounded somewhat familiar. The funeral was the next day and was only attended by Shannon, his mom and a couple of old ladies, neither of whom they knew. There were no flowers in the church, no special singers. The service was pleasant but fast and the Walsh's were home within the hour. They both felt sad about their loss. Eddy may have come to the funeral if he had been home, but he was off on a road trip some where. It was too bad that all people, especially older people, didn't have more friends. It seemed so sad that

The Empty Net

after living on this planet for over seventy years, there were only four people who were effected by this lovely ladies life and death.

On the way home from the funeral Shannon and his mom talked about life and death and the importance of family. His mom told him that even though he and his brother sometimes fought and didn't get along, that they both loved each other deep down, had shared history and roots, and should always look after each other no matter what.

Shannon asked his mom about death, why it happened, where people really went and if everyone would be together again some day. His mom assured him that people that lived a good life, that didn't hurt people and did the odd good thing for others, would go to Heaven. She was confident that eventually all of them would meet up and be together again there. Shannon wondered about the details, would you always be the age in heaven that you died at? What if you didn't get along with some of your family members, would they be segregated from you in Heaven? And the most frightening, what if someone you loved was not a very good person and didn't make it to Heaven, would you remember them and be sad or what? They were all good questions that really had no answer, at least no answer Mrs. Walsh could provide. "Some things we have to leave up to faith, we believe they will happen and act accordingly." Mrs. Walsh further explained.

The whole conversation made them sad and they gave each other a big hug. It was perhaps the first time that Shannon realized that his mom and father would not be around forever. It scared him. Ms. Dunn was the first person that he had known who had died. He had never known his grand parents, they died before he was born. His uncles and aunts were the same age as his parents and had never even been sick, not that he knew of. The death of Ms. Dunn had matured Shannon in a way he wasn't quite ready for. As they made their way home, the mom told Shannon to promise her that he would always look after his brother, Eddy, no matter what. That caught Shannon by surprise. He always thought of Eddy as invincible and figured that if any one would need taking care of, it would be him, not Eddy. He promised his mom and they hugged again.

At dinner that night Mr. Walsh was uncharacteristically kind to Shannon. Usually, he would tease him about "going down to see the old broad, or have a nice time with your old girlfriend." There was to be no teasing today. The father asked about the funeral and what was going to happen to her house. They speculated that it would be put up for sale and some young family would move in to it. Shannon wondered if the new people would keep the tulips, but the parents both doubted that would happen. It took too much time to grow those kinds of flowers, the time young families didn't have. Despite the fact she lived alone, the Dunn house was large and had a grandness about it. It was larger than the Walsh home, had a double garage and larger lot. The back yard was huge and backed on to some green space with large trees. It was one of the first houses to be built on the street and was probably the most expensive one.

A couple of days after the funeral, the lawyer, Mr. Green, called and asked if he could stop by and speak to Shannon. He suggested that it might be good if both parents were there also. Mrs. Walsh thought that was odd and wondered if Shannon was in trouble.

When Mrs. Walsh opened the door for Mr. Green, they both laughed. "How are you doing, nice to see you again, how is your boy Eddy?" "Fine, fine and how is Susan? The tight look in Mr. Green's face told of something amiss. The phony smile and cheery disposition faded in a heart beat. "May I sit down, Mrs. Walsh." "Of course, Mr. Green, is something wrong?' "Yes, yes, I am afraid there is. Susan as you may have heard got hooked up with Rahib, the religious fellow. She dropped out of grade twelve because she got pregnant and now the three of them live in a commune in California, we think." Mr. Green was almost in tears and so Mrs. Walsh didn't ask any questions.

Mr. Walsh came bounding into the room and was surprised to see the only lawyer he ever knew socially sitting in their living room. Names being a difficult area with Mr. Walsh he simply asked "how you doing guy?" Before Mr. Green could answer, Mr. Walsh asked "how his little princess was doing, she must be all grown up now." Mrs. Walsh tried to give him a signal to shut up but he didn't get it. Mr. Green repeated his problems with Susan and this time started to cry. As it turned out, Susan had turned against the parents affluent lifestyle and now essentially had disowned them. The parents had never seen the baby and only talked to Susan once in the last three years. They didn't even know exactly where she was anymore.

When Mr. Green had composed himself, Mr. Walsh asked if Shannon was in trouble. "Oh, no, no, no, I'm sorry if that's what you thought." "I am the Solicitor for the Estate of Ms. Dunn and wanted to get the process moving." "My firm prepared Ms. Dunn's Will and we have known her for many years. As you know Ms. Dunn had no relatives or even close friends, other than you Shannon. Her Will leaves everything to Shannon." Mr. Walsh was turning red with excitement and anticipation, so much so, that Mrs. Walsh suggested he get a glass of pop or water or something. He went to the kitchen humming.

Mr. Green continued to explain the process. It would take about five months to complete the estate process, what with the valuations, taxes to be filed and other stuff. Shannon could have the house right away, but it would have to be registered to him with the parents as the trustees. "You mean she left him her house." Mr. Walsh wanted to be sure. "Yes she did." "How much of a mortgage is there on it?" Mr. Walsh suddenly had a lot of questions, as if it was all a dream, game, charade or something. Was there a hidden camera somewhere he wondered? "There is no mortgage on the property and after taxes, fees and everything else Shannon should receive the house and approximately $ 250,000.00 cash, of course it would be in trust until he was eighteen, which was only over a year away. Mr. Walsh luckily landed on the couch after he passed out. The excitement was just too much. His kid was now rich and pretty much set for life. He had worked thirty five years, hard work, and had no where near that amount. Shannon was reserved, but pleased, but really missed Ms.

Dunn. She had become his friend, his grand mother, his mentor. She was very intelligent and they had great conversations together.

Shannon thanked Mr. Green and told him that he would keep up the tulips. Mr. Green didn't know what he was talking about.

Eddy called home that night about 11:00, just after they got back to their Hotel Room. The game hadn't gone too well, a 4-2 loss, but Eddy got both goals and was the third star. Eddy hadn't spoken to the family since before Ms. Dunn had died and didn't know of her demise. Mrs. Walsh didn't know where to begin. "Eddy, Ms. Dunn died." "Yah! Good mom, so what else is new?" Eddy didn't care about her when she was alive and cared less about her now that she was dead. "Eddy, that's not very nice, she was a lovely lady and besides she left your brother her house and a quarter of a million dollars." Eddy sensed his mom was a little miffed in his attitude and that she was not kidding. "Are you serious, she left all the dough to the weasel monkey dog?" "That's right Eddy, everything she had goes to Shannon." There was a long silence, Eddy must have been in shock. His seventeen year old brother was now rich, set for life, all because he cut some old ladies grass. He wondered why he hadn't thought of that scam, so that he could now be the rich one. "And there is more Eddy, the lawyer is Mr. Green." "Did he say how Susan was doing?" Eddy still had a soft spot for Susan despite the fact that she had never given her all to him, she was still his first love. Their break up had been difficult, but not cruel. Mrs. Walsh explained her circumstances to a stunned Eddy. Eddy laughed and laughed, while he felt bad for Susan he felt good that it happened to the Green's. A simple hockey player wasn't good enough for them, so he hoped they were happy with their religious freak "son-in-law".

Shannon had a year left of high school and wanted to finish it. He thought if he over loaded with credits he could finish early. His marks had always been very good and the extra work would not be a problem. He would simply scale back his photography for awhile. He

The Empty Net

was anxious to finish school and more anxious to turn eighteen. Eddy couldn't sleep that night, thinking over and over about the good fortune of his brother. He wished it was him, he dreamed that it was him, but it wasn't, it was Shannon. Eddy dreamed what it would be like to never have to work or worry about money your whole life. People like his father had gotten up every day to go to a job they hated, just to make money. Eddy wondered how much a person could accomplish and how much better society could be if people didn't have to work. People would have the free time to pursue athletics, academics, whatever they wanted. Maybe there would be a cure for cancer and aids, maybe there would be no poverty, maybe there would be no more wars or class struggles. What the hell was he thinking? He didn't care about all the world issue stuff, he cared about himself not having to work in a lousy job all his life. He was suddenly very jealous of Shannon, Eddy thought maybe they should split it, maybe that is what the old lady really wanted.

Eddy phoned Joanne and told her the news, his two goal game, the death of Ms. Dunn, Shannon now rich. She was more interested in hearing about Ms. Dunn and her death rather than the money or the score of his game. Joanne knew the woman and had met her on several occasions, usually with Mrs. Walsh. Joanne remembered her tulips and the nice lady sharing stories over tea. As she spoke she got upset. Eddy couldn't believe what he was hearing. Why would someone like Joanne be getting upset about the old neighbour. Joanne got angrier at Eddy as they spoke. "Maybe if you were as nice to people as Shannon was, without there being some angle to it, nice things would happen to you." "Whatever, I don't care, Shannon will just blow it any way." They both sort of laughed at that one, they knew Shannon would never blow it and probably would double it at some point. If there was one thing he was good at it was money. He would work hard to earn it, and he was disciplined to spend it wisely. Eddy was tired of all the death and money talk and wanted to change the subject. "Did you ever want to have sex with me Joanne?" "What is that all about?" "Sorry, I was just thinking and wondering, you know I always had a dream to marry

The Empty Net

you." "No, I didn't know that Eddy, I thought your dream was to marry Anna." "Well, that is what it may have looked like, but you were always my dream, from the day I first met you in class." "Even though I'm gay Eddy, I probably would have had sex with you on a couple of occasions, when we had been drinking or out late dancing, but I never would have jeopardized our relationship." "You are a great guy Eddy, a very attractive guy, you just have to work a little on your compassionate side, you can't treat every body like a useless jerk." Truth made Eddy tired and he thanked Joanne for her insight and said good night.

Chapter Eighteen

Eddy wanted to chill out and forget about the night. It was the first two goal game of his junior career, but it went un-noticed because of the death. At least at home it went un-noticed. Eddy had called from the privacy of the hotel lobby and now made his way back to his room. When he went into his room it was dark and quiet, Eddy thought his room mates must have gone to another room to watch a movie or something. He was too tired to find out and walked in the dark towards his bed. He bumped against the side of the bed and gently rolled in to it. Guys could always find a bed in the dark and Eddy was no exception. He pulled the blanket over him and put his head down on the pillow. As he did, he felt something cold and weird feeling on his neck and ears. It smelt like lemons, but was odd. He jumped out of the bed to turn the light on. His room mates started laughing as Eddy ran to the bathroom. He looked into the mirror and saw that his head was covered in shaving cream. The guys had emptied two cans of shaving cream on his pillows. He laughed and thanked them. It was a reward, a recognition of his two goal night. His team mates respected him and took the time to play a prank on him. It was positive team building were no one got hurt, Eddy appreciated it. The next day the team was on the bus to complete a weekend of games in eastern Ontario. Eddy got dressed for the morning skate like he had many times before. When he put his skates on and pulled his laces, they came out. Some one had cut his laces down the middle. "Yikes, hey who cut my laces?" Of course no one came forward, except Jimy who threw him a new pair of laces. He scrambled to put them in his skates, but wasn't quick enough to escape the $ 25.00 team fine for being late. It was another prank by the team in response to his game the night before. It was fun to be the centre of attention and recognized by the guys, even if did cost him $ 25.00.

It was late at night when the team arrived back in the Falls from the road trip, but Donna Brady was up and pleased to see Eddy return safely. She gave him a big hug and welcomed him home. It always made Eddy uncomfortable when she gave him a big hug, while only wearing a t-shirt. She was pretty hot and he was attracted to her. He knew she was lonely because her husband was always gone. The two sat downstairs, drinking juice and talking. She congratulated him on his two goal game and asked him about the trip. He told her some of the things that happened, but not everything. He finally told her about Joanne and Anna. She was not surprised and suspected early on that Joanne was gay. Eddy couldn't believe it, was it only him that didn't see the truth. Donna spoke of how great a person Joanne and Anna were and that it shouldn't change their relationship. Eddy had heard that people didn't like gay people or lesbians, but ever since the news broke, he couldn't find any. Every body spoke of the two girls in glowing terms. No one was offended or even surprised, let alone concerned. Donna was very interested in their relationship and how it would be continuing. She was curious if they had sex and if so, how it was. Eddy could feel some magic in the air and could sense that Mrs. Brady was becoming a cougar. Eddy made up sex stories and enthralled her with his triumphs and skills. She was moving around on the couch like a hamster on a wheel. It seemed like her t-shirt was getting shorter and shorter and it was obvious that she was excited by his stories. Eddy could sense that they were on the verge of something and he didn't know if he wanted to go there. He thought about the two kids sleeping up stairs, the husband away on business, all those thoughts that he hoped Donna would have thought about.

  Eddy popped up and told Donna he was exhausted and had to go to bed. She had a look of disappointment in her face, but understood. She gave him a long embrace, but he was still exhausted. Eddy went upstairs while Donna remained in the basement. Eddy didn't hear her come upstairs all night.

  When Eddy came down the next morning for breakfast Donna was sitting in the corner sipping on a coffee. "Eddy, I'm so embarrassed, I'm so sorry." "Donna, what are you talking about, sometimes you think too much." Eddy gave her a kiss on the cheek

The Empty Net

and a reassuring wink as he went back upstairs. Donna smiled at him and thanked him. They never spoke of the evening again, but each knew what could have happened if Eddy hadn't been so strong.

With Eddy and Anna in agreement that their relationship was now just a platonic one, Eddy had to explore some other opportunities. He had been remarkably faithful during his time in the Falls, and he now felt bad about that. There was a lot of work to do to catch up to some of his team mates. He starting hanging around the team and going to team functions. Earlier he would beg off saying he was busy with Anna. His team mates would see him with Anna and Joanne and their jealousy would surface. They would kid Eddy about the two beautiful girls that always clung on to him, of course the kidding had stopped as soon as the news of their sexual orientation spread throughout the dressing room. Every place the guys went as a team, a posse of girls seemed to follow. Some girls looked to be as young as eleven or twelve, some looked like they were in their thirties, even though they probably weren't. The girls were collectively known as puck bunnies or dirties. They existed in every hockey city and were never shy in their pursuit of players. Eddy wondered what the deal was. Maybe they were girls that were looking for a hockey player to enhance their own status with their friends. Maybe they were they looking to marry a player and use the player as their ticket out of town. Eddy couldn't figure it out and it bothered him. He thought of Tara and Tina and how he would kill them if he ever saw them hanging around looking for these guys.

As much as he disapproved of the girls hanging around and throwing themselves at the players, there were certainly times when they worked their charms on him. Some of the girls were great looking with great bodies and would do anything, no strings attached. It was hard for a guy to say no, especially when pursued. Every once in awhile the stories would make there way around the league about some puck bunny getting pregnant, or a player getting charged with sexual assault, but it really had no impact on anyone's behaviour. The girls would leave notes on the players cars, call them at their billets, send them letters at the arena, attend practices and hang around the arena after games. Eddy tried to be strong in his resistance but as the season wore on his resolve was seriously challenged on a daily basis. He never took any of the puck bunnies home to the Brady's and would not speak to them on the telephone. After all, he had certain standards.

Eddy was constantly tormented by Tara. During the day at school she would flirt with him every chance she got. At home she would hang around him as close as she could. At night she would make a lot of noise in the bathroom, and then leave the door to her room from the bathroom open. When Eddy would go into the bathroom he could see her lying in her bed, sometimes in very provocative positions. She wanted him to come in but never actually invited him. Once when he went into the bathroom he could see through her open door that she was lying on her chest naked. He found a condom on the sink. He never kept them around and could only assume that Tara had placed it there for him. As inviting as she was, he couldn't. It got so bad that he finally set Tara up with Zak. It was against his better judgement but it was better than him ending up in a relationship with her. She didn't seem to mind and pretty soon her and Zak became inseparable. They were on the phone all the time, she hung around the rink and waited for him after the games, while her mother waited for Eddy. It worked and she started to leave Eddy alone. Her bathroom door was no longer left open and there were no more condoms left in the sink. At times he regretted setting Zak and Tara up, but he knew it was for the best.

Chapter Nineteen

Stan Jones was not a man to be toyed with. Eddy was hesitant to go to the arena after receiving the call that Mr. Jones wanted to see him. Eddy had only met him once since being drafted. Mr. Jones did not hang around the dressing room and did not mingle with the players, he was known to be aloof and not overly concerned about the feelings of the players or coaches. It was rumoured that with another team in his previous job he fired the coach on December 23 rd. Eddy figured the only reason that Mr. Jones would want to meet with him was to tell him where he had been traded to. Eddy was getting sick of the Falls and all that had happened and welcomed a change of scenery.

Mr. Jones wanted to know how Eddy felt about playing in Niagra Falls and for that the matter the league. Eddy stated the expected, that he was pleased to be given the opportunity and enjoyed the team, the city and the league. Before Eddy was finished, Mr. Jones interjected and said "that's great Eddy, your mother called to let us know your father has had a heart attack, but that he is okay." "We have arranged for you to take the bus home this afternoon to be with your family."

The bus ride home was the longest of Eddy's life. It was too much time to be alone with nothing to do but think, and think the worst. He worried that his dad would be dead by the time he got home. He worried how his mom would handle it. He thought of his dad and how he had helped him develop as a hockey player and as a person. His dad was always at the rink for him, no matter what the time of day or night, he always made sure the family had what it needed and he always made time for his kids. Eddy never thought of his dad as being vulnerable. To him he was a giant, an indestructible giant who would always be there. Eddy never thought of his parents as being old, even though they obviously were. Eddy wanted the chance to tell his dad that he loved him, something he had never done. If only his dad could hold on until he got there. Gerry Walsh had gone to bed after getting home from work. He skipped dinner, which was rare and told his wife he didn't feel good and would go to sleep. The next morning he was still tired but felt a little better. He had some pain in his left shoulder but decided to go to work, just like he had every day for the last thirty five years. It was cool in the mill that early morning and so Gerry was surprised by how much he was sweating. By 9:00 a.m. his left arm was giving him a lot of pain, he was still sweating, had trouble breathing and couldn't focus. At 9:15 a.m. he passed out on the floor in front of five of his co-workers. One called an ambulance, one started C.P.R.. The ambulance arrived quickly and rushed him to the hospital. They knew he was having a heart attack and gave him the appropriate drugs. He stabilized in the ambulance and was awake when they arrived at the hospital. They took him to a cold sterile room where they told him they would be putting him out and doing some tests.

    Mrs. Walsh was called by the plant foreman and told of Gerry's health problem. The foreman hadn't seen her husband and didn't know how he was. Shannon was still at home and so he drove his mom to the hospital. Shannon had needed the car later in the day to do a photography shoot and had driven his dad to work that morning. If he hadn't have done that, they probably would have had to take a cab. They arrived in the cardiac wing of the hospital just as Gerry was undergoing an angioplasty. The doctors explained that they would be putting a needle and a small tube in the vein in his groin running it up into his heart where they could see what damage was done. They would be shooting dye through his blood stream so they could see if there was a blockage. The procedure took about two hours to complete after which he was moved to a private room where his wife and son waited for him. He was in some pain but alert. They all hugged each other and he assured them that he was okay. Three hours later the doctor came into the room to tell them that Gerry had a blockage close to the heart and a couple of blocked arteries. He would require a shunt and a by-pass operation which would be done the next morning. The family was scared about the possibilities but relieved that the doctors knew what it was and that they could fix it. Eddy took a cab from the bus terminal and got to his dad's room just as his mom and brother were leaving. His dad had to get rest before his big day, but Eddy wanted to see him for a few minutes first. Shannon and his mom went out of the room and Eddy went to the bedside of his dad. His dad was groggy but knew it was Eddy and was glad he was there. Eddy hugged his dad and told him he loved him and thanked him for every thing he had done for him. His dad pulled him closer and told him he loved him too, was proud of him, but that he wasn't going to die. Eddy was getting upset and didn't want his dad to see that, his dad had enough to worry about. Eddy told his dad to go to sleep and stood by his bed until he did. The Walsh family went home, had something to eat, talked, tried to get some sleep, changed their clothes and then headed back to the hospital. It was a long day as they paced the hospital waiting room floor anxious for any news. The procedure was a long one and so no news was good news but it was hard to just sit and do nothing. Eddy and Shannon talked about how things were going with them and what they wanted to do in the future. They talked about Miss Dunn, not that she had died, death talk was taboo, but about the fact that Shannon now had a house and some cash. Shannon said he was pleased with his new found wealth but reminded Eddy that he wouldn't see it for another year, so it still didn't seem real. Shannon told Eddy that it would be their house some day. Eddy laughed and said he would be rich and have two or three houses of his own. The boys kidded some more and tried to keep their mom positive. It was very difficult for her. Her husband and her boys were her whole life. She had relied on her husband for most of her life and wouldn't know what to do if anything happened to him. She thought that if he was to go then she wanted to go as well. She knew that was selfish because her boys still needed her, and the thought of her selfishness made her more upset. The doctors finally came out to the waiting room around 3:00 p.m. The operation had been a success and Mr. Walsh was doing fine. He would be in recovery for the rest of the day, but back in a room where they could see him tomorrow after lunch. They told Mrs. Walsh that he was strong, his heart was good and with the blockages by-passed, he should have a good recovery.

The Empty Net

The family went home but despite their exhaustion could not fall asleep. Shannon had begun to doze off a little bit when the door bell startled him. The door opened and in came Joanne and Anna. Mrs. Walsh ran to them and squeezed them hard. She was very happy to see them. It had been a long time and she missed them dearly. Eddy was surprised but very thankful they had made the long trip. They said as soon as they heard what had happened they got the next bus home. They loved the Walsh family and were concerned about the father. The two girls would offer what assistance they could. Joanne gave Shannon a big hug and talked to him quietly for about twenty minutes. Shannon was obviously upset and Joanne was very comforting to him. It was then that Eddy realized how much they loved him and his family. Joanne was like his sister. Shannon treated her that way and she reciprocated. Eddy wondered why he hadn't figured that out a long time ago. She truly was his sister and filled a large role in their family. Anna was busy in the kitchen making the family something to eat. She was so thoughtful and helpful. Eddy hadn't seen her in that way before. She really was something and came up big when she was really needed. He was proud they were his friends. The girls and Mrs. Walsh went to the living room to talk, Shannon and Eddy fell asleep. Together they all went to the hospital together, united, strong and prepared to help the father deal with what he had to deal with in his recovery. The nurses told them that the father had a good night and was getting stronger. He was still tired and could only see two visitors at a time. The mom went into the room with Joanne in tow. The father was very happy to see Joanne and gave her a big hug. They talked for awhile and then came out to give the others a chance to visit. Eddy and Anna went in next. The father gave Anna a big hug and told her howhappy he was to see her. He squeezed Eddy's hand in a knowing way. The father had hoped that the two would get married some day, but had adjusted to the news of the break up very well.

    Eddy told his dad that he had been in touch with Jimy who told him that he should get back to the Falls. As much as he didn't want to

The Empty Net

he also knew it was time. His dad was out of danger and the season was almost over. His dad told him that there was nothing that Eddy could do for him at the hospital and that it would be good for him to return and finish the season. His parents fully understood and encouraged his return and basically forced Shannon to drive him to the bus terminal. The girls would wait it out a few more days and help when they could. Eddy got back on the Thursday evening, just in time for a road game the next night. Eddy was starting to hate buses, he had been on them far too often. The bus ride to Kitchener had a different feel to it. The guys were loose, too loose. There were only a few games left in the season and the Flyers had no hope of making the play offs. That in itself was difficult for Eddy to take. There were only ten teams in the division and eight made the playoffs. How embarrassing, if anyone cared.

The Memorial Auditorium in Kitchener was a classic arena that every one loved to play in. The facilities were first rate and the crowds were always five thousand strong and loud. It was like playing in an N.H.L. arena, just on a smaller scale.

The Rangers, who were in a rebuilding year of their own, quickly opened up a four to nothing lead. In other games that might make the guys angry, but not that night. Even when the score was seven to nothing, none of the Flyers seemed to care. Mid way through the second period the ref made a horrible call on Tom Chapman. Chapman was a rather slow defenceman, but never seemed to get caught out of position. He blocked a shot at the blueline and tried to skate away. If he was able to break through the clutches of their defenceman he would have a break away. Their defenceman put his stick around Tom's waist and pulled him down. Tom thought he might be awarded a penalty shot, but instead was given a penalty for diving.

Jiggs Smith had taken all he could take. He was angry and needed an outlet, the lousy call by the ref was just the excuse he needed. The garbage can sailed over the players heads landing on the ice just a couple of feet away from the referee. It startled him and he turned to look at the bench, just as a water bottle bounced off his shoulder. The ref immediately tossed Jiggs from the game. Jiggs hadn't gotten his money's worth yet and decided to stay. The spare sticks were the next things to hit the ice, followed by more water bottles and some pucks. The local police finally made their way to the bench and politely escorted Jiggs to the team bus. The game was delayed about fifteen minutes while things were sorted out and the sticks were re-stacked next to the bench. The momentum of the game did not change and the Rangers had squeaked out a very impressive nine to nothing win. Jiggs had a meeting with the Commissioner the next day and ended up suspended for the rest of the season, the team was fined.

    The next practice was painful. Jiggs skated the team harder and longer than he had all year. Guys were swearing at him under their breath as they did laps around the arena. After the practice he was still angry and tossed things around in their dressing room. He was calling the players chickens and gutless pieces of shit. There wasn't a swear word that went unused. He threw a helmet against the wall so hard it broke in two pieces just above a players head. The bottom line was that he felt the team had quit a month ago and just wouldn't compete anymore. He reminded the players that this was a stepping stone to the pro's and only the best and the toughest made it. Guys that came out of teams that did not compete and were known as having bad attitudes did not make it. The players got his point but no one really cared. Jiggs was suspended and was not supposed to have anything to do with the team. Eddy was secretly hoping that someone would call the Commissioner and complain. He didn't want Jigg's skating them to death when the season was already a write off.
    Bob Williams a tough forward told Jiggs that he thought they were not being taught enough and that the practices were use less. He complained that they did simple drills from another era and weren't schooled enough in proper systems that would allow them to compete on a regular basis. A few guys applauded and made some comments. The coach screamed at Bob that he didn't know his ass from grass,

The Empty Net

whatever that meant, and that he should leave, they didn't need a cancer on the team. The team was advised the next morning that Bob Williams had been sent home, that he would not be released and he would not be traded. Basically his hockey career was over. The guys got the message loud and clear. Fortunately, the last two games of the year were against teams that had wrapped up playoff spots and were playing rookies and resting their better veterans. The Flyers were able to get two wins to end the season and at least that was somewhat of a positive. It really wasn't as they were nothing games, but in the world of hockey coaches were always looking for something positive to build on. Sometimes a team would lose a game seven to three, but if they had outscored the other team in the third period, then they had won the third period and that was something to build on.

The end of the year banquet was not a happy one and every body was happy to just go through the motions and get it done with. The awards were handed out, but when you play on a last place team that doesn't make the play-offs, they don't mean much. Sure someone might be the best right winger on the worst team in the league, but what did that really signify.

When they called Eddy up to collect his trophy for best rookie defenceman, he almost didn't go. Donna and Tara clapped and pushed him out of his seat. He was almost embarrassed to win the award. He was just glad there were no speeches. The Brady's were very happy for him. They told him how good an accomplishment it was and that some day he would appreciate it and feel good about it. He doubted it but thanked them.

Tara cried the entire trip home from the banquet. The banquet was symbolic in a number ways, one of which was that it meant the players would be all going home within a day or two. She did not want Zak to go and she did not want Eddy to go. She didn't know what would happen the next year and wanted things to remain as they were. That night Eddy heard Donna crying in the basement. He went to comfort her. They spoke of how much they would miss each other and that they would stay in touch. It was very difficult for the host families. They got to know the player as a person and went through the ups and downs of the season with them. The billets were always important people in the life of a junior hockey player. Many players would keep in touch with their billets for their whole life, some would never be heard from again. Eddy was sad to leave the Falls but was anxious to get home. It had been a long season. His dad was home from the hospital and recovering well. He was strong, felt better than he had in years and was doing lots around the house. The operation was a success and would probably add years to his life. He was always nervous to do anything physical and that was a problem. His doctor said it was natural that after having a heart attack the person would not want to do anything physical for fear of having another one. It was a very painful, scary experience that most people did not want to repeat. The father was encouraged to try things and eventually did start to do physical activities with no problems. He soon became comfortable enough to take up skating again, something he hadn't done in twenty years. Mr. Walsh had a disability pension and decided not to return to the mill. The family was happy about that choice but hoped he would get some hobbies so he wasn't just hanging around the house all the time. Both his parents promised to travel more and go to see Eddy play in a game. They had never seen him play junior hockey. His father would have been at every game if he could have been, but in the past, with work, it was impossible.

  Joanne had left the Falls and moved into the Walsh's basement. It was good to have her there on a regular basis. Her dad was driving across America in a sports car trying to find himself, and the mother was living in a commune in India, trying to find herself. Eddy never understood what exactly they were looking to find, but thought that each of their journey's was pretty cool. To Joanne it was just an embarrassment that she didn't often talk about. Anna stayed in the Falls as she was going to take some courses over the summer so she could finish early. There were a lot of telephone calls between her place and the Walsh's place during the summer, sometimes she would

The Empty Net

call for Joanne, sometimes for Eddy, sometimes for the mom, sometimes for whoever was there.

Chapter Twenty

Eddy worked out ever day in the summer, worked at a hockey school for a month and hung around with Shannon. Shannon was doing a lot of photo shoots and often Eddy would tag along to help out. Shannon appreciated his help and said they made a good team. Shannon was very busy and making some serious dollars. Eddy thought Shannon should quit school and do it full time, but Shannon always retorted that there was lots of time and a good educational foundation was the cornerstone to success. Eddy respected his brother and the work that he did. He was amazed how good the pictures looked when Shannon developed them. They were pieces of art.

In July a big brown package arrived from the high school. Eddy had passed all of his courses and was awarded his grade twelve diploma. His parents were very happy and very relieved. His dad cried and his mom smiled. Grade twelve was still a big deal and not every one graduated. They were pleased that at least Eddy would have that. He told them he was not interested in going to school any further and they didn't push. They wanted him to get his grade twelve, he did, now the rest was up to him. Joanne and the family went out to the local restaurant to celebrate. With Mr. Walsh better and Eddy a graduate there was a lot to celebrate.

In early July Mr. Jones was in town scouting a couple of players and decided to stop in at the Walsh house. After some pleasantries and small talk, Mr. Jones said that Eddy had been traded to the Peterborough Petes for some draft picks. The Flyers were still rebuilding and were a couple of years away from competing. The draft picks were good for the organization and the change would allow Eddy to play on a winning team. Eddy thanked Mr. Jones for all he had done for him and asked him to thank every one else for him as well.

Eddy was excited about going to Peterborough, it was closer to home, they were a winning team, and he had heard they always treated their players well. It wasn't until his mom mentioned it that he realized he would be playing on the same team as Bobby Gage. He had no idea how that would work out, they had barely spoken to each other the last time they were thrust together. How would it be playing a season together.

    Eddy went to Peterborough with Joanne in mid July to meet the coach, some of the players and check out the town. The feel inside the Peterborough Memorial Centre was much different than the one at the arena in the Falls. Even a stranger to the game could feel the intensity. This was not a place for pretenders, this was a place for champions. It had that arena smell that came from years of character building wins and the fans that went along with them. It was a feel that the new buildings, with no tradition, could not duplicate.

    Peterborough was a nice mid size Ontario City. It had its mix of industry, some high tech, some business and a University. With its canal system and waterways it was a natural tourist destination, but not in the plastic way that Niagra Falls was. There were no tacky stores to buy porcelain, candles or cheap t-shirts. The people seemed more rugged and perhaps that was due to the climate. Winters were cold and snowy and hockey ruled. It was a working class town with ambition and it fit Eddy perfectly.

    There was a long downtown street with stores on both sides of the road. Some of the stores had long been closed up, some were thriving. Eddy loved to walk down the street for a couple of miles just looking at the windows, it was a stress reliever that worked for him. He also enjoyed walking down by the water watching the boats chug past. There were some boats that were bigger than his house, floating palaces for the rich and near rich. He hoped that someday he would own one, or at least know someone that did. It was hard to say goodbye to his family again, but in late August he had to report to his new team. He loaded up all his stuff in boxes and moved down to Peterborough.

The Empty Net

The first meeting with the team was an interesting one. The Petes didn't make a lot of changes so there was some reluctance to new guys coming in. The Petes had worked hard at building their team through the draft, using trades sparingly, only to complete the puzzle. Eddy was introduced, most of the guys knew him somewhat from playing against him.

The coach was Ted Lane, a young, University trained man, with some minor league playing experience. He was a student of the game who knew all the latest systems and how to motivate players. He treated the players like adults and expected adult behaviour in return. He told the team that every one that was on the team would play. He was a coach that would roll four lines, unlike Jiggs who usually went with two lines, wearing them out long before the game ended. The coach said he would meet with each player individually on a weekly basis during the season, and he never broke his promise.

Eddy was pleased that he would be in a place that he knew where he stood and what his role on the team was. He looked forward to the coming season and had high hopes for it. The Petes had lost in their Division final the previous year and had much of the same team back for this season. It was said that Eddy was the missing piece of the puzzle and that excited him.

Bobby Gage brushed past Eddy after the first meeting. There was obviously still a problem between them and it would have to be resolved or it would impact on the rest of the team. To make matters worse, Eddy would be living in the house of Dave and Tammy Butler, an elderly couple with no children, who had another player living with them, Bobby Gage. As a veteran Eddy was pleased he didn't have to live in a hotel for training camp, he had made the team and was placed in his billet home right away. No hotel room jammed packed with rookies for him. He just couldn't believe that he would be sharing the house with Bobby. At some point they would have to talk things out but how. Training camp was much different than what he had experienced the previous year. As a veteran who had made the team there wasn't that same pressure to prove yourself. As a league veteran there would be no initiation to worry about either. The Petes approached things differently. The pre-season was a time to work in systems, develop line combinations and defence pairings, not just skate the players mindlessly. By the time of the first exhibition they were in pretty good form. The first game against Cornwall was a seven to nothing blow out. Eddy had three assists, two on goals by Bobby Gage. The next game against Kingston was closer, five to nothing, with Eddy getting one assist. Eddy was at home resting when he was awakened by Mr. Butler and told there was someone at the door to see him. Eddy wasn't expecting anyone, didn't really know anyone in town, and was surprised someone was looking for him. When he saw Anna at the door he was happy, sad and confused all at the same time. They went downstairs to talk. Anna had switched her school and would now be attending in Peterborough. Eddy was amazed. "Why would you want to come to Peterborough to go to school, I thought you loved it where you were." "I did Eddy, but I miss you and want to be near you." "I still love you and want to be close just in case you need me." "Joanne is staying at home with your parents and helping them." "So are you just coming here so that you will know someone?" "No Eddy, I really love you and want to be near you."

They spoke for a little longer before Bobby came downstairs. Eddy introduced Anna as his girlfriend, Anna smiled and Bobby was impressed. Eddy didn't get into the complicated history of him and Bobby, or the more complicated history of him and Anna. He simply said that they had all grown up in the same town. That was enough to get Anna and Bobby talking for about half an hour. They seemed to get along well and each said they looked forward to seeing each other again. Anna unknowingly chipped away at some of the ice between Eddy and Bobby.

Bobby was jealous of Eddy because of Anna and told him so. "This is my second year in this place and I can't seem to meet any one nice, anyone that thinks of me, and not just as a hockey player." Eddy told him that he understood and the two spoke for about an hour about the demands on them, the puck bunnies and normal relationships. They both felt better afterwards.

Eddy phoned Joanne to see if she could offer any insight into the Anna situation. She told him that they had cooled off a long time ago, and that even when they were together Anna always spoke about Eddy. Joanne was convinced that Anna was not a lesbian and just had a sort of experimental phase. Anna was in love with Eddy and nothing would change that. Joanne suggested that Eddy give Anna another chance. Eddy thanked her for her advice, but was clear that he didn't think he would give Anna another chance. He was tired of getting hurt and being lied to.

The first game of the regular season was against Niagra Falls, in the Falls. Eddy had known that since he was traded and had checked the schedule. He had dreaded it from that time but knew he had to get over it and get the game done. He went through so much with these guys, how could he play against them. He was nervous on the bus ride to the Falls and thought about last season and everything that happened. He was anxious to see Tara and Donna again but that was about it. During the introductions he was cheered and booed. That sort of summed up the experience in the Falls for him. The first shift of the game the puck went into the corner for Eddy, he was reluctant to go in and take out his old friend and team mate Trevor Day, but knew he had to. He hesitated for a second and then went in to get the puck. His delay allowed another Flyer to come in behind him and hit him just as he hit Trevor. Eddy went flying against the boards. He had a sharp pain in his shoulder and thought he might be injured. He wasn't sure if he was hurt bad or not and stayed down on the ice, waiting for Fred Tanner the trainer. The delay had cost him a chance to get the puck out of his zone and could have cost him an injury.

With Eddy down on the ice and appearing hurt, there was a quick gathering of players from both teams. Bobby grabbed the player that had hit Eddy and punched him a few times good. He swung him

The Empty Net

around and hit him some more. The other player got free and quickly returned the favour. It was a good tilt between two middle weights. Eddy was pleased that Bobby had stood up for him. Other than that one incident the game was not very physical. It was always funny how players never knew how a game would go. Sometimes people thought there would be a real physical game because of something that had happened in the past between the two teams but the game would turn out to be very tame. Sometimes two teams may not have played each other in a year and the game for some reason would turn out to be a blood bath.

    The game ended in a two all tie with Eddy getting both goals. He was second star of the game and got the same reaction that he got at the beginning of the game. After showering, Eddy went around from the dressing room to where the parents were waiting. Tara came running over to him and jumped into his arms. She gave him a big kiss and told him how much they missed him. They weren't going to have a player this year but were still going to all the games. Donna came up to him and gave him a big hug and a kiss. They had brought him some cookies and other stuff. He appreciated it as they didn't have much in the way of snacks back at the "senior's" home, as he called it. The three talked for awhile until the bus was ready to pull out. They said good bye and promised that they would talk on the phone soon. Eddy really missed them and wished he was still living with them. It was so much different living with Dave and Tammy Butler. They were nice people, went to bed early, never asked about hockey and minded their own business. They were older than his parents but had nothing in common with them. Their house was old, smelt old and had none of the toys that he had grown accustomed to. He wanted to live with and be part of a family, not share space with some geriatrics. Tammy was a good cook however, and there was always lots of sensible food in the house. Eddy couldn't have any one over to the house because the Butler's went to bed at 9:00 p.m. each night. It was hard for Eddy and Bobby to even talk once it was tucky-tucks for the Butler's. When

The Empty Net

Eddy and Bobby would get home from a game they would have to tip toe in the house trying not to wake them. Eddy felt bad if he did wake them, but it also made him angry. What the heck were they supposed to do, sleep in the garage. Eddy thought it was a mistake that the billets should be that old, but he never complained. It was something for anyone to open up their home to strange young hockey players, and Eddy was thankful that some did. When you had young billets, with young families there was always the possibility of disruption to the family. When you had a billet family with teenage girls, there was a different kind of disruption possible. At least Eddy was sure that he wouldn't find any condoms in the sink of his bathroom. Not unless Bobby had taken a different direction in life, but that was very unlikely.

The first home game of the season was against Oshawa and the Walsh family would be in attendance. It was no big deal now these opening nights, but Eddy was a little nervous about his parents, particularly his mom seeing him play. He just hoped there wouldn't be too many fights or any injuries. The family had gotten in later than expected and so Eddy wasn't able to show them around the City or even to show them around the rink. The family walked around the rink looking at the pictures of all the previous teams, the murals on the wall of the present players and all the other trappings of the rink. It was a great place. Shannon was impressed for cultural reasons and not for athletic reasons. He wanted to do a study on all the people that were there. He wondered why they were there, what they hoped to get out of the game, who they were. He was always fascinated by the concept of the fan and why someone would devote allegiance, and passion, to a team, a player or to a sport in general, he didn't get it. He was impressed that there were a lot of people there to watch his brother play hockey, people that actually paid to see his brother play hockey. The father was impressed by the number of food concessions and washrooms. It was just like the Gardens that they had seen several years ago, just smaller. They found their seats and watched as the

The Empty Net

players warmed up. They could not believe how big every one was and how fast they moved. Mr. Walsh shed a tear wondering when his boy became a man and a hockey player, the time had gone too fast. Mrs. Walsh was concerned about how big the players were and how fast they were. She shed a tear wondering how her boy could avoid getting roughed up by these men. Shannon shed a tear after he realized they played three twenty minute periods with intermissions between each one. They were going to be held captive for at least three hours.

The game got off to a fast start with lots of action at both ends. Oshawa was a good team and were hoping for a good season. The teams exchanged a number of opportunities in the scoreless first period. During the intermission, while the Walsh family grabbed some hot dogs, Coach Lane went over a diagram showing the players how Oshawa was closing down the neutral zone with a left wing lock. It was a designed play used to slow the other team from making its way into the other teams end. The coach showed the team the adjustments he wanted them to make. Sure enough with the adjustments in place the Petes were able to open the neutral zone a lot more and get the puck into the Oshawa end much easier. Eddy made a rush down the right side with a forward, he passed the puck over to the forward and drove to the net where he got the return pass. The pass was a beauty, right on his stick and then in the net. It was a pretty goal and set up by the smarts of Eddy knowing he had a play and continuing with it. He saw his parents clapping loudly a few rows up from the Petes bench. He winked at them, but didn't know if they saw him. The third period opened with the Petes leading one to nothing. It stayed that way until about three minutes remaining in the game. Eddy made the blueline and put a perfect pass onto Bobby's stick just outside the other teams blueline, he was in full flight and flew by the defenceman and went in on the goalie all alone. He faked right, went left and put the puck in the top corner of the net to give the Petes a two to nothing lead. The team stepped up its defence and the game ended two nothing. Eddy was the first star of the game, Bobby was the second star.

The Empty Net

After the game, the parents, some of the billets, along with the odd puck bunny waited outside the players dressing room for the players to come out. Eddy came out and was pleased to see his parents and Shannon. Shannon took pictures of Eddy and the various goings on, but didn't take any of him on the ice. The boys talked about Shannon's emerging business. Shannon told him he loved the photography part of it but hated the business side of it. He didn't want to look after the books, do invoicing, chase down accounts, market or anything else, he just wanted to take pictures. Mr. and Mrs. Walsh told Eddy how impressed they were with him and that he was like a real pro. They liked the fact that the fans yelled his name and he seemed to be popular with the fans and his team mates. Bobby Gage made his way out of the dressing room and over to where the Walsh's were standing. He said hello to them and asked if they remembered him. They said of course they did and told him how nice it was to see him again. They told him what a good hockey player he was and wished him well. Bobby then made his way over to a group of people that wanted to say hi to him. It was too late for the players to go out, so they agreed to meet the next day to have lunch.

After the late morning skate, the Walsh's picked Eddy up at the rink. Anna was with them and together they went to a nice restaurant in the downtown. There was something about an honest blue plate special consisting of meat loaf, mashed potatoes, mixed vegetables, gravy and a roll that you just couldn't beat. They talked about the dad's health, hockey, Anna's school and photography. When they got tired of the coffee they left for a tour of the city. It wasn't much of a tour, they simply drove around looking at things. Eddy had not seen a lot of these sites as most of his time was spent at the rink. The parents thought that it seemed like a nice place and were pleased that Eddy seemed to like it as well. They spoke some more before Eddy announced that he had to take a nap. Shannon couldn't believe that Eddy was going to take a nap and called him a baby. Eddy explained that he had a very structured day with eating, sleeping and working out all figured out to the last minute. "When you are a fine tuned machine

The Empty Net

you don't leave anything to chance." Shannon said he was still a baby but asked what time he wanted up. Bobby was also home and was going for a nap. After about a fifty minute sleep the boys woke up feeling refreshed and ready to tackle the rest of the day. The two players went to the gym to work out for an hour before dinner. When they returned home Mrs. Butler had made a feast for every body. Mr. Walsh smiled at the boys and said they were lucky to have such a good cook. They all agreed and continued to eat.

    The Walsh family had to get home and wanted to get a jump on the day. It was hard, like always to say goodbye, but now that Mr. Walsh was retired they would see each other more. At the time Eddy didn't know how much more, but by Christmas his parents had been down three more times to watch him play. It really helped Eddy adjust and cope with his life as a hockey player. The home sickness could mount, especially when the hockey part was not going well. It was compounded by the fact that he was in a strange city living with an old couple and a guy that would sometimes talk to him, sometimes ignore him.

Chapter Twenty One

The Christmas break was a mixed blessing. Eddy was on a good roll and wanted to keep it going. Hockey players were like that, if a player got on a good roll they wanted to play two or three games a day. If they were in a slump, one game per week was too many. At the break Eddy was second in scoring for defence man on the team and sixth overall. He was putting together a pretty good season and hockey people were taking notice. This was an important year for him and all of the other junior players that were eighteen years old. In June the N.H.L. would hold their draft where each team would select twelve players, with thirty teams, that meant three hundred and sixty players from all over the world would get drafted. It was very difficult to get drafted, but if you were one of the better players in your junior league, you had a good chance. If you didn't get drafted you could still get invited to a pro training camp but the odds were much greater of actually making the team. Bobby was the second leading scorer on the team and almost a guarantee to be drafted. Eddy didn't worry a lot about it because other than work his hardest, there was nothing he could do to enhance his rankings.

    The holiday was a nice rest. The bus ride home wasn't as long as the year before and the break was two days longer. It was great to spend time with Joanne again, he missed her a great deal. They went out a lot and spent a lot of time together talking and laughing. Eddy would joke to her that maybe they could get married any way, even if she was a lesbian. Joanne would joke back that Eddy had gone through so many girls that he was now reduced to lesbians as there was no one else left. Eddy couldn't believe it and would mockingly ask her what she meant. Joanne reeled off a bunch of names. She knew about almost every girl he had ever been with in high school. Eddy was impressed with her information but wondered how she got it. She told him that she kept her ears open and spoke with a lot of the girls who would brag about him. She felt bad sometimes because she wanted to protect him, but couldn't, not against himself. Joanne shocked him with her

The Empty Net

own list of conquests in high school, some of the names appearing on both lists. Eddy's eyes opened wide, he didn't think there were any lesbian's or gay people at high school. He was surprised to learn that there were quite a few. Some he kind of suspected, most he had no idea. It was a curious world that intrigued him at some level.

    Shannon was busy over the holidays with sessions. He continued to do work for the local newspaper and also tried to get some pictures done for his high school. His professional bookings kept him busy and so the high school newspaper work was becoming less and less. Eddy helped out around the make shift studio in their house and in the dark room. He liked helping his brother and it was easy work. It was different than the physical work he did during the season. Eddy was anxious for the Christmas break to end so he could get back to the task at hand. When Eddy got back to Peterborough he got called into the office of Julian MacDonald the general manager of the Petes. He was nervous and thought he may have been traded again. He never met with the general managers and usually when he did it was bad news. Mr. MacDonald told him that they were pleased with his performance over the first half of the season and hoped he had a productive second half. The reason for the meting was that the Petes tried to develop the whole person and not just the hockey player. The team had let him go the first half of the season without going to school or working, so that he could settle in. They were not going to let that happen in the second half of the season. The team had enrolled Eddy in a business college. It was a private type of school, that was both expensive and fast. His course would finish about the same time as the hockey season did, depending on how far they went in the play-offs. At the end of the year he would have a certificate and some business skills. Eddy didn't really know anything about business, but had no choice in the matter, so he knew he was about to. The next day he enrolled and was given a bunch of text books and hand outs. He would be learning about computers, book keeping, management, advertising, banking and accounting systems. It looked impossible but he was assured that they did everything to ensure that the student learned the

The Empty Net

material and graduated. He would have to attend every day for five hours. At least he would have some focus during the day.

He called home to tell his parents the good news. They were pleased and even Shannon was excited. Shannon yelled to the phone that maybe someday they could work together. Eddy retorted by asking his mom to ask if Shannon was now a hockey player too. Every one got a chuckle out of that one. Eddy worked diligently every day at the course and found before too long that it was to his liking. There was a sense of satisfaction in learning, it was comparable to the feeling after scoring a goal, an accomplishment. While his career goal had not changed, at least Eddy was thinking that knowing some stuff about business wouldn't be bad when it came time to negotiate a contract. The Petes were in first place in their Division and had locked up a play-off spot by late February. The games still had meaning as position was at stake but there wasn't that pressure of having to win just to get to the post season. Eddy had not been on a winning team in a long time and it was a different experience. Every time they played someone they wanted to learn about them, that way if they met in the play-offs they would be ready. In early March the Petes had a home and home series with Sudbury. The Wolves were a big team and liked to intimidate their opponents. While many of their opponents may have truly been intimidated , it rarely reflected in the score and the Wolves were a last place team. The first game was Friday night in Sudbury. It was the game of the week and featured on television across the Province. Every player loved to play in front of a big crowd and there was no bigger crowd than the television audience. Parents, friends, girlfriends and players from other teams would all be watching. As soon as the puck was dropped, Sudbury enforcer Terry Clarke grabbed Dennis Beam, one of the smaller forwards on the Petes. It was as one sided a fight as Eddy had ever seen. It reminded him of the beating Bones threw into him years ago, except he was conscience long enough to say he saw this one. Coach Lane was livid, yelling at the Sudbury bench. He wanted to go over to their bench and discuss it

The Empty Net

with their coach but the police held every one apart. There was an unwritten rule in hockey that enforcer's fought enforcer's, that freed up the game for everyone else to play, with out worrying about getting gooned. If someone challenged the enforcer that was different. To have your enforcer grab a small player that was known not to be a fighter was a disgrace. After order was restored, Coach Lane sent out the biggest guys and strongest guys, including Eddy. When the puck was dropped two other fights broke out right away. These were much more even and arguably the Petes came out on top of both of them. Eddy sensed a long game. Dennis was out for the game with cuts, bruises and a suspected concussion. Terry Clarke was back in the game after serving a five minute fighting major and a two minute penalty for being the instigator. It didn't seem like justice, but this was after all hockey. On the street Terry Clarke might be looking at some jail time, here he got a standing ovation when he skated back to his bench. He spent the seven minutes taunting the Pete's as they skated past the penalty box. The only consolation was the two goals they scored with him in the box. He seemed oblivious to it though, his grin and yapping never changed, or stopped. It wasn't until the second period that Terry Clarke saw the ice again. He wasn't going to pull the same stunt twice. Coach Lane moved Jim Reiker, a defenceman, up to the wing to line up against him. As the puck was dropped Jim said "wanna go" and away they went. Jim was much tougher than Dennis, but Terry was a specialist. Jim got some early punches in but then Terry took over and finished it. He was too tired to swing at the end and waited until the linesman came in to break it up. Because Terry hadn't started the fight he wasn't kicked out of the game. He was exhausted as he killed his time in the penalty box and didn't grin so much or yap so much as he had in the first period. It was a tough job fighting and quickly wore a player out. Two fights in a game was a busy and tiring night.

  As the two players came out of the penalty box, Terry started to regain his yapping. Eddy had heard enough and skated towards him. As the players came together they both dropped their gloves at the same time. Terry got a couple of early punches in, but he was spent. Eddy kept spinning around keeping Terry off balance. Eddy landed about five good shots to the face of Terry, knocking off his helmet and cutting him badly over the left eye. There was no need to review any score after that one, Eddy had smoked the slightly bigger goon. The Petes all banged their sticks against the boards and saluted their new champion. Eddy went to the penalty to serve his time, Terry went to the dressing room to get stitches and get changed, his night was done. In the penalty box some fans tried to throw pop at Eddy, but he just smiled and blew them a kiss. It made them crazy and more determined to get at him. Two fans managed to fall down from their seats into the penalty box. One came at Eddy, the other was more interested in trying to scramble back to his seat. Yelling at a player was much different than standing toe to toe with one in the penalty box. The fan was about five feet nine inches tall and about two hundred and thirty pounds. Eddy was about six foot four, three inches taller on skates, two hundred and twenty five pounds and in the best shape of his life. Eddy laughed at the guy as he darted towards him swinging wildly. Eddy backed up, threw two punches and knocked the guy out. The guy was bleeding and not looking too well when the police finally made their way into the penalty box. The joker had not come to the game by himself and his beer buddies obviously weren't too pleased about his present condition. Several of them tried to get at Eddy, but none did. The ref opened the door to get Eddy out of the penalty box until the ambulance could remove "Mr. Brave" and the police and security could settle down the crowd. The game was delayed about thirty minutes before everything was looked after. Eddy made his way back to the bench after his penalty was up to a chorus of boo's. He didn't even get a chance to sit down on the bench before the first projectile hit him. Fans behind the Petes bench threw what ever they could in the direction of Eddy and his team mates. The police made their way into the crowd and ejected about thirty fans. For the rest of the game the first two rows behind their bench consisted of security people, police and rink personel all standing up, looking into the crowd. It was a weird feeling for all of the players. The players on both sides joked about it on the ice. They hoped that there weren't any snipers in the crowd and were thankful it wasn't puck night or some other giveaway that could be thrown back onto the ice at them. Mercifully, the game ended, the Petes picked up two points and the police escorted the team bus onto the highway. The police needed a statement from Eddy before the team left, but assured him he wasn't in any trouble, unless the guy died. Eddy had never thought of that. What if the guy really died? Eddy knew the guy was too drunk to die and didn't give it another thought. It was only on the bus that the players remembered it was a television game. Yikes! Not exactly the kind of game the league wanted people to see. The television footage of the drunks falling into the penalty box and the subsequent pounding was shown on most news casts across North America. In Sudbury and some other parts, they characterized it as two drunks innocently falling into the penalty box where the one was attacked by an out of control player who almost killed him. Other news casts were a little more accurate. None of them had the background on the game or the events leading up to the altercation in the penalty box. The latest news said the guy was a thirty five year old out of work truck driver with no family, by the name of Dan Benson. He was in a coma but was expected to live. Eddy heard that one in the middle of the night and almost went crazy. He asked Bobby if he should pack his bags and run or if he should call a lawyer and just turn himself in. He was scared and Bobby wasn't much help. The phone had rung off the hook since the incident and the Butler's were now seriously sleep deprived. At one point they told Eddy he was a fugitive and should move out. They were frightened by it all and didn't want the madness in their home. Someone had awoken them from their sleep and by the time the weary bus made it's way back to Peterborough, they had seen the replay about a thousand times. Around 5:30 a.m. the phone rang for Eddy. It was Terry Clarke. Eddy wondered how he got the number but knew that every team had guys that knew other guys on other teams and so it probably wasn't that hard to find a guy if you wanted to. "Nice fight you had tonight kid, you destroyed me." "Thanks Terry, it was just the moment, you know." "Hey, don't sweat it, you did great, I just wanted to let you know I was at the same hospital as that piss tank you mauled and that he is okay." "Really, the news said he was in a coma and might die." "Don't believe everything you see on the news kid, some of his drunken buddies may be in a coma, but he's awake and yapping about kicking your ass the next time the Petes come to town." Eddy thanked Terry so much for calling. He couldn't believe that after what happened that the guy would go to the trouble of finding him and then giving him the information. The police called in the morning to tell Eddy that the guy was fine, had sobered up and been charged with a handful of criminal offences. Eddy made it clear he did not want to go back to Sudbury to testify at any trial. The officer laughed and told him he wouldn't have to, that everything was on tape. Eddy spent the day convincing the Butler's that he was not a terrorist, and telling his story to the local media and all his buddies that were calling. Tara and Donna phoned to see if he was alright, as did Zak McDougall and Mrs. Fiset.

  Eddy received a loud ovation when he stepped onto the Peterborough ice that night. It was obvious that pretty well everyone in the building had seen at least highlights of the previous game and came expecting a war. It was funny to most players that the fights almost always got more response and more noise from the crowd than the best goal ever did. Terry Clarke hadn't made the trip with the team as he was nursing a deep cut over his eye and wouldn't be able to fill his usual role. The Wolves weren't anywhere near as brave with him out of their line up and the game was pretty tame. A lot of players made comments to Eddy, but they were all positive. They thought it was great that he gooned the guy. Most players took more than their fair share of abuse from a handful of fans in the different rinks, and so they were pleased to see it when one got filled in. It sent a message and shut some of the idiot's up for awhile. Eddy was pleased to get the game out of the way and get another win for the Petes who were on a serious roll. After the game there were about thirty people that wanted to talk to Eddy, usually there might be one or two. One scuffle in the penalty box and he was a celebrity. Eddy hadn't planned what happened, he wasn't even particularly proud of what had happened, but it did happen and now people viewed him differently. Even the coaching staff viewed him differently. They spoke to him and encouraged him to play more of a physical game. In hockey talk that translated to fighting more. As much as Eddy enjoyed fighting, he did not want to be reduced to a role player that could only fight and not play. He wanted to be a hard nosed defenceman that could stand up for himself and not shy away from the physical side.

Dennis Beam never recovered from the beating he took in Sudbury. His concussion symptoms had gone and he had no physical effects, however the mental scars were ever lasting and prevented him from playing the game as he had before. It was a shame to see his game fall apart so quickly and so much, but he wasn't the first and wouldn't be the last. Some players that had been injured, blocked a shot in the wrong place or were hurt in a fight could never get past it to continue playing, they were puck shy and their careers were over. Within a few games it was painfully obvious that Dennis could not turn it around and so the coach sent the once forty goal scorer home.

Windsor had a good season going and were chasing the Petes in a futile attempt to catch them. The Spitfires were a mix of skill and brawn, were well coached and worked hard. Mid way through the second period of a tie game, Bobby Gage got jumped in front of the Peterborough bench. The Windsor player was beating him pretty good and the linesmen weren't doing anything to break it up. Eddy decided to take things into his own hands and jumped off the bench and into the fight. He grabbed the guy and spun him around allowing Bobby to get free. Eddy would have put a beating into the guy but the benches had emptied and there were three or four guys holding onto him. There were about eight separate fights going on at the same time which made it hard for the referee and linesman to control. The best they could do was to keep skating around pulling guys off if they had too much of the upper hand. Eventually the players got tired and just sort of held on to one another waiting to be escorted to the penalty box or the dressing room. Eddy and the guy that jumped Bobby were still out on the ice and managed to get together with one another at centre ice. Eddy got several shots in quickly which stunned the guy, the fight was over quickly. Fights usually didn't last too long and so if a player could get in some shots quickly they were bound to do okay. None of the game officials had seen Eddy come off the bench and so he was only given a fighting penalty. The guys howled about it in the dressing room between periods. They couldn't believe Eddy didn't get nailed. Coming off the bench was equivalent to a mortal sin in hockey and would call for a lengthy suspension. During the intermission Bobby came over to Eddy and thanked him for helping him out, it meant a lot to him. Bobby was not a fighter and did not like that part of the game. He had done nothing to provoke the guy and wasn't sure why the guy grabbed him.

  The third period was a rough as the second. Eddy had only been out for one shift after his penalty was over before a guy grabbed him and started to punch him in the shoulder, arms and finally his face. Eddy had his arm caught and couldn't get free. It was not good to have a hand caught during a fight. The guy landed a couple of good shots before Eddy broke free. He hit the guy several times before the coup de grace. Eddy hit the guy square on the mouth, cutting him and knocking out some chicklets in the process. It was a hard shot that also made a weird noise. Eddy looked down and could see that his hand was bleeding pretty badly, it was also swelling up pretty fast. Eddy had seen this before and did not like it. Fred Tanner the trainer took Eddy to the hospital. The good doctor removed a couple of teeth from his hand and stitched him up. Later that night the x-rays showed that Eddy had badly broken the hand and done some damage to the tendons. He would require another surgery on his hand. The doctor wasn't out of the room when Eddy started crying. He was afraid his season was over and maybe even his career. He hated surgery and just wanted the pain and everything else to go away. If only he could set the clock back, but he couldn't.

The Empty Net

The surgery went well, two screws, a plate, countless stitches and three months recovery. The hand was much worse than the last time and the doctor warned Eddy not to rush back. With his hockey season over Eddy was toying with the idea of packing it in and heading home. If it hadn't have been for the business course he probably would have. He was determined to finish the course and so he stayed with the team. Being an injured player was like being an outsider of the worst kind. Guys were friendly to the injured player, but didn't really want them around. Fans were friendly to the injured player in the stands, but they were already yesterday's news. Coaches were friendly to the injured player, but couldn't use them, so didn't have much use for them.

Eddy was no longer required to attend at team meetings, be at the rink for practices or attend the games early. As an injured player he did not go on any road trips. Before long none of the guys called him up to go to movies or do anything else. It was again a harsh reminder of the life of the athlete. People were either athletes or they weren't, there was no category for injured athlete. Bobby felt for Eddy and was the only one on the team that continued to do anything with him. It was a little different of course, since they lived together, and the Butler's encouraged them to stay out as much as they wanted. The two tried to make it as easy on the Butler's as possible. They had come pretty close to asking the team to move the boys after the last incident but had relented when Mrs. Walsh spoke to Mrs. Butler. Although the boys did not necessarily enjoy living in the house with two older people, the parents took comfort that he was well looked after.

One night after the boys had attended a movie, Bobby broke down and apologized to Eddy. He was sorry that they had stopped being friends and that he had not forgiven him. Bobby said that his arm had hurt really bad and he thought Eddy had done it on purpose. His parents had convinced him that only one player from their town could make the N.H.L. and so Eddy had tried to injure him so he could never play again. He did not want to believe it but the parents kept saying things like that over and over. They also told Bobby that he

The Empty Net

could no longer talk to Eddy on the phone or see him. Bobby said he knew it wasn't right but there was nothing he could do, his parents controlled him. After Bobby's second year of junior he had a huge falling out with his parents and had not spoken with them since. Bobby thought that they may attend the odd game but had never actually seen them in the rink. One of the reasons, the main reason that Bobby's father had taken the job in Toronto was so that Bobby would be exposed to better coaches and better players. Although he may have had different coaches there was never the amount of ice time available that he was used to back home. He did not like Toronto, never developed any real friendships and pretty much lived a hockey life dominated by his parents. His goal was still to play pro hockey but he didn't like the person he had become to accomplish it. His parents would not let him have other players over to the house unless they were goalies. They didn't want other players that were not as good as him to have any effect on him and they never thought there was anyone better than him on the team. Goalies were safe because he did not compete with them directly. His coaches were never right, the referees always favoured the other team and the parents and his team mates were all jealous of him. His father told him all that on a daily basis. In his second year of junior his father didn't think he was getting enough ice time and complained to the coach and manager. They basically told him to get out of the office and never call them again. He then demanded that his son be traded. The team told him he could take Bobby home, that they would not trade him and that he could not play anywhere else. They were not going to be dictated to by the parent of an eighteen year old hockey player. Bobby didn't know anything about the demands of his father until the coach called him into his office to basically tell him they were sending him home. Bobby went crazy and told the team that his parents would not ever call them again and if they did just to hang up on them. Bobby confronted his parents and laid it out for them. If they were ever to get involved again he would not talk to them ever again. His parents told him that they had given their whole life for him and that he would do what they told him to do. The discussion got no where and Bobby told them he never wanted to see them again. He refused to answer their phone calls, sent their mail back to them not opened, and didn't go back home in the summer or at other breaks. Eventually the cards and phone calls stopped. Bobby felt a great deal of independence after the confrontation and was glad it had happened. He could now live his own life. Part of that was fixing things up with Eddy. He was afraid to at first and then didn't know how to do it, or what to say. He was not good at personal relations, a trait he shared with Eddy. Bobby admitted that after he heard about the trade, he had asked the coach to put him and Eddy in the same billet house.

Eddy was surprised and moved by the revelations, especially the last one. He thought that Bobby hated living with him. He was surprised that Bobby had shut his parents out of his life, but had known something was up because they never called and never went to the games. Eddy thought maybe they were dead or something but hadn't wanted to say anything. If Bobby wanted to talk about it he could have brought it up. Eddy had missed Bobby and regretted the incident. He reassured Bobby that the stick swinging incident was carelessness and nothing more. He never wanted to hurt him, he never even thought about the possibility. The two agreed to never let anything come between them again.

The only advantage of being injured, if there was one, was that the radio guys loved to interview the injured player, not because they were any good, but because they were available. After the end of a period or the game most players liked to go into the dressing room to first get a drink, cool off and maybe take some equipment off. By the time they got out to do an interview, the air time would be almost over. The first couple of times that Eddy was interviewed the questions were all concerning the incident in Sudbury and his fight with the fan. They asked if he had been in touch with the fan to discuss it. Eddy explained that a drunken alcoholic who had previously sprayed him with beer and pop had jumped into the penalty box and tried to assault him. Eddy wanted nothing to do with the guy but the guy wouldn't back off. He swung a few times trying to hurt Eddy, Eddy then subdued him by knocking him out. When Eddy asked the announcer exactly what they would have spoken about, the station took a commercial break. The next time he was asked to guest on the post game, the Petes had lost four nothing. The announcer asked him why they had lost the game and he answered that the other team had scored more goals than they had. The announcer was not pleased, pushed it and asked if Eddy thought the score would have been different if he had been in the game. Eddy responded that it might have been three nothing. Exasperated, the announcer finally asked what the team had to do to win. Eddy replied that they had to score more goals than the other team. That was the end of his radio experience, the third string goalie, who wasn't hurt, but hung around every game was the new darling of the post game show.

    The Petes season did not end as planned. They were supposed to be a play-off team that would go very deep. Instead they got knocked off in the first round four games to one. The Manager and the coaches were not pleased and looked for answers every where but in the mirror. The players let the City down, they quit. It sounded good in the papers and deflected the attention from the coaches. The team just wasn't ready to play, and didn't. Eddy didn't care, he didn't feel a part of the team anyway. He felt some remorse for Bobby and a couple of the other guys who he wanted to see do well. The end of the year banquet was like all the others. The powers that be put a positive spin on some things that went well and looked forward to next year. For the majority of teams in amateur sports and professional sports the rhetoric is the same. There is only one winner in every league, one Grey Cup winner, one Stanley Cup winner, one Queens Plate winner and one Memorial Cup winner. The rest of the teams were just filler, rounding out the field and giving the champions their foil. Most teams don't win, most are not winners. As long as the fans think that there is some positive, some hope, they will continue to support their teams. Hockey,

The Empty Net

like many sports, had become almost a therapy for certain people. Where else could they pay ten or twelve bucks, have a few beers, if they felt so inclined, and then scream at the players, berate the officials, and disturb their neighbours. Sometimes they would use obscenities, sometimes they would throw things on the ice, sometimes they would assault fellow spectators. Any where else they might be arrested, but not here, not if it was in the name of sports. It was a curious relationship, that between the players and the fans. They needed each other to exist but were never overly comfortable with the other. Fans would turn on yesterday's hero as soon as they screwed up. Players would wave to the fans, sign autographs, but maintain their distance from the fans. If fans did not support the team, then the team would not exist. The fans were more important than the players, but neither group knew it. The players were interchangeable cogs in the wheel. Most of the players realized that but refused to really acknowledge it. They thought they got paid for who they were, the reality is they get paid for what they do. When they are no longer able to do what it is they did, they are gone. For some that is a harsh reality. Eddy hated the business side of sports and realized that truism only too well. An athlete needed to build a reputation, a personality that would sustain them for a couple of years of pay cheques after their skills had diminished. Eddy was trying to figure out his.

    With the season over, school was just about over as well. Eddy wrote a few exams and was told very quickly that he passed them all. He was awarded a business certificate at a little ceremony the school had. The newspaper did an article on him and his pursuit of education. They intimated that he was looking for something to fall back on when his career was over, which may be sooner than later. There were some flattering comments but most of it was a typical article written by a small town sports reporter. The local scribes all thought they were great writers and once in a while would be given the okay from their editors to do a personal piece on a player instead of just reporting on the most recent game. Most of their insight was way off, but they wrote in such flowery terms no one cared. Some towns had supportive press, some had press that ripped the team even when they were winning. Eddy thought it was funny because the two needed each other. If the press was always negative eventually the fans would start to stay home. If enough fans stayed home, before too long a franchise would be in trouble. If the franchise folded or was transferred to another town then the local newspaper would not need a reporter to cover the departed team. Eddy's biggest problem with the local press was that they had never played the game at a high level and didn't really have a feel for it. They would print what juicy tidbits of information they were fed by the team, or by an anonymous source close to the team, and then pretend that they were on the inside, which they were not. Negative headlines seemed to capture more attention than positive ones and the reporter would get trapped in their own ratings trap. They would have to lower themselves continually to sink below the depth they had already sunk. The only one to get hurt would be the player and they were disposable anyway, so to the reporter it didn't matter.

   The Butler's were sad to see the two boys go, at least that is what they said. Within ten minutes of the boys departure however they were on the telephone with Mr. Julian MacDonald explaining that they would not be able to billet for the team any more.

Chapter Twenty Two

Bobby Gage had no where particular to be, so he accepted Eddy's invitation and went to the Walsh's to stay with them for the summer. The boys were excited about the N.H.L. draft that would happen the third week of June. It was in Buffalo that year, but Eddy had planned not to attend. Where he was once courted by scouts, he was now forgotten. A couple of incidents and a bad injury could have that effect on scouts. Even though he had played decently and put up some good numbers when he was healthy, this was the N.H.L. The best eighteen year old players in the world would be drafted. Each team only had a few rookies per year so there weren't that many new jobs available. Bobby had been consistently rated to go in the ninth or tenth round all year. His play was consistent and his ranking changed very little. He hoped he would be drafted, but anything later than the fourth round didn't really mean much. Sure he would be invited to training camp, but he had virtually no chance of making the team. A player was better off not to be drafted then they could at least try to arrange a try out with a team that they thought they had a shot of making. Eddy came home from the gym early one night to hear a scout from a pro team talking with Bobby. They were talking about Eddy, which was always an interesting topic to Eddy. The scout told Bobby that he doubted that any team would take a chance on Eddy because of the injury and that he was a head case. The scout said everyone had seen the television clip of him and the fan, and had heard of his other suspensions. He was a loose cannon that no one needed. Bobby on the other hand could fit into their system nicely and probably make it to the big team within a year. Bobby told the scout that if he wasn't prepared to sign Eddy then he could forget about drafting him. The scout told him that was a very foolish position to take and that he should reconsider. The scout also told him that they could draft him and then he would be their's. Bobby told him that they could waste a draft pick on him if they wanted to but that he would never report to them. The scout was taken aback and didn't know how to respond. Most players took the shit dished out in

The Empty Net

the hopes of getting the glory and big pay cheque that came with playing pro. This kid had integrity, he was different. Eddy snuck into the house and the two never mentioned the conversation.

Anna was also home and living in the Walsh house. It was a bustling, happy place. The parents loved it when there were lots of people there, especially the girls who were such great help. The boys basically did their own thing, working out, eating all day long, sleeping until noon or later and never really available when there was something that needed to be done.

It took Bobby a month but he had finally convinced Eddy to attend the N.H.L. draft. They decided to make a weekend of it and enjoy the best that Buffalo had to offer. The two invited a couple of their buddies, non hockey playing buddies, and headed off to Buffalo. Despite living only a half an hour away from Buffalo when he was in the Falls, Eddy had never been to Buffalo. As soon as they crossed the border they sensed the difference. Everything seemed bigger, the buildings, the roads, the flags, everything. There was a particular smell to the place as well. It smelt like American cigarettes did when combined with rotting garbage. It wasn't overwhelming but it was distinctive. The City looked busy and foreboding. The grey buildings with their large flags waving compelled and repulsed the boys at the same time. Once the facade was penetrated the boys felt better. The streets and stores seemed like streets and stores in every other town they had been in. There seemed to be a few more bowling alleys than in most places and an abundance of chicken wing places, but everything else was pretty much the same. Not wanting to be too organized the boys had refused, despite the pleadings of Mrs. Walsh, to book a hotel room in advance. Besides the draft there were a lot of other events happening that weekend as well. Buffalo was a happening place. After inquiries at seven or eight places they found one that was perfect. An indoor pool, parking, two double beds and a bar. The boys decided to settle in and have a few drinks before exploring the town. In the hotel bar Eddy and Bobby ran into a few guys they knew or recognized from junior. The two figured that everybody that could

The Empty Net

skate and was eighteen years old was going to be in Buffalo that weekend, just in case. The two buddies that had joined them thought it was great to meet potential millionaires. They had nothing to do with the hockey world and so everything was exciting to them as fans.

The arena in Buffalo was huge. The boys had played in some large venues but this was different. This was just like on television, it was pro hockey. They found seats about half way up from the ice. The ice of course was gone, replaced with a wood covering that supported the hundreds of tables occupied by scouts, managers, coaches, computers and phone equipment. The rink was a beehive of activity. The boys heard various conversations taking place in about ten different languages. This was not just about them, it was a world wide event. Seeing all the players from all over the world was discouraging. Many of these guys they had read about or seen on television. Eddy and Bobby didn't think that they belonged and wanted to go home. Their buddies were caught in a fantasy world and refused to even consider leaving. They would take a bus back home if they had to, but they weren't going to miss this.

With the arena packed the draft began. There were speeches from the President of the N.H.L., the Mayor of Buffalo and some other people that the boys didn't recognize. The first team to draft took about twenty minutes, they announced the player with his stats, weight, height and every other detail you could think of. They then took pictures in numerous combinations, some with the player and the coach, some with the player and the scouts, some with the player and his parents, some with the player and other hockey officials. Finally, they either got tired or their photographer ran out of film and it was time for the second pick. The pattern continued for the rest of the day which only saw four rounds being completed. The rest would be completed tomorrow, with far less pomp and ceremony. The boys knew a couple of players that had been drafted in the first four rounds, but none that they had played with. There was definitely a European and Western Canada flavour to the first day of the draft.

The Empty Net

Sitting in an arena all day watching a handful of guys and their families celebrate was not the best way to spend a day in a new City. The boys decided that a night on the town would be more to their liking and proceeded to find the seediest dumpiest looking bar they could. Buffalo being Buffalo, they didn't have to look far. The antlers over the door and the giant beer sign next to the door was all the enticement they needed. Inside there were what looked like dirt floors, lots of women and a haze of cigarette smoke. They mingled with the locals and met some nice girls, unfortunately they were too nice and things didn't progress the way the boys had hoped. They tried a couple of other bars and found them to all be pretty much the same. At 2:20 in the morning they decided to end their safari and head back to their room. It was rough getting up the next morning but arise they did. They dragged themselves through the shower, forced down some left over donuts, got dressed and dragged themselves back to the arena.

The arena looked like it had been looted overnight. The television cameras were gone, the bright lights were turned off and the people that remained were not all dressed up. Day one of the draft was for the television audience, day two was simply business. The good thing was that the rounds went much quicker, no speeches and fewer photo's made sure of that. Eddy and Bobby started to recognize a lot more of the names being called. They even had a team mate drafted in the fifth round. He wasn't there because of other commitments and so the boys decided that it would be a good idea if one of their buddies went up to accept on his behalf. It didn't take much to convince their buddy Johnny that he was perfect for the role. Johnny had followed the home town heroes so he knew the names of the coach and many guys on the team. Johnny was probably fifty pounds overweight and not very tall. The team was in shock as he rolled up onto the stage to shake hands with the brain trust. People in the crowd snickered and other teams were laughing. The team that drafted him didn't know what to do. They didn't always meet the players before they were drafted, maybe they made a mistake, maybe this was the wrong kid. They went along with it even to the point of taking a couple of pictures. Johnny

The Empty Net

thanked them and made his way back to the seats, the boys were howling, almost falling out of their seats, the team was huddled around their table deep in conversation. It was at least an hour before any one from the team made their way up to where the boys were seated to confirm that Johnny was not the kid that they had drafted. The scout seemed very relieved and even appreciated the prank a little bit. Eddy and Bobby had so much fun with that one they didn't even care if they were drafted. They wondered what other stunts they could pull off, without getting kicked out or arrested.

It was the ninth round and the boys were bored. As they got up to leave for the long journey home their concentration was broken. "The San Jose Sharks are pleased to select from the Peterborough Petes centre/left wing Bobby Gage." The boys could hardly believe it. Bobby wasn't even sure it was him. He finally made his way up to the stage where he met the team brain trust and had some pictures taken. They took him to their table and loaded him up with some paper work and team souvenirs. It was very exciting for all the boys to share in Bobby's special moment.

When they got to the border and the customs agent asked them if they had anything to declare, Bobby proudly told him he's going to San Jose. The customs agent nodded like he knew what they were talking about and sent them on their way. The ride home seemed much shorter than the ride down. Bobby would report to the main camp in San Jose the second week of September and he couldn't wait. When the boys got home there were messages from three different N.H.L. teams for Eddy to call them. He wondered what they wanted and his curiosity forced him to return their calls. All three teams wanted to sign him but could not guarantee him a spot on the team or even in the minors, he would have to earn that. They all said that he was one of the best defenceman not to get drafted and were sure it was because of the two incidents. Eddy had dreamed of playing for the Montreal Canadiens all of his life. Even though they offered less money than the other teams as a signing bonus, he decided Montreal was where he wanted to be. Bobby was a little jealous that Eddy got more signing bonus than he had gotten, and he was going to be a Montreal Canadien. Bobby was regretting that he had been drafted and wished he was in the same position as Eddy.

The Walsh's were very pleased that a team with such a rich tradition wanted their boy to play for them. The neighbours were ecstatic and came over to the house to congratulate Eddy. The two boys were interviewed for the newspaper who ran a nice page and a half story on them complete with pictures, compliments of Shannon. Eddy and Bobby worked very hard over the summer. If they weren't on the ice then they were in the gym trying to get stronger. They also worked out with the local track club to help with their foot speed. Anna was the new coach for the local track club so it wasn't too bad. The drills were sometimes pretty ridiculous but in time they realized they were getting faster and stronger. She was a big help to the boys and really knew her stuff. The newly found foot speed they developed off the ice translated to better quickness on the ice. It wasn't such a big deal for Bobby who was already pretty fast but it greatly benefitted Eddy. Eddy's hand felt good, stronger than it ever had been and he was pain free. He was physically and mentally ready to play hockey again.

Chapter Twenty Three

Eddy decided to finally part with some of the cash he received for his signing bonus and the money he had invested from the sale of the motorcycle, to purchase a car. He decided to go Toronto hoping he would get a good deal. He took the bus down with Joanne as support, but hoped they wouldn't have to take the bus back. They talked about cars on the bus ride down, but Eddy could not figure out what type he wanted. He liked trucks, he liked the sport utilities, he liked sports cars and he liked big luxury cars. He decided to travel from dealership to dealership and test drive various models. The first dealership had mostly sports cars and more expensive cars. It was well lit and had a very nice decor. The salesman that approached them seemed kind of stuffy and almost annoyed that they were there. He scoffed when Eddy asked if they could test drive a forty five thousand sports car. "And how were you planning on paying for this vehicle?" Eddy was pissed off at the guys tone of voice and told Joanne they were going to go some place where all the sales people were not jerks. As they left the dealership Eddy brushed by the salesman and said, "I was going to pay for it in cash pal, I'm a pro hockey player." The salesman said he was very sorry and asked him to reconsider. Eddy knocked over the brochure rack as they left.

  The next dealership was also very nice but had mostly family type cars, some trucks and some sport utility vehicles. Two salesman approached at the same time. It was like a feeding frenzy and Eddy and Joanne were the meal. They had a few words with each other and one left and went back to his office. Eddy said they would be interested in test driving a sport utility. As he winked at Joanne, the salesman said that was an excellent vehicle for a young family. The car, truck, whatever it was, was very nice. It had good pick up, looked sporty and drove nice. It was thirty two thousand dollars and available in many different colours. Eddy took a brochure with the information the guy had written down on it and promised to be back. The third dealership was dumpy looking from the outside but had a lot of different cars displayed inside. The female sales person introduced herself to them and asked them what they were looking for. Eddy admitted he really didn't know but would when he saw it. The salesperson took them back to her office and asked them a bunch of questions. She wondered what he was going to use it for, was there storage issues, how many people would be in it, would it be used in the winter and other piercing questions that Eddy had never considered. He was pleased that she had asked the questions that she had. It made him think that a sporty luxury car that looked like a truck was his ideal vehicle, unfortunately they didn't yet exist. Eddy and Joanne decided to have dinner and think about it over night and then look again the next day. After dinner they realized they had no place to stay. They had taken taxi's all day and were sick of them. The hotel across the street from the restaurant wasn't a fancy four star facility but it certainly looked comfortable enough and inviting. Eddy checked in and got the key card. It wasn't until they got in the room and turned on the lights that they realized it was a room with only one double bed. They looked at each other and laughed. Joanne called down to the desk only to find that there were no other rooms available. Joanne said she was fine with it as long as Eddy was, and the two agreed it wasn't too bad.

    Joanne had a bath while Eddy watched television. When she was done she slipped into the bed and watched television while Eddy took a shower. After such a busy day both were anxious to get some sleep. Eddy climbed into the bed and they turned the television off. Neither had closed the drapes properly and the glare from the downtown lights was streaming into the room. Joanne got up to close them properly. Eddy could not help but notice that she was naked and had a fantastic figure. With the room darkened they tried to fall asleep. The bed was small and it wasn't long before they were rubbing up against each other and competing for the blanket. Joanne rolled on to Eddy in search of the blanket and it was all he could take. He pulled her closer to him and their lips met. Years of pent up sexual tension between them was being freed. They rolled around on the bed hugging, kissing and caressing each other. Before long they stopped and simply laid on the bed. At the same time they started to talk and confess that it wasn't right. They laughed at the same time. Naked they sat up in the bed and turned the light on. Joanne was certainly a knock out and Eddy was in the best shape of his life, but there was no real chemistry between them. They loved each other very deeply, but not in a sexual way. With that realization made they turned out the light and quickly fell asleep.

    The morning came early with the noise of the awaking city just outside their window. They got dressed and went for breakfast. Eddy had a vision during the night that he should get a domestic luxury car with two doors. He liked the feel of a big car, especially in the winter, wanted a leather interior, room in the trunk for his hockey sticks and something that would last for a long time, just in case. He decided a sporty Cadillac would be the answer and so they made their way to the dealership. The sales people were very nice and showed them several different models that filled the bill. Eddy decided on a dark blue model with a light gray leather interior. It was a great looking car with a lot of luxury and safety features and all for just forty one thousand dollars. His hockey sticks would fit in the trunk and that sealed the deal. The salesman did the paper work and Eddy arranged for payment in cash. Unfortunately the vehicle was not available immediately but would be delivered to Eddy at his home in one week. The salesman was good enough to drive them to the bus terminal where they got the next bus to the North. Eddy hoped that the trip home would be his last bus trip.

    A small crowd of neighbours came out of their homes to get a better look at the beautiful blue Cadillac parked in the Walsh driveway. It wasn't every day or even every other day that a new car showed up in their neighborhood and when one did, it was an event. The dealership in Toronto had arranged to have delivery right to his house. The dealership must have figured if he was young and rich it wouldn't be the last car he would purchase and they wanted to be there for the next time. Mrs. Walsh cried when she saw the car glistening in the sun. She could not believe how beautiful it was and that her son had been able to afford it. Mr. Walsh was very excited and pleaded with Eddy to drive it. Joanne jumped in the back seat with Eddy, Mrs. Walsh sat in the front seat and her giddy husband drove. They drove for about an hour before Eddy was able to convince his dad to take them home. The rest of the day was spent staring at it, polishing it and just sitting in it.

    Training camp meant the end of summer and a return to the grind of hockey. The more training camps that Eddy endured, the more of a grind hockey became.

Chapter Twenty Four

The two boys reported to training camp in Peterborough in style and in the best shape of their lives. In practice they were head and shoulder above every one else on the ice. They were clearly the two best players on the ice all the time. Even the coaches thought they would not benefit from another year of junior hockey but desperately wanted them back on the team. With those two players the team could go all the way. They were only in Peterborough for a couple of weeks before it was time to report to the pro camps. Eddy was off to Montreal to compete at the famous Montreal Forum, Bobby was off to San Jose to compete in the not so famous Cow Palace, or "palais de bouf", as some affectionately called it.

Eddy cried the first time he walked into the Forum. It was beautiful, it was a shrine. He had seen it so many times on television but the lens could not do it justice. The place was the perfect place to play hockey. The rich red, blue and white colours, the famous "CH" logo, the trophies throughout the building, the wall of fame, the pictures of all those that had gone before and the living legends walking around the building. The rookies checked into their hotel rooms before the first meeting, the veterans mostly owned or rented homes in Montreal so it was not very disruptive for them. Eddy had gained more weight and added another inch to his already imposing frame over the summer. He was one of the bigger players in the room, but not one of the strongest. He was almost nineteen, some of the guys were in their late thirties. They had families, expenses and a burning desire to keep their positions, on and off the ice. While the veterans were cordial, they were not overly friendly. Training camp was the most anxious time of the year for a professional hockey player. In two weeks a player could be injured, traded, demoted to another league for much less money or released outright. It was a hard transition for most players to go from celebrity, earning a celebrity income, to former sports celebrity earning no income. Many players had not trained for any other occupation which only complicated the transition that much more.

The team was put through a battery of drills before they even hit the ice. They were fitness tested, they were weighed, they were measured, they had mental tests that would be used later as a baseline if they suffered a concussion and they were photographed. The tests were simple ones like in the past. These tests involved being hooked up with wires that relayed information to a computer and wearing a breathing apparatus to determine oxygen levels, usage and fitness. Each player was then given a print out and new targets were determined. Some veterans that hadn't worked as hard in the off season as they should have didn't do as well on the tests and were scorned, it was strike one for some of them.

The first workout was just skating, lots of skating. Speed drills, agility drills and endurance drills. Eddy did well and did not look out of place. Some of the veterans waltzed through the drills like they were nothing. Eddy could not believe how good these guys were. It was a huge jump from junior to pro, especially for an eighteen year old. Eddy figured he would be sent back to junior but wanted to stay as long as he could in Montreal. His goal was helped along by the fact the team had two veteran defencemen that were holding out for new contracts and one that was injured just before training camp. There were four others with pro experience and five rookies that had none. Eddy thought he was the best of the rookies but could not be sure. A week into camp the team had it's first exhibition game. Eddy was heart broken when the list went up and his name was not on it. He wondered if his pro camp experience was over. A veteran told him not to worry about it that it didn't mean anything. He told him it was probably better not to play in the first exhibition game, but he never explained why that was. Eddy watched the game from the press box. He learned a lot watching from up high, but had spent too much time in various press boxes over his career to enjoy this one. The game was brutal. There were so many fights, bad plays and missed chances that you lost track. One of the rookie defenceman, got brave with a veteran tough

The Empty Net

guy and got destroyed. The kid was a mess when Eddy saw him in the dressing room. He went back to junior the next morning. The afternoon after the game another list was put up with the names of those that would be remaining in camp. Three rookie defenceman were sent back to junior, Eddy had so far survived. There weren't that many more cuts to make and Eddy for the first time really started to believe that he would make the team.

The second exhibition game was against the Detroit Red Wings, a great traditional rival, but superior to the habs for the last couple of seasons. The flight to Detroit was an adventure, the drive to the rink, the arrival at the rink and entering the visiting teams dressing room were all adventures in themselves. Eddy was in awe of everything. He thought he was going to be sick or pass out or just make a complete fool of himself out on the ice. His legs were weak and shaking, his head hurt, his heart pounded. He wanted to go home and forget about it all. The dressing room was huge and more like a busy club house at a golf course. People were walking around doing all sorts of things while the players got ready. Some players would get dressed and then just sit with their head down thinking for an hour or so about what they were going to do on the ice. Some players stretched and stretched and stretched and then got dressed at the last minute. Reporters mingled with the players until an hour before the game, stick boys and trainers made sure everything was set up properly for the players. Eddy was not comfortable with how freely people could move around the dressing room, in junior it was just the players in the room before the game. The dressing room had a television, stereo system and a clock that counted down how much time was left before game time. Eddy got dressed and sat at his stall thinking. He was almost overwhelmed by emotions but had to keep them in check so he could get through the game. There would be plenty of time to rehash the experience later. It was show time, time for business, to show everybody what he could do. The coach came into the dressing room briefly before the game but said little. The lines and defence pairings

The Empty Net

had been on the board in the dressing room since they arrived, so there was no surprise or discussion necessary. The buzzer inside the dressing went off and it was game time. The guys had a ritual of who went first, second and last. Some guys knocked gloves, some guys knocked sticks or hit the other player on their shin pads for good luck. Whatever the ritual it would last the season, sometimes a career. Eddy hit the ice and prayed he would not fall over, trip a team mate or some how make a spectacle of himself. He didn't dare look into the crowd for fear of being distracted. He would scan the crowd from the bench. He took his place on the bench for the National Anthems and looked around. In the first row of the second tier of seats he noticed Joanne and Anna. He had no idea that they were going to be there and he had not provided any tickets for them. He nodded at them and hoped that they saw him. He was glad he didn't have to watch the game from where they were. He had the best seat in the building. The play went past the bench very, very quickly and with no protective glass in front of the bench the players had to watch the game all the time, or at least be aware of where the puck was.

At the ten minute mark of the first period Eddy made his National Hockey League debut. His legs felt heavy and he was breathing heavy before he even got on the ice. It didn't take long to get involved in the play. The Red Wings fired the puck into his corner and he had to get back quick to retrieve it. He spun around with it and looked up just as the freight train hit him. Eddy could not believe how fast the forward got to him. In junior hockey he would have had ten seconds or so to make a play, here it was immediate. After his fifth or sixth shift of the game Eddy settled down. He actually enjoyed the experience and had the confidence that he could he play with and against players at this level.

The third period saw the Red Wings leading three to one with emotions starting to rise. Mid way through the period, one of the Detroit tough guys, and they had many, started to push a veteran who

The Empty Net

rarely fought. Eddy didn't like that and stepped in. The two players hit each other about twenty times before getting tired. The Detroit player said "good go rookie" and the fight was over. There was sort of a code that when a player said it was over, it was over. The player had a role to play, a job to do, but also a career to protect. No one tried to really hurt the other player seriously, but no one wanted to be embarrassed either. Eddy's team mates appreciated the gesture of sticking up for a veteran and were impressed with how well he did against a legitimate heavy weight tough guy. They all made comments to him, as did the coach. The guys were starting to accept Eddy into their exclusive brotherhood. Eddy's hand was very swollen and he iced it immediately after the game. He tried to hurry showering and changing so he could find Joanne and Anna. They smiled at him as he came down out of the dressing room and down the hall to where the fans were waiting. He gave them a big hug and tried to walk down the hall with them, but was interrupted several times by autograph seekers. He thanked the girls for coming to see him. They said they would not have missed his first professional game for anything. The three didn't have much time to talk as Eddy had to be on the bus to the airport and a flight back to Montreal. He had lost his first game as a pro, but Eddy thought he had played well and considered it a successful debut. The coach walked by him on the airplane and said that he had played a good game. Eddy felt good about that.

  A few days after the game Eddy was called into the General Manager's office. He was scared and didn't want to go but knew he had to face the music eventually. The G.M. greeted him warmly with a big smile. "Ed, we like how you are making the adjustment and have decided that you will start the year with the team, congratulations." "Which team Sir?" The G.M. laughed loudly, "the Montreal Canadiens." Eddy hugged him, catching him off guard, and ran to find a phone. He called his dad first and told him the news, he could hear his mom asking questions and then crying in the background. Joanne and Anna were very happy for him. Shannon told him he would like to go to see a game and take pictures of Eddy.

The Empty Net

The first regular season game was against the Toronto Maple Leafs in Montreal. The family arrived on Friday morning the day before the game. His parents could not believe how beautiful the Forum was. They shared the emotion that Eddy had felt the first time he had walked into the building. Shannon was also impressed with the building and took a couple rolls of film trying to capture its majesty. Eddy also got permission for Shannon to take pictures inside the Forum and of Eddy on the ice in uniform. The brothers spent about an hour doing what they each did best and then went for lunch. Shannon and Eddy drove around Montreal looking at the buildings and spectacular Churches. Shannon fell deeply in love with the City and wondered why he had never been there before. The architecture, the parks, the feel, but most of all the people, were compelling.

Saturday was the greatest day of Eddy's life. He was playing for the Montreal Canadiens against the Toronto Maple Leafs with his family and friends in the crowd. One of the perks was getting a certain amount of free tickets for the games. Eddy had also managed to grab a couple of other tickets from a veteran that didn't have any friends or family attending the home opener.

The Walsh gang included the family, Joanne, Anna, Donna and Tara Brady, Bobby Gage, who had been sent back to Peterborough, and two other friends. They filled a whole row of seats about ten rows up from the players bench. The Forum was always alive, but when the Leafs were in town there was electricity plus. This was one of the greatest rivalries in pro sports. Each time they met it was special, regardless of where the teams were in the standings.

After the opening ceremony the players were introduced. Eddy was starting on defence, if he didn't pass out before the game started. Despite the previous game, many practices, years of junior and a life time of games, he still had trouble controlling his nerves before each game.

The Leafs were a big physical team and liked to intimidate other teams. The game was twenty seconds old when Terry Clarke, the former Sudbury tough guy and second year Leaf guy, grabbed and starting throwing punches at Eddy. Eddy grabbed on to him and they exchanged blows for over two minutes. Exhausted they tapped each other on the head and the linesman intervened. It was a great fight and everyone in the Forum was on their feet cheering. Eddy had a reputation that he could handle himself, but that was not his role. Many of the Forum faithful were surprised at how well he had handled himself. Terry winked at him as they went to the penalty box. Eddy noticed his hand swelling bigger and bigger. He recognized the feeling and didn't like it. At the first stoppage he skated to the bench and went to the dressing room. The trainer x-rayed his hand in the dressing room and could tell immediately that it was broken. Eddy got changed quickly and went to the hospital. Luckily, surgery was not necessary, but the hand would have to be immobilized.

    The doctor put the hand in a cast and sent him home. Eddy was still living in a hotel room, the same hotel he had put his family up in. He got back at about 1:30 a.m. and went directly to their room. As expected they were waiting up for him. His parents hugged him and told him how proud they were of him. His dad told him that his life was now complete. They could tell from the cast that his hand was not well but no one mentioned it. Eddy finally told them that it was broken but he didn't know how long he would be out until he spoke to the trainer.

    Eddy figured that he would be out for at least two months and figured it would cost him a return trip to Peterborough. The next day the trainer met Eddy in the dressing room and they went to the medical room. The trainer said that he had been in touch with the doctor and thought Eddy would be able to play in a couple of weeks. If he needed they would fit him with a new glove so they could tape his hand better. Eddy was surprised and questioned the trainer about the time frame. The trainer was sharp in his retort and basically asked if Eddy wanted to play or not. The trainer gave Eddy a fitness regime that started that day. The trainer laughed as he left him to work on some other players. Eddy was amazed but was learning. He saw his team mates, particularly the veterans playing on cracked ankles, with separated shoulders, broken noses, broken fingers and cuts and bruises of various magnitude. Some of the injuries that he had seen would keep a regular employee off work for a month, the hockey player might miss a game. Every player knew the sad reality that for every spot in the line up there were fifty guys ready to fill it. Injuries were just part of the equation and had to be minimized and played through. Eddy worked at keeping his strength and aerobic capacity high. His hand hurt him all the time but he learned to block the pain out. Ten days after being injured he was back in the line up with a specially fitted glove and a frozen hand. The warm up was discouraging, he couldn't feel his hand and couldn't feel the puck on his stick. The hand was throbbing and hurt every time he moved it. He got a couple of more shots to freeze it during the game but it didn't help. Every time he got the puck he got rid of it. He couldn't do much with it and didn't want to make any mistakes. He had to back down on several occasions from guys that wanted to fight. At least players had the respect to leave a guy alone that was hurt.

  The weather in Montreal was getting colder and snow was starting to accumulate on the ground. Eddy had settled into a nice apartment in the downtown within walking distance of the rink. He loved driving around the City at night and did so every chance he got. He had been to the West coast twice but did not enjoy it. He learned early that he hated to fly. It wasn't a fear of crashing or dying or anything like that, it was more of a claustrophobic feeling that made him dread road trips. He spoke to some veterans about it and one put him onto some medication that was somewhat helpful. The trainer got him his own prescription but he couldn't use it if they played the same day they flew. The practices, travel, games and the pain were wearing on Eddy every day. When he dreamed of playing professional hockey he never thought of the other parts associated with the game. Some guys played for the love of the game but for many it had become a business. Eddy noticed that it seemed like some guys played on auto pilot getting through game after game and keeping themselves healthy. Not exactly the dream he had as a kid.

One night Eddy was walking the streets of Montreal when he heard the familiar sound of skates tearing up the ice and pucks being fired off of boards. The sound drew him into a park that had a nice little out door rink right in the middle of it. Eddy stared in amazement as he watched a group of men in their sixties and seventies play the game as it was meant to be played. They skated hard on every shift, as hard as they could at their age, and came off the ice smiling. They were having the time of their lives with not a worry in the world. Eddy wished he could join them and never have to go back to the other game that he now hardly recognized. This was hockey at it's purest. That is the game Eddy wanted to play. He watched for an hour until the cold forced him to move on. He dreamed of the day that he could play on the ice with men like that, in that type of game. It made him happy to think that hockey, fun hockey, didn't end with being a kid.

Bobby Gage called Eddy often trying to lift his spirits. Bobby was still playing junior but wanted to be in the N.H.L. Eddy was not having fun but didn't want to go back to junior. The money was good but there was not the same camaraderie between the players that had existed in junior. Most of the players were married and went home after games. On the road everyone did their own thing. Sometimes they would go out for dinner together, but that was about all they did together. Eddy had met a couple of the wives and some of his team mates children but had never been to a team mates house. There were three other rookies on the team but one was engaged and two didn't speak any English. Sometimes they would go to a movie together, but the other two could not understand the words and would want to leave half through. Eddy saw about ten movies that Fall, but never saw an ending. The other players would kid him about it and try and fill in the endings for him.

The only saving grace for Eddy was that Shannon loved Montreal and was there almost all the time. The boys appreciated each others company and explored the City together when they got the chance. Joanne had stayed for a couple of weeks and promised to visit again after Christmas. Shannon had turned eighteen and had decided to buy a condo in Montreal. He had the money and wanted a base in the city. Eddy was pleased because it gave him a place to stay that was like home. Eddy had tired of the hotel he was staying in and supported Shannon's decision to buy the condo.

Eddy enjoyed every minute of the games he played in the N.H.L. The thrill of going into arenas that he had seen on television, playing against players that were household names, and the great pay days were certainly a rush for a young guy.

Playing in front of 18,000 loud people every game was exhilarating and sometimes overwhelming. Eddy felt pressure to perform on every shift. There were no short cuts at that level. Eddy loved to watch the other players at practice and marvel at their skills. He was impressed with how fast guys were and how well they could control the puck. At times it was hard for Eddy to remember he was one of them.

Eddy got lots of mail from his fans, particularly those in Peterborough, Niagara Falls and his hometown. He tried to keep up with the requests and had help from the team. They provided him with a stack of glossy photos to sign, then they would do the rest. Montreal was a great place to play, as long as the player had thick skin and a short memory. Everyday there would be about eight pages of coverage, in each of the three local newspapers, in both French and English. The press would scrutinize a player's every move, on and off the ice. It was difficult to take at times, but also a positive because every player knew they would get lots of ink spilt over them.

Eddy had a lot of stories written about him in junior, but not of the detail and quality of the three Montreal papers. The reporters were good writers and knew the game very well. They also had lots of access to the team, travelled on the road with the team, and knew every player's secrets.

The Empty Net

Eddy was tired of the practices that were tougher than anything he had previously experienced. He was always nursing an injury and in pain, which started to wear on him mentally. He didn't have any real friends on the team and no one to talk to that knew what he was going through. The coaches didn't talk to him and the press would eat up a story like Eddy wanted to tell. He was smart enough to know that and never mentioned his feelings about the difficulty he experienced. He knew they would label him a quitter or a head case and try and run him out of town. It was an honour to play for the Canadiens, doubts about commitment to the cause would be unforgivable.

It was confusing for Eddy. He had worked his whole life to get to where he was, but now he didn't like being there. The advice his father had given him weighed heavily, he did not want to let people down. Every game he played, Eddy thought it might be his last.

The Hab's played five games in seven days with the last three all on the road. By the last game before a three day break Eddy was exhausted, bruised and mentally drained. He had no jump and wanted to go home. He could not understand how guys played whole seasons or entire careers all beat up. He had picked up three points so far in the season, all assists and felt good about how he had played considering the adjustment from junior and the injuries that he had.

The third road game of their short swing through the South was the toughest. Dallas was one of the best teams in the league and had not played in two days. Late in the second period Eddy got the puck at his own blueline, skated up the ice to the Dallas blueline before he fired it into their zone. As he let go of the puck his skate caught a rut in the ice. He twisted badly as he went down in pain. The pain was similar to the pain he felt in high school when he had been blind sided in a game. The trainers came out onto the ice and after about thirty seconds helped him to his feet. Two players helped him off the ice and two team equipment guys helped him to the dressing room. He got changed and they took him to the hospital. Because he was a hockey player he had an M.R.I. performed within the hour. The M.R.I.

confirmed damage to his knee similar to the damage he had suffered five years previously. He would require extensive surgery but that would wait until he was back in Montreal and the swelling had gone down. He was done for the season so there was no real rush. Eddy didn't know if he could take another surgery or if he was mentally strong enough to go through another round of rehabilitation. Eddy spent the week before knee surgery on the phone with Joanne and drinking, drinking heavily. He was depressed and wanted to escape his reality.

    The surgery went as well as could be expected. The doctors were guardily optimistic about his chances of playing hockey again, but the reality was that it would be up to Eddy based on how hard he was prepared to work. Eddy was pleased that he hadn't been sick with the anesthetic like he had been in the past. He was very positive and optimistic and most concerned with when he could start drinking again.

    Mr. And Mrs Walsh visited Eddy in the hospital and said how sorry they were for him. Eddy said it was the best thing that could have happened to him and that he had no regrets. He assured his parents that he would be okay mentally and financially. His parents didn't understand why he was so excited. Eddy's demeanor only served to heighten their concerns. They thought maybe he didn't understand that his hockey career was probably over. The family, Anna and Shannon decided to stay in Montreal until Eddy could come home.

    The injury occurred during the game and so he would receive insurance money if he couldn't play again. It was not the amount of money that Shannon had received in his inheritance, but it would serve him well for a couple of years and give him a good start on his next career. Joanne and Eddy spoke regularly and she understood how he was feeling. She never judged him and was always supportive of any decision he made. Eddy took his parents, Joanne, Anna and Shannon out to the same great restaurant in Montreal that they had gone to months earlier to celebrate his signing with the Canadiens. After the

The Empty Net

main course was completed Eddy explained to the group that he had decided to retire from hockey but that he had no idea what he would do next. His parents were a little surprised but seemed pleased. The family was all very supportive of his decision to retire. Anna was angry with him and couldn't understand how he could throw it all away. She thought that he should wait until the re-hab was completed and then see how the knee responded. Anna told him he was throwing away a lot of money and prestige and should reconsider his decision and try and play for a few more years, at least. He explained to her that he had accomplished his dream of playing in the N.H.L., had been interviewed on national television, had signed thousands of autographs, toured North America and made some money. He had done what few others would ever have the chance to do, but he was tired and beat up. He had nothing left in the tank, nothing left to give back. Anna could not understand and it bothered her. Anna and Eddy had not been close in a long time and decided not to see each other any more. It was difficult for them on some level, but they knew it was the best decision for the long term. Just like with hockey, Eddy had given everything he could to the relationship and had nothing left to give.

The relief felt was immediate. Eddy felt as if he had his life back and could now do whatever he wanted to do without having to get prior approval from someone else. A couple of weeks after surgery he was back home for good. He bought his dad a car similar to his Cadillac, his mom some furniture, a dishwasher and some other goodies and bought Shannon a telescope, computer and some other trinkets. Shannon didn't really need them but appreciated the gesture of his big brother. Shannon now had more money than Eddy and better earning potential, but that was not the point.

Even before the injuries Eddy had doubts about how long he could last as a pro hockey player. He loved hockey, but not how it was played in the N.H.L. Eddy met with the General Manager for over an hour. The G.M. liked Eddy personally and appreciated his talent. The G.M. wanted Eddy to re-hab and come back next season. Eddy explained to him that he already had two major surgeries on his knees, surgery on his hand and too many stitches to count. He was physically and mentally spent. He could not go through another re-hab and try to regain his present skills.

The G.M. had trouble understanding Eddy's position. He had played hockey before getting into management and told Eddy he would give anything to be able to play one more game. Eddy wanted to share that feeling, but couldn't. It just wasn't in him.

The G.M. appreciated Eddy's honesty and respected his decision. Because he was injured during the game the team would make sure that Eddy collected insurance money and anything else he needed. The money would give Eddy two years salary, which would give him a good start on a new life.

Chapter Twenty Five

Eddy was more content with life than he had been at any other time in his life. He rarely watched hockey on television and didn't miss it. Many guys he knew from junior were playing pro hockey, but only a few were in the NHL. Most were playing in the minor leagues earning little more than a living. Some of them would get traded three or four times in a season. It may have been an exciting lifestyle for a player twenty one years old, but not that attractive for a married guy in his thirties.

Eddy was asked to speak to the Crusaders at a pep rally but graciously declined. He would speak to the team privately and even go to a couple of practices, but did not like speaking in public and did not want to be billed as the former hockey player. He enjoyed talking to the guys and telling them about the life of a hockey player. Most of his stories involved fond memories from junior hockey, not from the N.H.L. He wanted them to know the whole picture but certainly not to discourage them from pursuing their dreams.

Shannon had turned eighteen and had the house and the money transferred into his name. He now had a big house, a condo in Montreal and a business. Not too bad for a young guy. He was the richest guy in the neighborhood, let alone the richest eighteen year old in town. He had rented out the house for the last year and a half and made a few bucks doing so. His money with interest had grown to over three hundred thousand dollars. He spent about thirty thousand dollars on renovations to the house which included a state of the art dark room in the basement, a reception area and a studio on the main floor. It was the perfect place. There were still two big bedrooms, three bathrooms, a sitting room, an office, a kitchen and the studio. Shannon was excited that he could work and live in the same place. His parents hated to see him move but at least he was only down the street. Joanne moved into Shannon's room so there was no escaping the move was a permanent step. Shannon was still doing some work for the newspaper

The Empty Net

but had started to do more portrait work and some magazine work. He had built a good reputation and did not have to advertise, people called him hoping to get work done. He had photographed the Premier and many business executives. He was getting more and more calls to do work in Toronto and Ottawa but had so far resisted. The only place he would accept jobs on a regular basis was Montreal. Even with Eddy no longer there, the City still had lots to offer and Shannon loved going there, staying in the condo downtown. He had been so many times that he knew the city intimately and had many friends there.

Eddy would often talk to Shannon about his career and how it ended. Shannon was sort of like a therapist for Eddy, but he didn't mind at all. Shannon didn't know all of the details or how hard his brother had worked to be a pro hockey player. Shannon suggested that Eddy write about his struggles and his victories in a book, but Eddy just scoffed at the idea. He was a retired hockey player not an author.

Shannon had finally convinced Eddy to come and live with him. It made sense as Shannon did not want to live alone, his parents did not want him to live alone and Eddy did not want to live with his parents.

It was fairly warm that May morning as Eddy lined up with four hundred other desperate men, all seeking the opportunity of getting a twenty second interview with the hopes of snatching one of the fifty low paying, hard labour jobs available at the mill. It was about a year and a half after he had played his last hockey game, but it might as well have been a hundred years. He was heavy, drinking too much and walked with a limp. His athletic days were behind him and he was having difficulty with the transition to a non athlete. He stood in line, telling hockey stories to some of the other guys, while proudly wearing his high school hockey jacket. It was his favourite hockey jacket and his oldest. Despite the fact he hadn't been able to button it up in years, he refused to wear one of the seven or eight other jackets he had. In that line Eddy was a celebrity and had many of the guys ask for his autograph. Most were confused and didn't know why Eddy was in

The Empty Net

line. Eddy knew why he was in line. He was young and willing to work hard and realistically needed a job. He hoped someone making the hiring decision would remember him as a hockey player and give him the job. Three hours after arriving Eddy made his way into the personal office. "Why do you want to work here" the interviewer barked. "Well, my father worked here and I remember the mill always treated him right and I need a job." "Thanks for your interest, we will let you know."

It was over quick but Eddy thought it had gone well. As Eddy arrived home he saw some young kid running from the front of the house. As he got out of the car he heard the first little explosion. The tulips were exploding before his eyes. He looked for the kid but couldn't find him. He was angry and spent twenty minutes in his hunt for the little fugitive with no success. When he went in the house Shannon asked him how the interview went. Eddy said he thought it went well, but that there were a lot of good guys trying to get the jobs. He told Shannon that some punk had blown up the tulips out front. He was confused and wondered aloud what kind of a little monster could do such a thing. "Yah what kind of a little monster would do something like that Eddy." The two had breakfast and talked about other, more pleasant happenings. Shannon continued to try and convince Eddy to simply act as his business manager. Shannon hated the business aspect and was getting too large and too busy to deal with it all himself. He wanted to focus only on what he did best. Eddy said he would think about it but was concerned that it would cause problems between the two brother's, especially since Shannon would be the boss. Shannon said there would be no boss, but Eddy could have the title of President, if he wanted. Eddy thought that was interesting and would think about it seriously. The two had been able to live together without any problems, maybe they could work together as well.

It was easy for the brothers to agree on the terms of their professional relationship. Shannon was earning a lot of money from his photographs and really didn't need the money. Along with the business side of things, Eddy would help out by driving Shannon to out of town shoots and by helping set up the equipment.

Walsh photography was a thriving, profitable business and the two brothers loved their life. The business never seemed like a job or hard work to them and they were both glad Shannon chose the school he had and joined the clubs he did.

Eddy's knee and hand only caused him pain when the weather changed and thankfully he was able to function normally. He tried to go skating twice a week and the knee held up fine. At times he would feel so good he would think about making a comeback. He would attempt a sharp turn on the ice or something else and would struggle. Any fantasy of a comeback would be quickly extinguished.

Bobby Gage was a regular at the home of Eddy and Shannon. Bobby had played one year in the minors, made no money, suffered injury after injury, and like Eddy, had decided to pack it in and get a real life, whatever that was. Bobby had gotten a job at the local sporting goods store and seemed to enjoy it. It wasn't much money, or any pressure, but Bobby enjoyed talking sports with the regular customers. Bobby was living at the Walsh home, in Eddy's old room, helping out with Eddy's aging parents.

Bobby and Joanne got along very well and the Walsh's loved having them in the house. The Walsh's couldn't imagine what it would be like to have an empty house and they weren't anxious to find out. While waiting for the rejection letter from the mill, Eddy bided his time helping Shannon out with his business.

Eddy quickly found he had a knack for business and enjoyed setting up the accounting and business systems for his brother. Eddy could work less than five hours a day and accomplish everything that Shannon needed him to do.

The Empty Net

A routine was established and Eddy wasn't even disappointed when he received the standard form letter rejection from the mill in late June. He didn't care, he had found his new pursuit.

Eddy was happy he could work and live with his brother and had a career he loved and was good at. He didn't have to worry about getting hit or playing through injuries. The boys would stay up late at night talking and watching television. They had the luxury of not having to get up early in the morning. Most of the photo shoots were in the late afternoon and sometimes Shannon would work in the dark room until the sun came up. Eddy liked to talk to Shannon about his career. "Shannon, I worked my whole life to be a pro hockey player. Unfortunately, when I achieved the dream, I found the reality much different from what I had expected. When we were young I would watch the games on television and wanted to be a part of what I saw." "Yah, I know, we couldn't watch anything else on television and I hated hockey." "You were a good sport Shannon." The bus rides, plane rides, practices, injuries, politics, mental abuse and all the other bull shit just became too much. My dream was to play hockey, to skate, to compete and be part of a team. I would have played the game for free if it didn't involve all the other crap. You know, I am almost thankful that I was injured because it gave me the excuse I needed to retire. I've never been a quitter and without the injury I would have had no excuse to quit. Besides no one would have understood my decision to just walk away from the game." "I would have understood Eddy. I hated watching the crap and hard work you had to go through. It was very exciting to see the crowd react to your play and to see you on television, but it was frightening to see the players always getting hurt." "I appreciate your understanding Shannon, it means a lot to me. You are a great brother."

The boys settled into their comfortable life of working when they wanted to and trying to work out at the fitness club three times a week. Eddy still had two life time memberships and wanted to get his money out of them.

Every chance they got, Shannon, Bobby, Joanne and Eddy would play road hockey.

Eddy Walsh loved to play hockey.

ABOUT THE AUTHOR

Michael David Lannan is a Family Law Lawyer practising in Kitchener, Ontario. He has been involved in hockey as a player, referee, coach, manager and executive at all levels, including Jr. "A" and Jr. "B".

Michael is the father of four active children, Eric, Jennifer, Melanie and Amanda, and enjoys their activities, writing, reading, and spending time on the beaches of Prince Edward Island.

Michael is a graduate of Fr. Henry Carr High School, Humber College, Wilfrid Laurier University, and the University of Windsor Law School. He has special training in Mediation that he obtained at the University of Toronto and The Ohio State University.

ISBN 1553694015

9 781553 694014